ALSO BY BERNARD O'KEEFFE

No Regrets
10 Things To Do Before You Leave School

The Garibaldi Series:

The Final Round
Private Lessons
Every Trick in the Book

THE MASKED BAND

Bernard O'Keeffe

MUSWELL
PRESS

First published by Muswell Press in 2025
Copyright © Bernard O'Keeffe 2025

Typeset in Bembo by M Rules
Printed by CPI Group (UK) Ltd, Croydon CR0 4YY

A CIP catalogue record for this book
is available from the British Library

ISBN: 9781738452880
eISBN: 9781738452897

Bernard O'Keeffe has asserted his right to be identified
as the author of this work in accordance with under the
Copyright, Designs and Patents Act, 1988

Apart from any use permitted under UK copyright law,
this publication may not be reproduced, stored or transmitted,
in any form, or by any means without prior permission
in writing from the publisher.

Muswell Press
London N6 5HQ
www.muswell-press.co.uk

For Jo

Prologue

He stood swaying in the living room, knowing he was drunk but, more importantly, knowing he was in love.

That was what mattered.

In fact, it mattered so much that he thought maybe he should give her a ring to tell her.

Yes, that's what he'd do. Impulsive, but romantic. She'd love it.

He reached for his phone, but the pocket of his jeans was empty. Strange. He always kept it there. He checked the other pocket. Wallet, but no phone. He took out the wallet, put it on the table and checked his jacket pockets.

Nothing.

He stood still, hands on hips, puzzled. Had he left it somewhere?

He checked his pockets again just to be sure.

Nothing.

What was it with him and losing things? First that package – not lost, exactly, but temporarily mislaid – and now his phone.

Where the fuck was it?

It could be anywhere. Literally anywhere. And if, by chance, someone had picked it up ...

He smacked his forehead. If someone had picked it up? Of course someone had picked it up! And it was obvious who that someone must be. All he had to do now was give her a call to see if she had it.

And to tell her he loved her.

His hand was almost in his pocket again when he remembered the pocket was empty and he didn't have what he needed to make the call – he was reaching for something he didn't have because he didn't have it ...

He shook his head. Yes, too much to drink, but what the fuck – he was in love!

He steadied himself and took a few deep breaths.

Be logical. Be rational. What was the problem here? The problem was he wanted to give her a call to tell her he loved her, but he didn't have his phone.

He took a few more breaths and then, as if from nowhere, a brilliant idea came to him.

The landline.

He picked up the handset and dialled her number. You hardly ever needed to remember numbers nowadays, just press the name in contacts, but her number was etched in his brain. Another sign that it was love.

He got ready to speak.

No luck. She wasn't picking up. Unlikely she would be asleep, so why wasn't she answering, especially if she knew she'd taken his phone by mistake?

Maybe she didn't have it after all.

What should he do?

Another brilliant idea came to him. He walked over to a table, sat down, lifted the lid of his laptop and googled 'how to locate my iPhone'. It took him some time to find the right search result but soon he had it – icloud.com/find-devices. All he had to do now was remember his username and password.

It took him about ten attempts (he couldn't work out whether he was using the wrong password or using the right one but entering it incorrectly), but he got in eventually and there it was!

A green circle pulsed on the map, showing the exact location of his missing phone. As he thought – she'd picked it up by mistake and taken it to her friend's. He hadn't realised it was *that* friend but, yes, it all made sense now. He changed the map to satellite view to make sure. Yes, that was definitely it. His phone was sitting in her bag or her jacket pocket while she . . .

What would she be doing? He looked at his watch. Yes, it was late, but surely she'd still be awake – he'd only just got in himself and she'd have travelled about the same distance. Chances were she'd be chatting with her friend telling her about the great evening she'd had.

Could his phone wait until tomorrow? He took a few breaths and tried to work it out. The truth was it *would* wait until tomorrow. He didn't need it that much. It wasn't like he was addicted to it the way so many of his mates were and couldn't bear to be without it. He could survive a few hours. And it wasn't as though there was anything on it he'd worry about her seeing. Nothing incriminating – or, at least, nothing he couldn't explain away. So, yeah, maybe he should wait until tomorrow.

Then another thought struck him. Surely she would have discovered that she'd picked his phone up by mistake and surely when she found out she would have . . .

He shook his head and laughed out loud. Surely she would have called him? She had his fucking phone!

What was he thinking of? He'd definitely had too much to drink.

He sat at the table, closed his laptop and held his head in his hands.

Then it came to him. Another brilliant idea. The best he'd had so far and one that refused to go.

The more he thought about it, the more it seemed the right thing to do. He knew where she was. It was within easy walking distance and, what's more, he did this friend she was staying with a favour recently: a big favour. And when he did that favour he did something else. He'd no idea at the time why he did it, but now it was going to prove useful. Very useful. The perfect way to spring a surprise.

He leaped up and headed out.

He ran the short distance, excited by what he was going to do. OK, it was rash and impetuous, but he was in love and he was drunk and nothing was going to stop him.

When he got there he was surprised to see so many lights on and to hear music and voices. Loud voices.

Something was happening.

What was it? Some kind of party? Had she gone off to a party without telling him?

Had she lied to him?

He shut the door gently behind him as he stepped inside and found himself in a side room off the entrance hall. He stayed there for a few moments, listening to the music, voices and laughter echoing from distant rooms as he worked out a plan of action. So what if someone was having a party? Why should that change anything?

He opened the door and put his head round. No-one was in sight so he crept into the hall.

It was then that he saw them.

What the fuck were they doing here?

And what the fuck was going on?

He heard footsteps. Someone was walking towards the hall. He looked around. There was no time to get back to the side room. What should he do?

He looked at them again and, as the footsteps came closer, he reached for one and ran upstairs.

1

Mick Jagger. Paul McCartney, Debbie Harry, Bob Dylan, David Bowie.

It was quite some band, and quite incredible to see them playing the Bull's Head in Barnes on a Sunday evening.

The audience were loving it. Dancing along to the sixties and seventies classics with the words on their lips and smiles on their faces, none of them wondered what had brought this supergroup to the Barnes pub and none of them questioned why Bowie, who had died several years ago, was there at all, let alone why he was playing drums.

Mick Jagger put one hand on his hip and the other on his forehead as he looked out at the audience. "You having a good time?"

Cries of 'yes' came from the audience.

Had the crowd been able to see the man behind the Jagger mask – Jagger as he was on the Stones 1972 tour – had they been able to see beneath the wig of flowing locks and the Ossie Clark all-in-one jump suit, they would have recognised the TV celebrity immediately.

Jimmy Clark had been in the public consciousness for so long, and in such a range of roles, that it was difficult to say with any precision what he was best known for. His first appearances as a youthful graduate were on children's TV but he soon moved into other areas. Before long he was a regular on quiz and panel shows, and soon he was hosting his own. And while doing this he was pursuing a writing career: a column in *The Times* followed by one in the *Mail* and a flurry of books (some destined for coffee tables or Christmas stockings, others, including a series of supernatural detective novels, for the remainder bin). Even now, in his mid-seventies, he was still making regular TV appearances — chat shows, more quiz shows, even the occasional documentary — and was a staple of many long-running radio shows where his plummy RP tones were instantly recognisable.

In short, there seemed nothing that Jimmy Clark couldn't do, and nothing that he wouldn't turn his hand to if there was enough money and publicity in it. And yet, despite a ubiquity that smacked of shameless self-promotion, most people loved him. Neither he nor his views may have been to everyone's taste (he had stood, unsuccessfully, as a Conservative MP on two occasions), but his charm and his winning smile guaranteed that he was a figure who commanded a great deal of affection. A one-off. A unique. There was (to the relief of those for whom he wasn't their cup of tea) only one Jimmy Clark.

"Can't hear you," said Jimmy from behind the mask. "Are you having a good time?"

More cries of 'yes'. A few 'take it off!'s.

"I still can't hear you," he said. "Are you having a good time?"

The cries of 'yes' seemed no louder than before, but Jimmy nodded as if they were.

"OK," he said. "Time to introduce the band!"

He turned to the drummer and held out his arm. "On

drums, and showing just how versatile a musician he is, David Bowie!"

From behind the Aladdin Sane mask with the red and blue lightning bolt flashed across the purple-washed face, underneath the spiky red wig and in the Yamamoto striped suit, Charlie Brougham looked at the audience with a dimple-chinned smile that no-one could see. Had he whipped off his mask he would immediately have been recognised as the actor who had played the floppy-haired hero in a string of British romcoms and classic adaptations, the man who had become synonymous with a certain kind of dashing, aristocratic English youth.

The floppy hair may have greyed and thinned, and recent TV and film appearances may have been as ageing philanderers rather than romantic leads, but Charlie liked to think, despite evidence to the contrary, that he was still very much in the public eye and a favourite of the gossip columns.

He gave a bow and a roll on the drums.

"On bass," said Jimmy, "the one and only Paul McCartney!"

The audience turned to the Sergeant Pepper McCartney, neatly moustached in the Noel Howard bright-blue satin suit with fringed epaulettes and army insignia.

Behind the mask Craig Francis smiled.

There were very few poets who could consider themselves household names and Craig Francis was one of them. Emerging in the sixties as part of the movement so memorably described by *The Times* as 'bringing poetry to the people', he had been one of the earliest performance poets. Not for him obscurity or difficulty. You didn't need a degree to understand a Francis poem. Nor did you need a dictionary. He wrote poems people could understand. Funny poems.

Sad poems. Clever poems. But, above all, accessible poems. For some in the poetry world this was not a good thing – he and his ilk were debasing the noble calling. But for many others this was just what they wanted and they couldn't get enough of it. Unusually for a poet, his collections sold. They may not have received favourable reviews but they struck a chord with the reading public. Soon, Francis was a regular on TV and radio, often asked to pen a topical response to what was happening in the news. And Francis was happy to oblige, becoming something akin to the nation's alternative poet laureate. Some said he should have been the real one.

Craig bowed and raised his hand to acknowledge the cheers.

"On keyboards," said Jimmy, "the one and only Debbie Harry!"

The crowd whooped and hollered. Underneath the brilliant blonde wig, behind the mask of Blondie's lead singer, and wearing the white dress she wore on the cover of *Parallel Lines*, Hazel Bloom smiled as she raised her hand to acknowledge the cheers. She was used to performing in costumes but, until the formation of the band, she had never performed in a mask – or, at least, not a literal one. How she wished she'd been able to wear one in her early days when she was making her first tentative steps on the alternative comedy circuit. Whenever she remembered those heckles and the times she was gonged off at The Comedy Club, she was amazed she had survived. Women comedians might now be something close to the norm but it seemed not long ago that they were very much a rarity. She liked to point it out in her act, adapting the old Doctor Johnson gag (he wasn't around to sue) that a woman doing comedy was like a dog walking on its hind legs – it wasn't done well but you were surprised to find it done at all. It never got any laughs but back then not many of her jokes did. Not that jokes were the thing. It was all observational and politically correct. It was only when Hazel started to do impressions that her career really took off. Suddenly she was in demand and, to her surprise, the demand had not dropped off over the last four decades. She still performed on TV and radio, often as an impressionist in topical comedy shows but also, in a sign of her success, as herself.

"And last but by a very long way not least," said Jagger, "on guitar, the legendary Bob Dylan!"

Loud cheers and renewed cries of "Take it off! Take it off!"

It was *Blonde on Blonde* Dylan, brown coat, scarf, and a shock of wiry hair.

Had Larry Benyon whipped off the mask the Bull's Head crowd would have seen the face of the former professional footballer who had graced the nation's TV screens for many years, most recently as a contributor to political debate. Quite how he had moved from professional footballer to the nation's liberal conscience many found difficult to grasp. Even Larry himself couldn't understand it. He had always regarded himself as more intelligent than the average footballer (the bar, or should that be cross bar, was admittedly low) and had always known that a career in sports presenting might suit his talents more than a career in management, but he had never imagined that his opinions on anything other than football might be sought or valued. Anyone viewing his first, stumbling, error-strewn appearance on the nation's screens would be amazed that the rookie presenter would one day become an articulate champion of many worthy causes, an outspoken critic of perceived injustice and folly, someone who many (the Labour Party included) thought would make an outstanding MP.

Larry raised his hand, acknowledging the cheers, and spoke into the mike in a carefully disguised voice.

"Ladies and gentlemen," he said, as if he were introducing Wimbledon or the Cup Final, "let's not forget the main man himself." He held his hand out in the direction of Jimmy. "The one and only Mick Jagger!"

"Take it off! Take it off!"

"OK," said Jimmy through his Jagger mask. "Here we go. One, two, three."

Dylan played the opening chords of 'Get off My Cloud'. Jimmy came in on the vocals and the audience started to dance again, joining in on the chorus, but changing the words:

"Hey (hey) you (you) take offa your mask!"

2

Doreen Amos knew she was in a for a busy morning as soon as she opened the door. The place usually needed no more than a routine clean, but there were times, and today was clearly one of them, when she let herself in to the huge seven-bedroom mansion to find the kind of mess you wouldn't associate with the image her employer liked to present to his millions of fans.

In all the years she'd worked for him Doreen had been the soul of discretion. Not a word to anyone. Not a hint of anything untoward. But that didn't mean she never speculated, and whenever she came across things – and people – that surprised her, she couldn't stop herself wondering what he got up to when he was out of the public gaze.

That was one of the reasons why she always liked to announce her arrival. By the time she arrived at 8.30 on a Monday morning he would usually be at his desk and would often have already been there for two or three hours. At his age you'd have thought he might have started to take it easy, or at least treat himself to the occasional lie-in. But no. If he was at home he would, more often than not, be hard at work when she turned up. And he would always answer when he heard her – though, given the size of the house, and given that he worked in his study behind a closed door, she might have to call several times before he responded.

"Hello?"

It was the second time Doreen had called and there was still no answer, so she walked down the hall to his study. She was surprised to find the door open.

"Hello?"

There was still no response, so she put her head round the door. The room was empty.

Doreen walked back down the hall and went upstairs, giving another 'hello' when she reached the first-floor landing.

Still nothing.

His bedroom door was, as always, shut. She walked towards it and put her ear close, listening for movement, and as she did so she noticed that one of the other bedroom doors was slightly ajar. This was unusual. One of the few instructions she had been given when she started was that the bedroom doors should be shut at all times. She'd never asked why – it wasn't her place to – but she'd often wondered why it was so important.

"Hello?"

She called again, edging towards the open door.

Nothing.

She paused outside the room and listened.

Nothing.

She gave the door a gentle push and it slowly swung back.

She tip-toed into the room, and sensed immediately that something was wrong.

The glass doors onto the balcony were wide open and in front of them a table lay on the carpet, the ornaments and photos it had held scattered around. A broken vase lay on the floor, surrounded by shards of glass.

Doreen looked at the door to the ensuite bathroom and slowly moved towards it. She crouched and put her ear close to the door.

She heard nothing.

"Hello?"

No answer.

She opened the bathroom door and put her head round. Empty.

Closing the bathroom door behind her, Doreen went back to the balcony doors, stepped out onto the narrow platform and looked down.

It was then that she saw the body.

It lay on the gravel directly below the window, legs and arms splayed at odd angles, and Doreen knew instinctively that it was dead.

Her hands went to her mouth and she leaned over the balcony to look more closely.

She shuddered when she saw the face.

Surely not. It couldn't be. What would *he* be doing here? And, more importantly, why would he be lying dead on the gravel?

She leaned further out and then saw something else. Another man. But this one was alive.

He looked up at her.

"I've called the police," said Doreen's boss.

3

Whenever Garibaldi introduced himself he had a habit, after giving his name, of adding, "As in the hero of Italian unification and as in the biscuit. You know, the ones we used to call squashed flies." Not everyone got the historical reference, but most (especially those of a certain age) got the one about the biscuits.

But making a Garibaldi biscuit gag was one thing. Dressing up as one, he had discovered to his horror, was another thing entirely.

What on earth had possessed him?

Why hadn't he thrown on a red shirt and a pair of breeches and come as Giuseppe Garibaldi? That would have been the smart thing to do. But no. He'd squeezed himself between two cardboard box sides peppered with clumps of raisins and come as the biscuit.

He'd always hated fancy dress parties. They may have been forgivable in your youth, the kind of thing you did when you were a student, but for a fully grown adult to send an invitation asking you to come dressed as something to do with your name was nothing short of embarrassing. Not as embarrassing, perhaps, as accepting it, and definitely not as embarrassing as turning up to it dressed as a fucking Garibaldi biscuit.

And then, when he'd turned up, who was there to greet him? A trio of country singers, no less. And not just any trio. *The* trio. Dolly Parton. Linda Ronstadt. Emmylou Harris.

That was the first big surprise.

The second one was that no-one else had dressed up. No-one at all.

As soon as he realised, Garibaldi rushed to the loo to try to get out of his gear. But when he got there it was locked and no-one answered when he called out and banged on the door. He tried to pull the cardboard off him as he stood outside, but it wouldn't shift. What had been held on by tied bandages now seemed to be secured by glue. It just wouldn't come off.

He had no choice but to return to the party.

When he went back into the room the crowd parted on either side of him to make a walkway. He looked down it and there, on a stage at the end of the room, stood Dolly, Linda and Emmylou, carrying guitars and waving at him to come and join them.

"Garibaldi!" said Dolly. "Come and sing with us!"

He looked at the people on either side of him. They were clapping and cheering and urging him forward.

"Sing with you?" said Garibaldi. "But I can't sing!"

"Everyone can sing," said Linda.

"But what's the song?"

"It's your favourite," said Emmylou. "Come on up."

Garibaldi looked around. The crowd were urging him to join the singers and it seemed he now had no choice. He walked forwards slowly and climbed onto the stage where the three singers stepped back, encouraging him to stand in front of them, facing the room.

"What's the song?" said Garibaldi, turning to them again.

"The Garibaldi Song," said Emmylou, as she started to strum.

"The what?"

Dolly and Linda joined the strumming and all three started to sing — perfect three-part harmony.

My currants ain't squashed flies
They taste so sweet — unlike your lies
Like Garibaldi's country let's be one
Let's make love and have some fun

Yeah my name's Garibaldi, take a bite.
Have a taste of me tonight.

Garibaldi looked at the party guests. They were all facing the stage and singing along.

"The next verse is yours," said Dolly, stepping forward and giving him a nod.

"But I don't know the words," said Garibaldi, smiling awkwardly at the expectant faces.

"One, two, three," Emmylou gave another nod and stepped back.

Garibaldi took a deep breath and opened his mouth. Words came out but he couldn't hear them. He had no idea what he was singing.

"Jim?"

He turned to the three singers behind him. Had one of them called him?

"Jim?"

It was louder this time, but he could see that the voice had come from none of the singers.

"Jim?"

It was above him now. Someone was speaking over his head.

"Are you all right?"

He looked up. Rachel was leaning over him.

"Why are you talking about biscuits?"

Garibaldi rubbed his eyes. The party was over. The singers had gone. And a touch of his body reassured him that he was no longer dressed as a Garibaldi biscuit.

Another anxiety dream.

"Biscuits?" he said. "What was I saying?"

"It sounded like, 'I'm a biscuit, take a bite. Have a taste of me tonight'. But it wasn't very clear."

"Was I really talking?"

"Yeah. Talking, singing. I'm not sure what it was."

"I'm sorry. I thought I'd stopped."

"You haven't done it for a while. Is everything OK?"

"What day is it?"

"Monday."

"Monday? What time?"

"8.30."

"8.30! Shouldn't you be at work?"

"It's half-term."

He'd completely forgotten. He sometimes struggled with days of the week and occasionally lost track of the month, but when it came to school holidays he had no chance. They came with such frequency it was impossible to keep up.

Garibaldi yawned, rubbed his eyes and stretched. "Half-term. Of course it is."

"So I was thinking," said Rachel, "maybe we could go out somewhere tonight?"

"Sure. What do you fancy?"

"There's some jazz at the Bull's Head."

Jazz at the Bull's Head. Garibaldi's heart sank.

One of the things that had attracted him to Rachel had been her love of country music – more specifically, the way she had picked up one of his Townes Van Zandt CDs the morning after they first slept together, nodded her approval and announced that she'd always been a great fan. Since then Garibaldi had discovered that her musical taste, like his own, stretched well beyond country. Folk, rock, blues, even a bit of classical – these were areas of taste where there was considerable overlap. Jazz, though, had for a long time remained a genre about which Rachel was considerably more enthusiastic than him. He enjoyed *Kind of Blue* and *A Love Supreme* but that was about as far as he went. When it came to the contemporary stuff Rachel liked he remained to be convinced.

"OK. Let's do that," he said, trying to sound keen.

"But I'm open to suggestions."

Garibaldi smiled. A week of no school nights and Rachel was open to suggestions. Things were looking up. "I'm easy," he said. "And I'm all yours."

"Great."

Garibaldi's phone rang on the bedside table.

He looked at the screen. Deighton.

"You know that 'all yours' thing?" he said.

"Yeah?"

"I might have spoken too early."

4

Garibaldi cycled along the High Street past the Sun Inn and Barnes Pond into Church Road, took a left at the Red Lion traffic lights and headed up Castelnau towards Hammersmith Bridge. Ever since the bridge had been closed to traffic the road had been quiet, but today it was busy. Police cars and a forensic van were parked outside a cordoned-off house on the eastern side and a crowd of onlookers had gathered on the pavement opposite. Garibaldi locked his bike to some railings, took off his helmet and walked towards Gardner, who was standing beside the cordon tape in a forensic suit.

"Morning, boss."

"What have we got?"

"A body underneath an open window at the back of the house."

"Don't tell me. Did he fall or was he pushed?"

"Could be. But there are a couple of odd things about it."

"Tell me."

Gardner turned to the house. "First thing is, this is no ordinary house."

Garibaldi looked at it. It seemed ordinary enough to

him, or as ordinary as a multimillion-pound mansion on the favoured side of Castelnau could ever seem.

"Or should I say," said Gardner, "no ordinary owner."

Garibaldi raised his eyebrows.

"Jimmy Clark."

"Jimmy Clark?"

"Yeah. He called it in," said Gardner. "Found the body this morning in his back garden."

"What do we have on him?"

"Clark? He's—"

"Not Clark. The body."

Garibaldi shook his head. Did Gardner do it deliberately?

"Male. Probably late twenties, early thirties."

"ID?"

"Not yet."

"Phone?"

"Nothing. No cards or wallet. Nothing on him at all apart from his keys."

"You said there were a couple of odd things. First is this is Jimmy Clark's house. What's the second?"

"The second is he's wearing a mask."

"Who? Jimmy Clark?".

"No. The victim."

"A mask?"

"Yeah."

"What kind of mask?"

Gardner hesitated.

"Are we talking a sex thing here? Is it that kind of mask?" He could already see the headlines.

"When you say sex thing . . ." said Gardner.

"Do you want me to spell it out?"

"I know how to spell it."

Garibaldi looked at his sergeant, unsure whether she was joking.

"This mask," he said. "What kind of mask is it?"

"Mick Jagger."

"What?"

"It's a mask of Mick Jagger."

"What's he doing in a Mick Jagger mask?"

"We don't know. Seems there was a party here last night."

"What kind of party?"

"No idea."

"And have we taken this mask off to have a look at him?"

"Yeah."

"And . . . ?"

"As I said, no ID or anything. No idea who he is."

"Where's Jimmy Clark?"

"He's inside. Pretty traumatised."

Garibaldi took out his card, showed it to the uniform on the cordon, pulled on a forensic coat, cap and shoes and went into the house. He followed Gardner into the entrance hall and reception room where SOCOs were at work and through the French windows that opened onto the garden.

"Morning, Doc," said Garibaldi to the figure crouched over the body.

"Ah," said Martin Stevenson, looking up.

"What have we got?"

"What we've got," said Stevenson, "is a dead Rolling Stone."

He moved back from the body to allow Garibaldi a closer look. Garibaldi crouched down.

"Must admit," said Stevenson, "it's a first for me. Never had one in a mask before." He held up a transparent bag which contained the mask and turned the face to Garibaldi. "Good likeness, don't you think? Jagger as he was, of course. Not as he is now. But quite an impressive piece of kit. Must have cost a bob or two."

"The cleaner looked out," said Gardner, "and was absolutely convinced Mick Jagger was lying dead on the gravel. She took some persuading that he wasn't."

Garibaldi turned and looked up at the window. "Did the cleaner find him?"

"No," said Gardner. "Jimmy Clark did."

Garibaldi moved closer and looked down at the corpse. Jeans. Trainers. Shirt. Fleece. It could have been anyone. Any young man. He thought of Alfie.

"Is it as obvious as it seems?" He pointed up at the window.

"Too early to tell for sure, but his injuries seem compatible with a fall from height."

"Not that high, is it?" said Garibaldi.

"High enough. Especially if you land on your head, which it seems is what happened." Stevenson crouched down beside the body. "It also looks like he's been in some kind of fight." He pointed at the face. "Here, just below the eye, there's redness, as if someone's hit him."

"And there are signs of a struggle in the bedroom," said Gardner.

"So," said Garibaldi looking up at the open window, "he could have been in a fight up there and fallen out."

"Could have," said Stevenson. "We'll have a better idea when we've had a look at him."

Garibaldi looked down at the body. "Poor sod."

It was always a shock. Not just to confront another life gone but to consider the way it went and what would follow its departure. The grief. The pain.

And, in suspicious cases like this, the questions.

*

Jimmy Clark never looked like this on TV.

On screen he had the chisel-jawed looks and the winning charm of a fading matinee idol. Always cool and controlled, he gave the impression in whatever he was doing – hosting, quizzing, opining, playing – that all was right with the world, that things were OK in a quaint, almost old-fashioned way.

Now, unshaven and shocked, he seemed someone else entirely.

"How long will this take?" he asked.

"I don't know," said Garibaldi.

"I have things to do," said Jimmy.

"I'm sure you do, but I'm sure you also appreciate that with a dead body in your garden, you might need to change your plans. Perhaps you could tell me exactly what happened this morning: how you found it."

"I've already told you." Jimmy pointed at Gardner. "I told her everything."

"I'm afraid you're going to have to tell it again. And you'll also, of course, have to give a formal statement."

Jimmy Clark gave a slow nod. "I can't tell you how shocked I am. I mean – I don't even know who he is. Do you?"

"Not yet, no," said Garibaldi. "Nor do we know why he was wearing a Mick Jagger mask."

"Ah, yes," said Jimmy. "The mask."

"Bit strange, isn't it?"

"It is, yes, but – look, detective—"

"Detective Inspector Garibaldi. As in . . ."

Garibaldi stopped himself. This was neither the time nor the place – even if it was the kind of joke Clark might make himself.

"Look, Inspector, before I take you through the events of

this morning, there's something I think I need to tell you. I know absolutely nothing about this man or what happened to him. I have no idea how he got into the garden and I have absolutely no idea how he died, but when it comes to the mask . . ."

Clark gave an exaggerated roll of his eyes and puffed out his cheeks — the kind of would-you-believe it expression he often wore on TV.

"The thing is, that mask is mine."

"It's yours?"

Garibaldi saw new headlines.

"Yes. I was wearing it earlier in the evening."

"You were wearing a Mick Jagger mask?"

"I was performing in the Bull's Head. Look, I need to tell you this but before I do, can you let me know what's going to happen—" he pointed towards the garden "—out there?"

"Your house is now officially a crime scene, Jimmy. We don't yet know what happened to the man in your garden, but until we do we have to treat it as a suspicious death. Scenes of Crime Officers will be here for some time."

"OK, well it's like this." Jimmy took a breath and looked from side to side before clearing his throat and addressing Garibaldi and Gardner as if he were talking to camera. "Yesterday evening I was performing in a band at the Bull's Head, a band called the Okay Boomers. There were five of us, and — look, do I have to tell you this? I mean, is there any way this can be kept quiet?"

"Kept quiet?" said Garibaldi. "We can try, but a man has been found dead in your garden in a Mick Jagger mask that you claim is yours. Might be difficult to keep a lid on it, don't you think?"

"I just think the others need to know. They need to know what's happened."

"The others?"

"The band. They were all here last night – we came back here after the gig."

"For a party?"

"For a few drinks."

"Who else is in this band, Jimmy?"

"I suppose you have to know."

"You suppose right."

Jimmy took a deep sigh. "There were five of us. Larry, Hazel, Craig and Charlie. And me, of course."

"Could we have their full names?"

"Of course. Larry Benyon, Hazel Bloom, Craig Francis and Charlie Brougham."

Garibaldi struggled to hide his surprise.

"We were all wearing masks," said Jimmy. "I was in a Mick Jagger mask and the others—"

"You were in masks?"

"Masks and costumes. We didn't want anyone to know who we were. We wanted to keep our identities hidden. I can explain it all."

"I'm sure you can, but before you do, let me get this straight. The band were all here last night after your gig?"

"That's right."

"And this band, the Okay Boomers, had played at the Bull's Head wearing masks?"

Jimmy Clark nodded.

"I see. So you were wearing a Mick Jagger mask, and the others . . .?"

"Larry was Bob Dylan, Hazel was Debbie Harry, Craig was Paul McCartney and Charlie was David Bowie."

Garibaldi scribbled down the names. "And these masks . . . where are they?"

"Well, as you know, the Jagger mask is outside in the

garden. As for the others, they're on a table in the hall, together with the costumes. I keep them after every concert."

"Every concert? You mean you've done this before?"

Jimmy raised his eyebrows and gave a tight-lipped smile. "Several times."

"OK," said Garibaldi, "so these other masks, the ones you wore yesterday. Could I have a look at them?"

"Of course."

Jimmy got up and walked to the door. Garibaldi looked at Gardner, gave a disbelieving whistle and looked at his notes to check he hadn't been imagining what he'd just heard.

"I don't believe it!" said Jimmy coming back from the hall. "They're not there. The masks. They've gone!"

5

DCI Deighton stood at the front of the incident room. Behind her on the board were two photos: one of the supine corpse in Jimmy Clark's garden in a Mick Jagger mask, the other of the dead man's face with the mask removed.

"This morning," said Deighton, "the body of a man was found at the house of Jimmy Clark, TV celebrity. Clark himself discovered the body at 8.00 am lying on the gravel by his lawn below an open first floor balcony window. No ID and we have yet to confirm the cause of death, but early indications suggest it may have been caused by a fall from the window. Marks on the face and body also suggest he may have been in a physical confrontation. Until we have the pathologist's report we won't know anything for sure but it looks as though the deceased was involved in a fight or struggle before falling or, as the old cliché would have it, being pushed. But there's something very odd about this victim. When he was discovered he was wearing a mask." Deighton turned and pointed to the picture on the board. "A Mick Jagger mask."

Garibaldi sensed the room's raised eyebrows.

"It's a mask that Jimmy Clark was wearing on Sunday

afternoon when he performed in the Bull's Head with a band called the Okay Boomers. They all wore masks and costumes and behind those masks were, wait for it ...four other celebrities. Larry Benyon. Hazel Bloom. Charlie Brougham. And Craig Francis."

Deighton paused, allowing the team to take it in.

"Difficult to believe, I know, but it seems that after the concert this band all went back to Jimmy Clark's. All five of them – and some of their partners — were there until late. Then this morning the man was found. Jimmy Clark claims never to have seen him before. So what we have is a secret masked celebrity band and a suspicious death at the house where the band were having a party. Once this is out, God knows what will happen." Deighton raised her eyebrows. "Any questions?"

Gardner's hand went up. "If the mask was Jimmy Clark's, what was it doing on the victim's face?"

"We don't know yet," said Deighton. "There will obviously be a close forensic examination of the mask. Whether that throws up an answer I can't say."

"Do we know what kind of party it was?" said DC Hodson. "I mean celebrities, showbiz ..."

"Yeah," said DC MacLean. "Like the one where that bloke was found in the swimming pool. Whose was it?"

"I have no idea what kind of party it was," said Deighton, "but we'll need to find out."

"And we have no evidence that this is murder?" said DC MacLean.

"Not yet. We're treating the death as suspicious."

"This band," said Gardner. "All sounds a bit weird, doesn't it? A whole load of celebrities wearing masks and costumes. A bit like *The Masked Singer*."

"The what?" said Deighton.

"*The Masked Singer*," said Gardner. "It's a TV show. There are these singers and ..."

She cast a nervous glance round the room, as if considering whether displaying her intimate knowledge of the peak time Saturday evening TV show would do much to enhance her reputation.

"Yes?" said Deighton. "There are these singers ...?"

"There are these celebrities who come on in costumes and wearing a mask and they sing a song and you, I mean the panel, they have to guess who they are." Gardner looked round the room again. "I've only seen it, you know, in passing."

"I've no idea whether it's like that," said Deighton, "not having seen it myself."

"I spoke to Jimmy Clark about the band," said Garibaldi, jumping in to rescue Gardner. "The masks and costumes were a way of keeping their identities hidden. The Bull's Head's pretty small and if word got out that that lot were playing there together you can imagine what would happen."

"Still sounds a pretty odd thing to do," said Gardner. "Famous people doing stuff like that. Asking for trouble, isn't it?"

"Exactly," said Garibaldi. "And that explains the disguise. Each of them wore a mask of a big pop star from back in the day. Larry Benyon was Bob Dylan, Hazel Bloom was Debbie Harry, Charlie Brougham was David Bowie and Craig Francis was Paul McCartney. Jimmy Clark, as you already know, was Mick Jagger."

"How do you sing through masks?" said DC Hodson. "Must be really uncomfortable."

"Jimmy Clark told me at great length," said Garibaldi. "Seems he's unable to tell anyone anything in any other way. He says the masks were no ordinary masks. Made at great expense – no surprise there, given the Okay Boomers' collective wealth. Specially moulded to fit each of them with ventilation, space to breathe. You name it, they had it."

"If the others are like Jimmy Clark's mask," said Gardner, "they'll be very convincing. Clark's cleaner saw the body from the open window and she was convinced a young Mick Jagger was lying dead on the gravel."

"So where are we on this?" said Deighton, turning to look at the two pictures on the board behind her. "Not very far is the answer. We've launched a house to house on Castelnau. We're checking Jimmy Clark's CCTV and other cameras. But it's all pretty thin at the moment. No ID. No phone. So we need to keep an eye on missing persons. And we also need to talk to the Okay Boomers."

"There's one other thing about these masks," said Garibaldi. "And that's that they seem to have disappeared. Not the Jagger one, that was on the body, but Clark can't find the others. It may be nothing, but on the other hand . . ."

"Exactly," said Deighton. "On the other hand. We keep an open mind and we assume nothing." She looked round the room again. "Right," she said decisively. "Let's . . ."

"Let's get on it," said Garibaldi, finishing the line under his breath.

6

"You know those Hollywood tours when you get to see all the stars' houses?"

Garibaldi looked at Gardner from the passenger seat. "What about them?"

"This is a bit like one of those, isn't it?"

Garibaldi laughed. "I don't think so. This is Barnes, not Hollywood."

"But all these celebrities..."

"Yeah, all these celebrities. Well, let's hope they can tell us something, because at the moment we've got nothing."

"Yeah, but you've got to be positive, haven't you?" said Gardner.

Ever since she had taken up with Chris, 'positive' had become one of Gardner's favourite words. Never had Garibaldi known his sergeant so upbeat, and although he felt nothing but sceptical derision for her new man's self-improvement claptrap he had the good sense to keep his opinion to himself and enjoy Gardner's new-found happiness. The bad days of Kevin (who cheated on her) and Tim (who made her feel inferior) seemed a distant memory, and, while stopping short of believing her claim that Chris could be The One, Garibaldi was glad for her.

"So that's where they played, eh?" Gardner pointed at the Bull's Head as they drove past it onto Barnes High Street.

"Yeah," said Garibaldi. "Famous for its jazz."

"You been to any there?"

"A bit."

"Not much of a jazz fan myself," said Gardner, turning down Station Road and taking a right into Vine Road.

Garibaldi was about to ask why, but the barriers at the two level crossings were up and they had soon pulled up on the gravel drive of a large house set back from the road.

Discussion of their shared aversion would have to wait.

Even though he had kept himself in shape and looked exceptionally lean and fit for a man in his sixties, it was difficult to think of Larry Benyon as a professional footballer who had performed at the highest level. Whenever Garibaldi had seen him play on TV he had always seemed large and even in his subsequent screen incarnations, first as a sports presenter and more recently as a political pundit, he hadn't seemed as small as he looked in the flesh. Maybe that's what TV did to you – made you larger than you actually were. From what he'd learned in his few dealings with the famous it seemed an appropriate metaphor.

"Thank you for finding the time," said Garibaldi.

"No problem," said Larry. In jeans, jumper and trainers, he sported close-cropped greying hair, a goatee beard and fashionably large glasses. He was trying to appear relaxed but Garibaldi could tell that a visit from the police had unnerved him.

"We understand that you were performing with Jimmy Clark and some others yesterday afternoon in the Bull's Head."

Larry threw back his head and laughed. "So our cover's blown! Is that what this is all about?"

"Not quite, Larry We also understand that after this event you were at a party at Jimmy Clark's house in Castelnau."

"That's right—" Larry broke off and looked from Garibaldi to Gardner. "Has something happened? Is Jimmy OK?"

"Jimmy's fine," said Garibaldi. "But the same can't be said for the body that was found at his house this morning."

"A body?"

"A man was found dead in his garden."

"What? I mean...who is he?"

"The victim has yet to be identified."

"What happened?"

"We're not sure. He may have fallen from a window but we're treating his death as suspicious."

"I don't understand. I—"

Larry looked around the room. He started to speak several times but stopped himself, as if he couldn't think of what to say.

He turned back to Garibaldi and Gardner, his expression one of wide-eyed innocence. "How does this involve me?"

"We're not saying it does. We're just trying to find out a few things. You see, there was something very odd about this man when his body was discovered this morning."

Garibaldi paused, examining Larry Benyon's expression in the silence that followed.

"What was odd about it?"

"The man was wearing a mask. A Mick Jagger mask. To be more specific, Jimmy Clark's Mick Jagger mask, the one he was wearing on stage at the Bull's Head when he performed with the Okay Boomers."

"What the f—?"

"Strange, isn't it?"

"I don't believe it. That's crazy. I mean, what—?"

"Did you see anything unusual at the party?"

"Like a man in a Jagger mask being thrown out of a window?"

Garibaldi fixed him with a steely stare. Benyon may have been regarded as the nation's liberal conscience, but he'd already taken against him.

"Look," said Larry, in a tone that suggested he realised his comment had been misjudged. "This is obviously a terrible thing. Absolutely awful. And I will, of course, help in whatever way I can."

"What time did you leave the party, Larry?"

"You don't think I'm involved, do you? I don't know anything about this."

"We'd just like to know what time you left."

"I can't remember exactly. When we finished the gig we all came back to Jimmy's, had some drinks and a bite to eat. I must have left at about one."

"Tell me, Larry, who was at this party?"

"What? You want all their names?"

"That would be helpful."

"It was the band—"

"The band," said Garibaldi. He took out his notebook and pencil. He always liked to jot things down. It made people nervous and he learned more from nervous people. "Just remind me again of who was in it, could you?"

"I don't believe it!" Larry waved his hands in front of him, like a ref turning down a penalty claim. "We were only doing it for a laugh. We didn't want anyone to know who we were. That was the whole point!"

Garibaldi waited, pencil poised. "The band, Larry."

"OK. Well it's Jimmy."

"Jimmy Clark?"

Larry nodded. Garibaldi knew it was Jimmy Clark, in the same way that he knew who else was in the band, but asking for information and confirmation of details was another way of establishing his authority. In his experience, the more important the person he was interviewing, the more he needed to do it.

"And there was Hazel, that's Hazel Bloom, Charlie Brougham, Craig Francis. And me."

Garibaldi jotted down the names. "So the band were at the party. Is that all?"

"Some partners were there as well."

"Partners. I see. Could you tell me who they were?"

"Jimmy's wife wasn't there, she was away, and Hazel's husband wasn't there either, but Charlie's girlfriend and Craig's wife were there. I ...I don't have a partner." He paused. "At the moment," he added, making it sound as though he was merely taking a temporary break, an actor resting between jobs.

"And these partners were at the Bull's Head?"

Larry nodded.

"So they obviously knew all about the Okay Boomers, the whole set up."

"They did, yes. It was just us and our partners. The whole idea was to keep our identities hidden."

"I see," said Garibaldi. "And it's remarkable that you managed it. How many times have you played?"

"That was our fifth."

"And no-one else had found out?"

Larry smiled. "It seemed not. We were pretty pleased. We decided right at the beginning that as soon as we were unmasked we'd stop. So I guess that time has come. No more masked band. Shame."

Garibaldi leaned forward. "I think the suspicious death of a young man is a higher priority for us at the moment than the future of your masked band."

"Of course it is. I'm sorry." Larry had the decency to look embarrassed. "This has come as a bit of a shock. I'm really not sure what to say." He tilted his head to one side as if he was weighing something up. "Look, I'm sorry I said that about it being the end of the band. Of course it's not as important as someone's death. It's just that it was a high-risk thing, some might say a foolish thing, but we all enjoyed it."

Larry's phone rang. He fished it out of his pocket, checked the screen and silenced it.

"I'm sorry. Look, I can't tell you how shocked I am by this. Anything I can do to help," he said. "Anything."

"Just to confirm, then. When you were at Jimmy Clark's last night after your gig you didn't notice anything odd?"

Larry shook his head.

"And the only people at the party were the band members and some of their partners?"

"That's right. You'll be talking to the others I presume?"

"We will."

"Poor Jimmy. What a terrible thing to happen in his house. Is he okay?"

Garibaldi shrugged. "A bit shocked, but then you'd expect that, wouldn't you? It would be odd if he weren't."

Garibaldi gave Gardner a nod and closed his notebook. "Well, thank you for your time, Larry . We were lucky to find you in."

"I'm working tonight but, yes, I'm free most of today."

"I'm sure we won't need to talk to you again today, but we'll be asking you for a statement."

"A statement? I see." Larry hesitated. "They're going to love this, aren't they?"

"They?"

"The media. The papers."

"We've said nothing yet, but I've no doubt it will receive some coverage. One more thing, this mask you wore yesterday. It was . . ." Garibaldi flicked through his notebook.

"Bob Dylan."

"That's right. Bob Dylan. Do you have the mask?"

"No. Jimmy keeps all the masks and the outfits."

"I see."

Garibaldi took a card from his pocket. "Well, if anything occurs to you, or if you need to get in touch, do give me a call."

Larry led Garibaldi and Gardner into the spacious entrance hall and opened the door for them.

As Garibaldi walked down the gravel drive he turned back to the house and saw Larry Benyon looking at the card he held in his hand, as if he thought it had been given to him by mistake.

7

It was difficult to tell whether Hazel Bloom looked shattered because she'd just been working out or because she had just been told about the body in Jimmy Clark's garden. Clad in Lycra, hair tied back in a ponytail and anxiously biting her lip, she looked more like a nervous schoolgirl than a famous TV comedy star.

"I don't believe it," she said. "And you have no idea who he is?"

"Not yet, no," said Garibaldi.

"And he was wearing Jimmy's mask?"

"Mick Jagger."

"It doesn't make sense. Why?"

"That's what we're trying to find out."

"And when you say it looks like he fell...I mean, are you suspecting anything else?"

"We're keeping an open mind," said Garibaldi. "At the moment we're talking to everyone who was at Jimmy Clark's last night after your..."

"After our gig. Looks like it's the end of that, doesn't it? Shame. There's something empowering about being behind a mask, don't you think? I guess I should know, having done impressions for so long, but the thing about impressions is there's always this tension. The audience knows it's you but it knows simultaneously that it's you being, or trying to be, someone else. With a mask all they see is the someone else. You're hidden. Sorry, I'm rambling, aren't I? Spouting off intellectual crap. I always do when I'm nervous."

"Tell me, Miss Bloom."

"Hazel, please. I hate Miss Bloom. Always reminds me of Molly Bloom. Whoops, there I go again. Couldn't resist a *Ulysses* reference, could I?"

"Tell me about these masks and costumes. When did you all put them on?"

Hazel looked out of the first-floor window of her house on The Terrace. It overlooked the Thames; Barnes Bridge lay to the left, the Bull's Head a short walk to the right.

"We were always going to stop, you know. As soon as people found out who we were we were going to put an end to it."

"The masks—"

"Of course. When did we put them on? Well, we all met at Jimmy's late Sunday afternoon and tried the masks and costumes on to make sure they fitted OK – which they did. They're impressive pieces of kit. When we were ready we ordered cars to take us down to the Bull. And before we left Jimmy's we put our masks on and we all wore hoodies with the hoods pulled up over our heads. No-one could see our faces at all. In fact, it would have been difficult even to see our masks. Then, when we were dropped off we slipped into the pub's side entrance and went straight to the Jazz Room. We knew the drill because we'd done exactly the same thing before. And when we were all there we got into our costumes and kept the doors to the music room locked." Hazel broke off and let out a sigh. "It all seems silly when you describe it, but if I'm honest it was all a bit of a thrill, like we were robbing a bank or something or like that Netflix show *Money Heist*, the one where they—"

"Where they all wear Salvador Dali masks," said Garibaldi.

Hazel looked taken aback, as if surprised by the quick cultural reference.

"Exactly. Anyway, we were in the Jazz Room having a sound check, still in masks and hoodies and then before they opened the doors we went backstage and stayed out of sight until it was time to go on. And then hoodies down and on we went."

"I see," said Garibaldi, making a quick scribble in his notebook. It was exactly that – a squiggle. He liked to make those he interviewed think they had said something of significance. "So what happened at the end of the concert?"

"We went backstage when we finished and waited for the room to empty."

"With your masks still on?"

"Yeah. Then when we knew the room was empty it was hoodies up again and we slipped out the side entrance and got cars back to Jimmy's place."

"And what about the gear?" said Gardner. "Who sorted that out? The drums, the instruments, the mics?"

"Jimmy paid people to do everything. They booked the venue, delivered the instruments, set them up. And they took everything down afterwards when we'd left."

Garibaldi looked at the squiggles in his notebook and then turned to the window. It was a great view of the Thames.

"Your partner wasn't there," he said, turning back to Hazel.

"No, he was away. Couldn't make it."

"Is he here?"

"I'm afraid not. He's at work."

Garibaldi raised his eyebrows. "What does he do?"

"He's a film producer."

"I see. Well, we may need to speak to you again and we will, of course, need a statement."

"A statement?" Hazel looked shocked. "You don't think I have anything to do with this do you? I mean, we don't even know who this man is. I find the whole thing...well, to be honest, I don't really know how I find it at all. I'm baffled."

"One final question. Your mask. Do you have it with you?

"The mask? No. Jimmy always kept them. He's got all of them. He's got the costumes as well."

"So you took them off when you got to his place?"

"That's right."

"And you gave them to Jimmy?"

"Not the masks. Not straight away. We were larking about with them throughout the evening."

"Larking about?"

"Trying each other's on, that kind of thing."

"So you put on each other's masks?"

"Yeah. We were in, let's say, high spirits."

"Drunk?"

"Not drunk, no."

"I see."

"And there were no drugs before you ask. We're all far too old for that kind of thing."

Garibaldi jotted down a note. "So, this Mick Jagger mask. You all tried it on?"

"I can't say for sure, but we were putting them on and doing impersonations. I remember doing 'Brown Sugar'.

And then I put on Bowie and did 'Starman' and then — but you don't want to know all that, do you?"

"Tell me, Hazel, what did you do with the masks when you'd finished larking about with them?"

"We left them with Jimmy. He's keeper of the masks. Or rather he was."

"Keeper of the masks? Was that an official title?"

Hazel smiled. "No, but I think he thought of himself as being in charge. Jimmy's like that. He thought the best way of keeping our identities secret was for all the stuff to be kept in one place. So he kept the masks and the costumes."

"I see. So when you left all the masks were where?"

Hazel furrowed a brow. "I think they were on a table in the hall, but I'm not sure."

"Is that all the masks?"

"I can't remember. Why do you ask?"

"I ask because Jimmy couldn't find them."

"Really?"

"He thinks they might have been taken."

"Taken? Who would have done that?"

"We're asking ourselves the same question."

"Well, that's a shame. I was very fond of Debbie. I was hoping to keep her."

"Hoping to keep her?"

"Yes, I mean – look, I didn't take it if that's what you're thinking. It's just that of all the masks I wore she was definitely my favourite."

"Of all the masks you wore?"

"We've performed several times."

"In different masks?"

Hazel laughed. "The Okay Boomers were our most recent incarnation."

"So what were you before?"

Hazel screwed up her face and looked to one side. "What were we before? Let's see. Well first of all we were The Presidents. And then ..."

Garibaldi reached for his notebook.

"What I don't get," said Gardner, as she drove back to the station, "is why they did it at all. Why do a series of low-key gigs wearing masks when if they'd been public about it they could have got a massive crowd? I mean, what did they charge to see them at The Bull? Fifteen quid? Jimmy said they were giving the money to charity but if they'd gone public they could have filled some massive place and given their charity a whole lot more."

"Maybe they liked the anonymity," said Garibaldi.

"If you're a star and you want anonymity you stay at home."

"Or you go out in disguise, which is exactly what they did. And now that they've been uncovered they're stopping, so maybe it really was all about the fun of playing rather than some publicity stunt."

"Publicity stunt? None of that lot need publicity."

Garibaldi nodded. "Exactly. Which makes me think it's what they've said it was. They wanted to play and have a bit of fun. And they went to one hell of a lot of trouble to do it. They've done it five times, each time under a different name and each time wearing different masks and costumes." Garibaldi took out his notebook and leafed through some pages. "First they were The Presidents – Obama, Clinton, Kennedy, Reagan and Trump masks. Don't know who the poor sod was who had to be Trump. Then they were the Comedians – Laurel and Hardy. Morecambe and Wise. Charlie Chaplin. Then The Players – that's players as in players of sport. So, George Best. Muhammad Ali. John McEnroe. Tiger Woods. Pelé."

"So, Larry Benyon didn't wear a mask of himself then?"

"Seems their sense of irony didn't stretch that far. And then, before they played as the Okay Boomers, they were The Animals. Not to be confused with the Alan Price sixties band of the same name but real animals. So, dog, cat, horse, cow, lion."

"A lot of effort," said Gardner.

"Yeah, all of the masks and costumes specially made. No expense spared. As you say, a lot of effort."

"Do you reckon they're linked to the death?"

"I don't know," said Garibaldi. "But there's something about these celebrities."

"What do you mean?"

"You can't work out whether they're talking or performing."

"Oh well, we all perform, don't we?" said Gardner. "We do it all the time."

"You're right," he said. "We do."

"Just like we all wear masks."

Garibaldi gave a sideways glance at his driver, struck by the profundity of her insight, and wondering what it was about the whole idea of masks that was making him feel uneasy.

8

Craig Francis's phone rang as he walked over Hammersmith Bridge.

He looked at the screen and took the call. "Hey, Jimmy."

"Craig, listen. There's something I need to tell you."

He could tell from the voice it was something serious.

"Have the police been in touch?"

"The police?" said Craig. "What's happened?"

"You're not going to believe this. This morning I went downstairs, looked out of the window and ...and there was a body."

"A body?"

"A dead body. A man."

"What?"

"On the gravel in the garden. It looked like it had fallen from the window."

"You're joking!"

"I've never seen this man before! The police made me feel like I was responsible! And they want to talk to everyone."

"Everyone?"

"Everyone who was at my place last night after the gig. They're treating the death as suspicious."

"But I don't know anything about it. This man – who is he?"

"I have no idea and nor do the police. But the thing is – and you're really not going to believe this – the thing is this man, whoever he is, was wearing one of our masks."

"What?"

"He was wearing my Mick Jagger mask."

"What? What was he doing in that?"

"It's a complete fucking disaster. My house is now a crime scene. It's crawling with police in white suits, photographers, all kinds of people tramping around."

Craig looked down at the river, his mind struggling to process what he had heard.

"What did you do with your mask, Craig?"

"I left it on the table in the hall like you asked me to."

"Are you sure?"

"Positive. Why do you ask?"

"I can't find any of the masks. I think someone's taken them."

"Taken them? Why would anyone do that?"

"Exactly. Why?"

"Have you looked everywhere?"

"Of course I've looked everywhere! What do you think I am, some kind of idiot?"

"No. I just—"

"I'm sorry, Craig. I don't mean to snap, but this whole thing—"

"I don't get it. Why was he wearing your mask? What the fuck's going on?"

"Look, give me a call when you've spoken to the police, will you?"

"Sure."

Craig hung up and walked to the end of Hammersmith Bridge.

Playing in the masked band had always been a high-risk venture, but he had never imagined a risk like this.

And he had never felt less like going to Birmingham, let alone going to Birmingham to address a conference of teachers.

Charlie Brougham knew the film was shit. He knew it as soon as he read the script and when he found out who he was starring opposite – not to mention who was directing – he should have baled.

But his agent had insisted it would be a good thing to keep himself in the public eye and Charlie, despite his protestations that he had no need to get involved in anything that was clearly so substandard, knew inside that his agent was right. In his darker moments, many of them in the middle of the night when he would wake up and be unable to get back to sleep, he found himself confronting a disturbing and unpalatable truth – that his fame now existed mainly in the past, that his reputation resided in films over thirty years old.

Everyone aged – of that he was well aware – and he knew that, short of pulling some Dorian Gray stunt, there was nothing he could do about it. He had to accept that the high-cheekboned, dimple-chinned, twinkle-eyed, floppy-haired stills that adorned the walls of his three-storey house next to Barnes Pond came from a different country. And he also had to accept that the boyish charm which had landed him so many romantic leads had been replaced by something more seedy – he needed no mirror to be reminded of how his face had puffed out, how the dimple was now hidden in folds of flesh and how what were once laughter lines now communicated something much sadder.

He liked to think his recent appearances as ageing villains and philanderers constituted some kind of reinvention, but critics had seen them as more of a degradation, and, as he stepped off the set of *Coming to Terms*, having just finished a scene in which his East End criminal had reunited with his old gang, he felt they could be right.

He checked his phone as he walked outside and saw a message from Hazel asking him to call.

He dialled her number.

"Charlie, thanks for getting back."

"Everything OK?"

"Actually, no. It's not."

"What's happened?"

"You're not going to believe this, but Jimmy woke up this morning and found a dead man in his garden."

"What? I mean, who?"

"We don't know yet, but there's something odd about the whole thing."

"Too fucking right there is. A dead man in his garden!"

"What's odd is that when he was found he was in one of our masks."

"One of our masks?"

"Jimmy's Mick Jagger mask."

"What the fuck was he doing in that?"

"I have no idea. But the police want to speak to all of us."

"The police? Why?"

"They're treating the death as suspicious."

"But I don't know anything about this."

"Nor do I, but they want to see us. We were all there last night, and the mask . . ."

"That doesn't mean we—"

"Do you know where your mask is, Charlie?"

"I left it at Jimmy's. Why?"

"Jimmy can't find them. He thinks someone's taken them."

"Why would anyone take the masks?"

"God knows. This whole thing – I really can't believe it. But, look, let me know how it goes with the police."

"Sure."

Charlie hung up. Another ridiculous scene in a crap movie suddenly seemed the least of his problems.

9

Whenever Garibaldi and Deighton caught each other's eye, especially at moments like this when it was just the two of them in her office, Garibaldi was acutely aware of what they knew about each other. He had no idea whether his boss ever regretted telling him so much about her private life, but he knew he regretted telling her so much about his.

He had no idea what came over him on those evenings when they went out for a drink together, but ever since the first one when he had told Deighton why he didn't drive they had become occasions for increasingly intimate revelations.

At work, Deighton had always been open with him about his problems – the depression that had led to his time off work a few years back – and, in the privacy of her office, she would enquire after his well-being. But in the discreet wine bar that had become their venue of choice, away from the constraints of the station and the possibility of interruption, her questioning had been more direct, and Garibaldi had reciprocated by becoming bolder himself. So, as Deighton discovered more about him so had he discovered more about her: in particular, about her relationship with Abigail.

That both he and his boss should be married to teachers

and that both should be some years older than their partners gave them much to bond over, and on their most recent night out, they had spent a good deal of time talking about how the levels of stress and irregular working hours in a teacher-detective relationship could have detrimental effects. When Deighton had suggested that such effects could be felt most obviously in the bedroom Garibaldi had not known where to look.

Maybe it was that disarmingly personal revelation, one that had sparked parts of Garibaldi's imagination into alarming productivity, that led him to make his own – a confession that he had regretted ever since.

Now, in Deighton's office, such wine-bar intimacies seemed a long way off.

Deighton hooked off her reading glasses, turned away from the screen and looked at him across her desk.

"You've spoken to the band?"

"Apart from Charlie Brougham and Craig Francis. I'm seeing them later."

"What did they all have to say?"

Garibaldi shook his head. "Nothing. No idea who he was and no idea why he was in that mask."

"Any suggestion he could have been a burglar?"

"No signs of forced entry. And Jimmy Clark says he doesn't think anything's missing. Apart from one thing, that is."

"What's that?"

"The masks."

Deighton furrowed her brow. "So the body's found in a mask and all the other masks go missing."

"Yeah," said Garibaldi. "Strange, isn't it?"

"Anything more from the scene?"

"Signs of a struggle or fight in the bedroom near the

balcony doors above where the body was found. A broken vase and glass on the floor. If there was a struggle that might explain the bruising on the body. And an early report on the mask says it's covered in prints and DNA, which is no surprise."

"Why not?"

"Hazel Bloom says they were all trying it on. They'd all had a few drinks and were, in her words, in high spirits. They were putting on each other's masks and doing impersonations."

"Impersonations?"

"Of the singer whose mask they were wearing. So Hazel Bloom put on the Jagger mask and sang 'Brown Sugar', then she put on the Bowie mask and sang 'Starman', and then—"

Deighton held up her hand. "OK. I get the picture. We'll need their prints and DNA for purposes of elimination."

"Sure, but that mask – I still can't work out why the victim was in it. First of all, how did he get hold of it? And, second, why did he put it on?"

"Anything from Clark's CCTV?"

"Nothing. Nothing from the camera out back trained on the garden and all we've got from the front one are the band arriving and going."

"Did they all leave at the same time?"

"No. Pretty staggered. The first left at about midnight, the last about an hour later."

"And no internal cameras?"

"Nothing," said Garibaldi.

"There's a side gate as well, isn't there? A tradesman's entrance."

Tradesman's entrance. Garibaldi couldn't remember the last time he'd heard the phrase – or at least not in its polite usage.

"There is," said Garibaldi. "Leads to a side door into the house and to the garden. But no cameras there."

"Anything from house to house?"

Garibaldi shook his head. "We're struggling. Sweet FA and dealing with the oldest cliché in the book."

"Which one?"

"Did he fall or was he pushed?"

"I see." Deighton picked up her reading glasses and turned to her computer. "Well, let's get on it."

"OK," said Garibaldi, heading for the door. "I'll go and see the last of the Okay Boomers." He paused at the door and turned. "Should be a film, shouldn't it?"

"Sorry?" said Deighton, her eyes on her screen.

"Last of the Okay Boomers. Great title for a film."

There was a knock on the door. Garibaldi opened it and stepped back. Gardner put her head round. "We've got a missing person report," she said. "The description matches."

Deighton stood up. "Who's called in?"

"A woman who hasn't heard from her son. Very unlike him. No answer on his phone. None of his friends know where he is."

"Where is she?"

"She's coming in. We'll get ready for an identification."

"Poor woman," said Deighton.

Poor woman, thought Garibaldi, but he knew that both of them, underneath the sincere feelings of sympathy, were also feeling a twinge of excitement at the prospect of a significant development.

Even after so many years, the emotions the job triggered still surprised him.

10

Craig Francis had given readings to all kinds of people in all kinds of places and had long ago come to the conclusion that conferences were the worst. And the worst conferences were those for teachers, especially when, as had been the case today, the reading was followed by a Q&A and he ended up fielding a string of silly questions. The truth was he loved reading his poems but he hated talking about them.

The same could be said of his experience with the masked band. He had enjoyed the performances (he wouldn't go so far as to say he'd ever loved them), but answering questions about it was a different thing entirely.

And that's what he was doing now, as he faced the two detectives in his living room – DS Gardner, a youngish woman with a nice smile and an older man who had introduced himself as DI Garibaldi with a weak joke about biscuits and Italian unification. Clearly a comedian.

"So," said Garibaldi. "You played in the band several times. Is that right?"

"That's right," said Craig, "but I'm not sure how that's relevant."

"A tricky thing relevance. It has a habit of surprising you. Sometimes you don't see it at first."

Clearly a philosopher as well.

"Look," said Craig, "I don't understand why we need to talk about that. A man's been found dead at Jimmy Clark's. Isn't that what we need to talk about?"

"Of course we do. But the thing is the man in question was wearing the mask worn by Jimmy Clark during your performance at the Bull's Head."

"That doesn't mean his death's linked to ...to us."

"I'm not sure, Craig, but at the moment we know that he was found in the morning at a house where the previous night there had been a post-gig party for your band. So asking about the band seems a logical thing to do, wouldn't you agree?"

There was something about his tone – a kind of irony-laced condescension – that Craig found difficult to take.

"The thing is," Garibaldi continued, "this story's going to be everywhere and I can't imagine that the two – your band and the dead body – aren't going to be linked. You know how the media works."

Craig let out a sigh. He knew only too well.

"This masked band of yours," said Garibaldi. "You've had several incarnations."

"That's right. The Presidents. The Players. The Comedians. Animals. And then the Okay Boomers."

"A lot of masks and costumes."

"Yeah. A lot of masks and costumes."

"And was it fun?"

Craig nodded. Now wasn't the time to share his misgivings. "It was, yes. Mainly because no-one knew who we were. We always said we'd stop the moment everyone found out. So I guess the fun's over now."

"A bit like that man's life."

"Look, I really don't know anything about this man. And it seems nor do you. We don't even have a name."

The man took out his notebook and flicked through a few pages. "I understand your wife was with you at the gig and at the party afterwards."

"Gina? Yes she was. And she's as shocked as I am, as we all are."

"Is she in?"

"Yes. Shall I get her?"

"Please, but before you do there's nothing at all about the events of last night that you feel you need to tell us?"

"You mean tell you before my wife comes in?"

Garibaldi nodded.

"What kind of thing did you have in mind?" said Craig, beginning to lose his patience. "I have nothing to add."

Craig got up and went into the kitchen to get Gina. He closed the door behind him so they couldn't be overheard.

"This is terrible," he said in a whisper.

"What's the problem?"

"They're making me feel guilty, as if I know something I'm not telling them."

"And do you?"

"Of course not! What could I possibly know?"

Gina's look was one with which Craig was painfully familiar; the raised eyebrows and knowing smile silently suggested all those times in the past when they had known things they needed to keep to themselves.

"They want to see you," he said.

"See me? Why?"

"Because you were at the party. You were at Jimmy's."

Gina threw her hands wide. "But what can I tell them? I know less than you!"

"Less than me? There's nothing I know that you don't."

Craig opened the door and led Gina back into the living room, where they sat down opposite the detectives.

"Gina," said Garibaldi, "you were at the party at Jimmy Clark's after the concert at the Bull's Head, is that right?"

Gina nodded.

"Did you notice anything unusual?"

"Unusual?" said Gina. "What do you mean?"

"Anything suspicious?"

Craig flinched. Asking Gina if she saw anything suspicious was like asking questions about the Pope and Catholicism or bears and wood-shitting. Suspicious was her default position.

"Like what?" Gina asked.

The woman detective leaned forward. "Was there anyone there who you didn't know?"

"Didn't know?" said Gina, glancing towards Craig, as if unsure how to answer. "I don't think so. There was the band – Jimmy, Larry, Charlie, Hazel and –" she looked at Craig again. "And Craig. And there was me and ...who else?" Another glance at Craig. "Oh, yes, Charlie's girlfriend. That was it, I think. It was just us."

"And was anyone behaving oddly at all?"

"What kind of a question is that?" said Craig. "Do you really think one of us has anything to do with the man's death?"

"That's what we're trying to find out."

"I don't know what to say," said Gina. "Everyone was drinking, fooling around. There was a bit of singing, a lot of laughter. A lot of mask swapping."

"Mask swapping?"

"Yeah, everyone was trying on the masks, doing impersonations. I mean *I* wasn't, but—"

"I see. So several people were wearing the Mick Jagger mask?"

"I think we probably all were at some stage," said Craig.

"It didn't fit too well as it was specifically made for Jimmy. All the masks were tailor made. So were the costumes."

"So you were all trying on each other's Okay Boomer masks?"

"That's right. Yeah."

"So you all had masks on at the party."

"Not all the time," said Gina. "That would be ridiculous, but we were fooling around with them."

Garibaldi paused and looked closely at Gina, saying nothing for a few seconds. Then he turned to Craig, still saying nothing.

"So," he said after a long pause, his eyes still on Craig, "people were wearing masks some of the time." He looked at Gina. "And you say that you knew everyone who was there. My question is . . ."

Craig saw it coming.

"My question is, if people were wearing masks some of the time, how can you be sure that, at any one time, you knew exactly who was there?"

Gina turned to Craig. He saw the alarm in her face, sensed her mind working.

"I understand your logic, Inspector, but if someone else was there in a mask, someone we didn't know, we'd have recognised them. It's not just the face, is it? It's the shape. It's the way you walk. It's how you talk."

"I'm not suggesting they might have *said* anything," said the detective. "I'm suggesting they could have been there."

"No," said Gina, "We'd have spotted them, of course we would. I mean we'd have noticed their clothes. No-one was in costume, remember."

"The chances are, if they were in a mask," said the detective, "you'd have looked at their face, not their body."

"I find this all very unlikely," said Craig.

"I'm sure you do," said Garibaldi. "In the same way that you would have found the idea of a dead man on the gravel in a Mick Jagger mask pretty unlikely as well."

Garibaldi nodded to Gardner and they both got up.

"Thank you for your time. We'll need a statement, of course, but in the meantime if anything else occurs to you, please get in touch."

He reached in his pocket for a card and handed it to Craig.

"The members of your band may be used to being in the papers," said Garibaldi heading for the door, "but I think this might be a pretty big storm."

Craig looked at the card in his hand. A pretty big storm.

He braced himself and thought of the best way to batten down the hatches.

The detectives had made him feel uncomfortable, especially the one called Garibaldi. Every question he'd asked had been loaded with accusation, as if he knew there were things he was choosing to keep from them.

The truth was there were many things Craig would rather the police didn't know about, and the prospect of being subjected to further investigation filled him with dread.

It also made him feel the urge to do things that would shock and surprise the many fans of the nation's unofficial poet laureate.

11

After another gruesome day on the set of *Coming to Terms* Charlie Brougham settled down in the living room of his house on The Crescent, beer in hand, to watch the football.

He hadn't been watching it long when the doorbell rang. It was late for anyone to call and, thinking it was a charity cold caller, he decided at first to ignore it, hoping, as often happened, that whoever it was would give up and go away. But the ringing continued, and when it was accompanied by a loud knock, he paused the game and went to answer.

He looked blankly at the man and woman on his doorstep.

The man flashed a card towards him. "Detective Inspector Garibaldi," he said, "and Detective Sergeant Gardner. Could we come in for a moment?"

"Of course," said Charlie, standing back and ushering them in.

He led them into the living room and offered them a seat.

The man pointed at the TV screen as he sat down. "Any score?" he said.

"Sorry?" said Charlie.

"The game. Any score?"

Charlie shook his head. "Not yet, no." He picked up the remote, turned off the TV and sat down. "But I'm sure you haven't come to talk about the football, have you?"

"Of course not," said the man, fixing Charlie with a stare that made him feel uneasy.

"I'm assuming this is about that poor man."

"That's right. The man found dead at Jimmy Clark's."

"I can't tell you how shocked I am."

"I'm sure you are."

"And however I can help—"

"We'd like to ask you a few questions."

"Of course."

DI Garibaldi took out his notebook and consulted it. "This band, the Okay Boomers. You played drums, is that right?"

"I did, yes."

"Wearing a David Bowie mask."

Charlie nodded. "Aladdin Sane."

"Bowie, of course, didn't play the drums."

"I was well aware of that," said Charlie. "All part of the irony."

"I see." Garibaldi consulted his notebook. "I understand that you all kept the masks on until you arrived back at Jimmy Clark's house."

"That's right. We really did want to stay anonymous. We all wore hoodies as well."

"So who went back to the house?"

"All the band, Craig's wife and Naomi."

"Naomi?"

"My partner."

"Is she in?"

"Do you want to talk to her?"

"If we could."

63

Charlie got up from his chair, walked to the open living room door and called. "Naomi!"

"So you knew everyone at Jimmy Clark's?"

"I did, yes, and I have no idea at all who that dead man might be. As I understand it, neither do you."

"What we do know is that he was found wearing one of your band's masks."

Charlie sensed a touch of aggression in Garibaldi's tone, as if he had taken the lack of identification as a personal criticism.

"I know that, but—"

"Good evening!"

Charlie turned to his partner. "Naomi, this is . . ."

"DI Garibaldi," said the man, standing up, "and this—" he pointed to the woman who had been sitting on the sofa beside him. "This is DS Gardner."

Naomi sat down. "Terrible news about that man. I can't believe it. I mean . . .do we know who he is?"

Garibaldi shook his head. "Not yet, but we're nearly there. Tell me, Naomi, you knew all about the Okay Boomers and their previous incarnations?"

"I did, yes."

"Do you know who else did?"

Naomi turned to Charlie. "I think it was just band members and their partners. That's right, isn't it?"

Charlie nodded. "We deliberately kept it a tight secret."

"And was it only the band and some of those partners who went back to Jimmy Clark's after the gig?"

"Yes," said Naomi. "It was the same with the other gigs as well, wasn't it, Charlie?"

"It was," said Charlie. "It became a tradition. A short-lived one as it turns out, given that we won't be playing the Bull's Head again."

"So no-one knew about either the identity of the band or these after-parties apart from band members and partners?"

Charlie shook his head. "No-one."

"Can you say that with confidence?"

"What do you mean?"

"I mean, how can you be sure that no-one knew your identities or that no-one knew you all went back to Jimmy Clark's after each gig?"

"I don't understand," said Naomi. "Are you suggesting that this ...this man came to the house knowing who would be there?"

"I'm not suggesting anything. I'm merely trying to establish the facts."

"Was he a burglar?"

"There's no sign of forced entry and it seems that nothing's been taken, apart, that is, from the masks."

"Jimmy told me about the masks," said Charlie. "Asked me if I had the Bowie one but I told him I left it on the table with the others like I always do. I don't get it. I mean, who would take the masks?"

"These masks," said Garibaldi. "I understand you were putting each other's on throughout the evening. Is that right?"

"Yes. We were playing around, doing impressions. I did 'Let it Be' in the McCartney mask, as I remember and 'Sympathy for the Devil' when I was Jagger."

"I put the masks on," said Naomi. "But I left the impersonations to the others."

"I see," said Garibaldi. He looked from one to the other, saying nothing for a few moments. "So a lot of you were wearing masks and you say you knew everyone there ..."

"I see where you're going," said Charlie, "we may have been wearing masks, but we'd have noticed if there was someone else there. Of course we would."

"How much had you all had to drink?"

"You think we were all too pissed to notice?"

"I'm just asking how much you had to drink."

"It wasn't excessive," said Naomi. "It wasn't as though—"

"And it was just drink. There was nothing else going on," said Charlie.

"I didn't suggest there was."

"I know. I just want to make it clear."

Garibaldi leaned forward. "I think you need to prepare yourselves."

"Prepare ourselves?" said Charlie. "For what?"

"The media will be all over this. All over you. So be prepared. And if there's anything you can think of, do get in touch." He held out a card for Charlie. "We'll need a statement of course."

"Of course," said Charlie.

When the detectives had gone Charlie went back into the living room, sat down and switched the football back on.

Naomi came and sat with him, but neither said anything.

They had been together for ten years but hadn't married. Given that each still bore the scars of bitter divorces, neither was particularly keen on the idea and this was fine by Charlie. He was happy with where they were – he liked to think they trusted each other and were prepared to make the accommodations and compromises needed at their time of life. They were both now too old and too wise for anything else. To Charlie, being with Naomi felt like easing into a comfy pair of slippers after a night out in fashionable tight-fitting shoes – an analogy he had wisely chosen to keep to himself.

But now, as they sat together, he didn't feel quite so comfortable. He tried to watch the football, but he couldn't concentrate. All he could think about was the detectives' visit and the possible implications of further police investigation.

When Charlie and Naomi had got together they had been open with each other about their pasts. Naomi had told him about her years as a hard-partying, fast-living socialite and he had told her about his own youthful indiscretions, most of which happened at the height of his fame and some of which, thanks to the tabloid press's relentless pursuit of his private life, had become widely known.

That he should have escaped so lightly had remained a great mystery to Charlie. As far as the public was concerned (and, given what he had chosen to keep from her, as far as Naomi was concerned), his alleged indiscretions amounted to no more than a string of affairs and moderate use of recreational drugs – hardly sensational stories and interesting at the time only because they concerned a national celebrity.

Now, in the wake of the discovery of the body and the unmasking of the band, the press would be after him again and while part of him perversely wondered whether that could result in a boost for him and his career, a larger part feared that such attention, together with a police investigation, might uncover things which, brought to light, would plunge both him and his career into permanent darkness.

12

www.bbc.co.uk/news

STARS IN MASKED BAND MYSTERY DEATH PROBE

A police investigation into the death of a man found at the house of TV star Jimmy Clark has exposed the activities of a secret celebrity band.

Enquiries into the man's death, which is being treated by the police as suspicious, have revealed that Clark, together with four other stars, have been performing in a band, disguising their identities by wearing masks and costumes.

On Sunday afternoon the band, calling themselves the Okay Boomers, played a concert at the Bull's Head in Barnes. No-one in the audience knew who was behind the masks, but now the band's identities have been revealed. Playing with broadcaster and writer Jimmy Clark were TV presenter Larry Benyon, actor Charlie Brougham, comedian Hazel Bloom and poet Craig Francis.

The surprise revelation has come after the discovery of the body at Clark's house.

An unnamed source has said that the dead man was himself wearing a mask, but the police, who have yet to name the man, have not confirmed this.

Another source said that previous incarnations of the celebrity band, whose gigs have all been at the Bull's Head, have included The Presidents, The Players, The Comedians and The Animals. Whenever they have performed they have played in masks to keep their identities hidden.

None of the band members was available for comment but a spokesman for Jimmy Clark said that all were shocked by the death and were cooperating fully with the police in their enquiries.

Deighton turned to the board behind her and pointed at the picture in the middle.

"Frankie Dunne. Twenty-six. Identified by his mother last night. Last seen by his mother on Sunday afternoon when he went off to play football for his club at Barn Elms. She expected him back that evening but heard nothing. Frankie always let her know if he was going to be late and especially if he was staying somewhere else. But he didn't ring and he didn't answer his mother's calls. Mrs Dunne woke up on Monday but still no Frankie. She rang round but no-one knew where he was. So yesterday afternoon she called us."

Deighton pointed at pictures of Frankie as he was found on Jimmy Clark's gravel – one of him in the Mick Jagger mask and one of him with the mask removed.

"Mrs Dunne, Eileen Dunne, says she has no idea why Frankie should have been found at Jimmy Clark's house."

Deighton pointed at the group of pictures at one side of the board.

"The Okay Boomers," she said. "Jimmy Clark, Larry Benyon, Craig Francis, Charlie Brougham and Hazel Bloom. They, and some of their partners, had all been at Clark's house the night before. Clark's house is here—" She pointed at a map. "The east side of Castelnau overlooking the Wetlands." She moved her finger across the map. "Here is where Frankie lived with his mum." Her finger rested on the North Barnes estate. "And here—" she moved her finger again, "—is Barn Elms where Frankie headed off to play football on Sunday. At the moment that's the last time we know he was seen. We don't yet know how Frankie died, but his body showed signs of bruising, and the bedroom from which he fell shows evidence of a struggle. Apart from that, we don't have much to go on, but we're treating his death as suspicious and there are a few obvious things we need to ask ourselves. First, what was Frankie doing at Jimmy Clark's house? And second, why was he wearing Jimmy Clark's Mick Jagger mask?" Deighton paused and looked round the room, her eyebrows raised. "Any questions?"

Garibaldi looked at Gardner, usually the first to respond. She didn't disappoint.

"Anything from forensics on the mask?"

"We await the full report," said Deighton, "but from what those at the party have said it seems that they were all taking turns to try it on, so their prints and DNA will be all over it."

"And this mask," said Gardner. "Do we know how long he'd been wearing it?"

"We don't know anything for sure," said Deighton.

"It could be," said Gardner, "that Dunne wasn't wearing it when he was pushed—"

"If he was pushed, that is," said Deighton. "We still don't know."

"OK, but it could be that someone put it on him after he—"

"Why would they do that?" said DC Hodson.

"Maybe to link it to Jimmy Clark," said DC MacLean.

"It's already linked to Jimmy Clark," said Gardner. "He was found in his garden."

"House to house has given us nothing so far," said Deighton, "but we're still going through CCTV security camera and doorbell cam footage from neighbouring residences."

She pointed at the Okay Boomers. "We've spoken to this lot and have their statements, but they have yet to learn the identity of the victim. So we need to get on to them again. And, needless to say, we need to find out all we can about..."

Deighton pointed at the picture of Frankie Dunne in his football kit.

"About Frankie Dunne. At the moment all we have is that he lived with his mum in North Barnes, he played football on Sunday afternoon and he was found dead in Clark's garden on Monday morning in Clark's Mick Jagger mask. We need all we can. Find out how the victim lived..."

And you'll find out how he died. Garibaldi, as always, finished the line under his breath.

"Do we have any idea of time of death?" said Gardner.

"We won't know until we get the post-mortem," said Deighton, "and even then I can't believe we'll get anything specific." She pointed at a pile of newspapers on her desk.

"Doubtless you'll have seen the coverage. As predicted, they're loving it, absolutely loving it."

She picked up the papers one by one and read the headlines. "'Masked Star Band in Mystery Death'; 'Stars unmasked over mystery death'; 'Man found dead at Clark's house'; 'Masks off as stars face investigation'; 'Take them off! Stars' secret exposed in Jimmy Clark mansion death probe'."

Deighton put the papers down with a sigh. "And, needless to say, social media's been busy. But our priority at the moment—" she turned and pointed again at the picture in the middle of the board, "—is the victim. A young man. Frankie Dunne. A mother's son."

A mother's son.

The words spun round Garibaldi's head as he got up from his chair.

Something about Deighton's manner this morning had struck him as odd, and he couldn't work out what it was. In one sense it had been business as usual – she had been her usual efficient self, steering the investigation, probing and directing with questions and instructions. But in another sense, she had been different – subtly different in a way he couldn't quite define.

Was he imagining it, projecting onto her his speculation about what might be going on in her personal life?

Or was his memory of what he had confessed to her on their last evening out affecting the way he saw her?

Garibaldi looked at Deighton again as she sat at her desk, head down, sorting through her notes.

A mother's son.

The words still echoed.

As he turned to leave Deighton lifted her head, hooked off her reading glasses and looked at him.

Garibaldi smiled and raised his hand, half in

acknowledgement, half in farewell. He had no idea why he did it and stood there awkwardly, his eyes still on Deighton and finding it difficult to look away.

Then, suddenly, he was looking at someone else.

He was looking at his mother.

Deighton was wearing a mask of his mother's face.

13

With Hammersmith Bridge still closed to cars, it was quicker for Garibaldi to cycle down to Barnes than it was for DS 'Uber' Gardner to drive him via Chiswick Bridge. This was fine by Garibaldi. More than fine. His bike rides gave him space and time to think, and today, as he wheeled his bike across the bridge, looking at the river stretching east towards Putney and west towards Chiswick, his thoughts were very much of Frankie Dunne lying on the gravel in the Mick Jagger mask. Even after so many years of being exposed to them, images of murder victims still had the power to shock – experience was no kind of anaesthetic – but something about this one had shocked him more than usual.

Maybe it was the mask.

Garibaldi had never thought much about masks, but when he'd fleetingly seen Deighton wearing one of his mother, he'd started to wonder whether he might be frightened of them. Had that moment been another instance of what had been happening to him for some time, or had it been the strange manifestation of some deep-seated fear?

A little research had reassured him that, if he was frightened of masks, he wasn't the only one. Fear of masks, according to Wikipedia, was very much a thing, and there was even a name for it. Masklophobia. An irrational fear of masks, people in costumes and mascots.

Maybe that's what he was. A Masklophobic. Without the costumes and mascots bit.

Lost in these speculations, he got back on his bike on the south side of Hammersmith Bridge, took a right into Lonsdale Road, passed St Mark's School and turned left into the estate. When most people thought of Barnes this wasn't the place that came to mind. For them Barnes was 'the village', the leafy avenues, bijou cafés and independent shops close to the pond – it wasn't a place of food banks and free school meals. But that didn't mean they weren't there, and in this North Barnes estate there was considerable hardship and deprivation. As in so many areas of London the close proximity of great affluence and acute social need was startling.

Garibaldi locked his bike at the Community Centre, sat on a bench and waited for Gardner to arrive, thinking of what they were about to do.

This part of the job had got no easier. If anything it had, over the years, become more difficult as, with the passing of time, Garibaldi became more aware of the sense of loss, the numbing grief that lay behind each statistic. When the case was up and running and he was immersed in the details of the investigation it was possible to bury that sense, or at least shove it to the back of his mind, but when he was on the doorstep of the recently bereaved, it was impossible to avoid. He may have seemed professionally emotionless, but at moments like this he was churning inside, putting himself in the shoes of the victim's next of kin, imagining the pain he himself would be feeling had the same thing happened to one of his own.

"I'm so sorry for your loss, Eileen," he said when he sat down opposite the woman who had answered the door.

The words were inadequate but they had to be said. Clichés were there for a reason, and at times like this there was nothing wrong with reaching for the nearest one.

Mrs Dunne, a petite, redheaded woman in her fifties, with blue eyes and freckled cheeks, cradled a mug of tea in both hands and looked from Garibaldi to Gardner with the confused expression of someone who's just been asked a question in a foreign language.

"I can't begin to imagine the pain you must be going through," said Garibaldi, "but I hope you don't mind us asking some questions about Frankie."

"Frankie, yes."

"Do you have any idea why he might have been at Jimmy Clark's house?"

"Jimmy Clark? I can't believe it. I like him. He's nice. Posh, of course, but nice. I like him on those quiz shows. Always funny, isn't he? Do you like him?"

Garibaldi gave a half-hearted nod. Eileen turned to Gardner, who smiled.

"So you don't know why Frankie was at his house?" said Garibaldi.

"Frankie never kept anything from me. Always let me know where he was. Always looked after me. Ever since he moved back here, that is."

"When did he move back?" said Gardner.

"About three years ago. Been here since."

"Just the two of you?" said Garibaldi.

"His brother lives in Hammersmith...his dad...he lost his dad when he was little."

"I'm sorry." Garibaldi shook away the memory that had flashed across his mind.

"And now ..." Eileen bit her lip and turned away. "He went to play football on Sunday afternoon and that's the last I saw of him."

She pointed at the photographs on a sideboard. "Always loved his football, Frankie. That's him. Barnes Lions. We thought – his dad and me – we thought he might turn pro. A few scouts turned up and took an interest, but nothing came of it. Who knows what might have happened?"

Garibaldi looked at the photos. "That's his brother?" he said, pointing at one of them.

"Sean, yes."

"And that's his dad?"

"Martin." Eileen pointed at a bride and groom. "That's us on our wedding day."

"Did Frankie have many friends?" said Gardner.

"He had some, yes. Football. Work."

"What was his work, Eileen?" said Garibaldi.

"Marks and Spencers." Eileen paused, as if she had remembered something. "They'll need to know." Her eyes popped wide with alarm, as if M&S not knowing Frankie's fate was a problem of great magnitude. "Will someone tell them?"

"Yes, Eileen," said Garibaldi. "Someone will tell them."

"He had all sorts of jobs," said Eileen, turning again to the photos on the sideboard. "He worked on the post for a while, then tried to do something with computers. He tried all kind of things, then when he moved back here he got a job down at Marks and he stayed. He liked it."

"Which Marks and Spencers is this?" asked Gardner.

"The one down in Barnes." Eileen pointed her arm towards the window.

"We know how difficult this must be for you, Eileen," said Garibaldi, "but we will do all we can to find out how Frankie died."

Eileen moved her head slowly from side to side. "I still don't believe it. If I hadn't seen him – there – lying there last night – I wouldn't believe it. So young. My angel. He might not always have seemed one to others but he always was one to me."

"We're here to help," said Garibaldi. "Anything you need, any questions, someone will help."

Garibaldi nodded towards the kitchen where the Family Liaison Officer had retreated on the detectives' arrival.

"There's one thing I don't get about it all," said Eileen.

"What's that?" said Garibaldi.

"Someone said – I can't remember who – they said he was found in a mask. Is that right?"

Garibaldi nodded.

"I just need to check because it's all a blur. I'm very confused."

"That's to be expected."

Eileen's eyes widened again. "Why would he be wearing a mask?"

"That's one of the questions we're asking."

"What kind of mask?"

Garibaldi wished he didn't have to tell her. To talk about a mask seemed somehow wrong. To utter the words 'Mick Jagger' seemed even worse.

14

Rachel pressed the remote, freezing the picture and silencing the *House of Games* theme music.

She looked at the numbers on the pad of paper on her lap and totted them up with her pencil. "So that puts me four ahead."

"Really?" said Garibaldi.

"Yeah, really. Do you want to check?"

Rachel held the pad of paper towards Garibaldi. He dismissed it with a wave of his hand and leaned back in the sofa.

"Early days," he said. "*University Challenge* still to come and then there's *Only Connect*, the triple pointer."

House of Games. University Challenge. Only Connect. The three legs of their weekly TV quiz competition, recorded and taken in ascending order of difficulty. Single, double and triple points. Garibaldi was convinced he was up overall, though Rachel's running total seemed to suggest otherwise.

"Ready for the next one?"

Garibaldi yawned. "I'm a bit tired."

"The case?"

"Yeah. You know how it is. Sorry, I've ruined your half-term, haven't I? We were going to go out."

"No problem," said Rachel. "Honest. I'm happy to take it easy. Telly, takeaways and lie-ins, that'll do me fine. It's good to slow down sometimes. Gives you time to think about things."

Garibaldi turned to her. "Is everything OK?"

"Yeah." Rachel's shrug was unconvincing. "It's nothing really, just—"

Garibaldi sat up. "Has something happened?"

"No, it's just that things have been on my mind."

"Anything you want to share?"

"It's work mainly. Maybe I'm not enjoying it as much as I did."

It came as no surprise. That Rachel had ever managed to enjoy her difficult and challenging job at Hillside Academy had always been a mystery to him.

"But you still like some of it, right?"

"I guess so."

"I mean, you're not thinking of chucking it in or anything?"

Rachel laughed. "You mean like go off to be a mature student? No, that's your thing."

Garibaldi still liked to imagine it – leaving the force and doing what he didn't do when he was young, when events turned his life in a different direction. He would often sit at his desk in the station and wonder what it would be like to sit at a desk in a university library, doing what Alfie had done a few years ago. Was it just a dream? Were those hours spent deliberating over which subject to study – History, Philosophy, Politics, Italian, English – anything more than a way of passing the time?

"So which bits aren't you enjoying?"

"I'm not sure. I think it's a more generalised thing. I keep thinking of a Townes Van Zandt song."

"Yeah?" Garibaldi smiled, remembering that morning after they'd slept together for the first time. "Which one?"

"Waitin' Around to Die."

"Crikey, things that bad are they? I know country music isn't known for its optimism, but even so . . ."

"You know the one?"

"Oh I know it all right."

"The one about not knowing where this dirty road is taking me and not seeing the reason why."

Garibaldi shut his eyes as he tried to remember the rest of the lyric.

"I mean," said Rachel, "it's not as if I think like that all the time but sometimes, I don't know, I keep asking myself, 'is this it?' We only get one shot, don't we?"

So that was it. The kind of existential crisis Garibaldi lived through each day, the questions that were never far from his own mind.

"One shot," he said. "Yeah."

"And I mean, I'm not that old, am I?"

"A spring chicken."

"So it's not like I can't do anything else, is it?"

Garibaldi sensed her need for reassurance. He reached out and took Rachel's hand.

"Of course not."

"The trouble is," said Rachel, "I can't think of anything else I want to do. I mean, I'd be lying if I said I hated the whole thing—"

Garibaldi remembered the time he had visited Rachel at her school, when one of her pupils was involved in an investigation. He had been struck by the way the head, and the pupil, spoke so highly of her.

"Don't forget," he said. "You're really good at it. You know that, don't you?"

Rachel faked an embarrassed smile. "Thank you, sir."

"I mean it."

"The thing is, though, whatever you do, wherever you are, you always think of other places you could be, other people you could be, other things you could do."

Garibaldi turned to her again as the rest of the Van Zandt lyric came to him. "Yeah, but that song, you know what it's about, right? All those things that are easier to do than waiting around to die?"

"Don't worry. I'm not going to do any of that. Drink, gamble, rob, run away."

"As I remember, it ends with the guy hooked on drugs and deciding dying might be a good idea after all."

Rachel laughed. "Funny what we like to listen to, isn't it?" She squeezed his hand. "I'm sorry, I'm being silly."

"You're not being silly at all."

"I just sometimes worry about...the future."

"Well, we all do that."

"I know, and I guess nothing's ever perfect, is it? You might think you want something else when what you should be doing is making the best of what you've got. Maybe I should listen to more Carly Simon."

"Carly Simon? From Townes Van Zandt to Carly Simon?"

"I think she's pretty good. You know her song 'Anticipation'?"

"Sorry. When it comes to Carly Simon 'You're so Vain' is where I begin and end."

"It's a great song. It says we can never know about the days to come but we think about them anyway."

"Right, so it's another cheerful one."

"Yeah, it is actually, because she says she's going to stop thinking about the future because it feels so right to be with her lover and feel his arms around her and because, and this is how the song ends, 'these are the good old days'."

Garibaldi smiled. "These are the good old days, eh? I must remember that. And as soon as we get the chance, jazz at the Bull's Head, OK?"

"Sure, but enough about me. Tell me about this case. It's everywhere. Read it in the paper, heard it on the radio, saw it on the telly. Quite a thing, eh? Celebrities playing in a masked band."

"I know. Ridiculous, right?"

"You think one of them killed him?"

"We don't even know if he was killed. In fact, we don't really know anything. We've only just discovered who he was."

"Shame we missed them playing at the Bull. Sounds like a laugh. And I do love a mask!"

"You love a mask?"

"Yeah. Everyone loves a mask."

Was now the time to tell her that he didn't?

"And these stars. You'll be talking to them, right?"

"I already have."

"And how was that?"

"They're not like you'd imagine."

"In what way?"

"They're smaller."

"Smaller?"

"Yeah, they seem big on TV. If not big then, I don't know, important, significant. They're stars, they're different from you. See them in the flesh and you realise they're, I don't know, human."

"What was Charlie Brougham like?"

"Charlie Brougham? Why do you ask?"

Rachel grinned. "I quite liked him back in the day."

"Well, I hate to disappoint you but he's, you know, got older and filled out."

"Oh well, I suppose it happens to everyone, doesn't it?"

Garibaldi sucked in his stomach.

"And what was Jimmy Clark like?" said Rachel.

"He was awful. Why? Fancy him as well, do you?"

"You're joking! I quite like Craig Francis, though. Love his poems. And Hazel Bloom's impressions aren't too bad. But Larry Benyon, he's the one who fascinates me."

"You're fascinated by Larry Benyon?"

"I like him. I like what he says, what he stands for. Seems, you know, decent."

Garibaldi grunted.

"You don't think so?"

"I'm not sure any of them is decent. Fame does strange things to people."

"Like make them want to play in a masked band?"

"Exactly."

"But Larry...those things he's spoken up about. The way he was once a footballer and now ...."

"If I'm honest," said Garibaldi, "I'm not really impressed by any of them. Seems like they're wearing a mask all the time, not just when they're playing in a band."

Rachel yawned. "Well, on that philosophical note, if you don't fancy *University Challenge* and if there's no school tomorrow ..."

She turned to Garibaldi with a brief raise of her eyebrows. Knowing exactly what it meant, he smiled, gave a measured nod, zapped the TV remote and got up from the sofa, holding out a hand and pulling her up.

15

Garibaldi leaned back in his chair. "What do you know about Barn Elms?"

"The playing fields?" said Gardner, standing by his desk. "Not much. Went to a sports camp there when I was a kid but can't say I've been back much since."

"So you're not a regular at the Sports Centre?"

Gardner put her hands on her hips. "Do I look as though I am?"

Garibaldi glanced at his sergeant and opted for tact. "You look as though you could be, yes."

Gardner smiled. "Don't you think I'd have told you? All those times we've been tucking into Gail's pastries and talking about how we should exercise more?"

"Yeah," said Garibaldi. "Those Gail's pastries. Maybe we should give them up."

They looked at each other for a few seconds then shook their heads and laughed. It was a ridiculous idea.

"How about you?" said Gardner. "Been sneaking down to the gym?"

"Do I look as though I have?"

"You look as though you could have, yes."

Garibaldi gave a knowing laugh, remembering the

look Rachel had given him when he'd told her Charlie Brougham had filled out. "Well, we're both OK then, aren't we?"

"So Barn Elms," said Gardner. "What about it?"

Frankie Dunne played football there on Sunday afternoon for Barnes Athletic. At the moment, that's the last we know about his movements."

"We're sure he played?"

"ABC, Milly, ABC. Don't forget the C."

"Check everything. Yeah, of course. I'll get on it."

"No need," said Garibaldi, holding up his hand. "Below my paygrade perhaps but, hey, old habits and all that . . ."

"And . . .?"

"I spoke to the coach or manager, he seemed to be both, and, yes, Frankie Dunne played for Barnes Athletic on Sunday afternoon. And guess what?"

Gardner looked at him blankly.

"They've got training down there tonight."

"You're going?"

"I think I will."

"Bringing your boots?"

Garibaldi smiled. "Might pay Barney a visit while I'm there."

"Who's Barney?"

"London's oldest plane tree. Planted in the 1680s. When last measured it was 115 feet tall and 27 feet in girth. And its home is Barn Elms."

"Fascinating."

"It is, isn't it?"

"Is that what you've been doing all morning, looking up trees on Wikipedia?"

"I'm just curious, Milly. Aren't you? Funny thing about

this job is you never know what's going to end up being relevant."

"So you think Barney the plane tree could be a key witness?"

"Assume nothing, remember?"

"Yeah, and believe nobody. Which is what I'm doing right now."

"OK." Garibaldi swivelled away from his screen. "Frankie Dunne. Where are we?"

"Still no sign of his phone at the crime scene or surrounding area but we've got a list of his calls from his phone provider."

"Anything interesting?"

"He made his last call on Sunday evening at 7.10 pm. No calls after that. No texts or messages. And the last call was from his mum."

"What about his bank cards?"

"Nothing suspicious overall, but we're still looking. Card was last used on Sunday afternoon in the Barnes Athletic clubhouse. After the match, presumably."

"What about his car?"

"An old Volkswagen. It's outside the house in Stillingfleet Road."

"Did he drive it to football on Sunday afternoon?"

"Doesn't look like it. His mum didn't see him again that day, so unless he drove back, parked it and went off without going inside, chances are he walked or got the bus. We're running his number through ANPR to see if we can get anything."

"Social media?" said Garibaldi.

"Doesn't seem to have been much of a fan. Instagram more than Twitter or Facebook. Last post was about four weeks ago. A picture of his football team. Didn't follow many and not many followed him."

Garibaldi leaned back in his chair, hands behind his head. "So our timeline's pretty blank. Football match at Barn Elms finishes about 4.00 pm. The coach says they go to their clubhouse on Queen Elizabeth Walk afterwards for drinks and some food. And he says he remembers Frankie being there. We don't know what time he left but at the moment we have nothing on his movements between then and being found dead on Jimmy Clark's gravel in a Mick Jagger mask the next morning. What about CCTV in Clark's neighbouring properties?"

"Nothing. None of them cover his house. We're looking at door cams but haven't picked up anything yet."

"So no sense of what time Dunne arrived at Clark's and no sense of how he got in. And Dunne seems clean, no trace of him on the system."

"Were you expecting to find something?"

Garibaldi held up his hands. "Not necessarily."

"Just because he lives on—"

"Exactly."

"On the other hand, his mum did say something about him when we visited. She called him her angel, but she also said—"

"He might not always have seemed one to others but he always was one to me. Yeah, I remember it as well."

"Could mean anything, of course and doesn't mean he'd necessarily have a record, but I wonder what she meant."

"Maybe we'll find out." Garibaldi looked at the notes on his desk. "What about his football team?"

"We've gone through the registered players. Some small stuff on a few. Nothing major. But I did discover something interesting about the team."

"What's that?"

"The club's honorary president is Larry Benyon."

"Really? You think it's relevant?"

Gardner gave a playful shrug. "Funny thing relevance, isn't it? You might not see it at first, but then . . ."

Garibaldi smiled, acknowledging the way one of his own favourite lines had been thrown back at him.

Gardner started to walk back to her desk but stopped and turned. "One thing worries me, though."

"What's that?"

"I'm worried we're treating Frankie Dunne like he's guilty."

"In what way?"

"It's like our starting point is that Frankie Dunne had no right to be anywhere near Jimmy Clark's house, so we're treating him as if he's the one who's done something wrong. But we don't know that, do we? We don't know anything."

"You're absolutely right. Assume nothing. We need to know more about how Frankie Dunne lived, angel or no angel. And we also need to know why he was at Jimmy Clark's."

He got up and hooked his jacket off the back of his chair.

"I'll get my bike."

Charlie Brougham had given up smoking years ago, but as he stepped off set he was tempted to take it up again. The film was getting no better – if anything, it was getting considerably worse – but he was now facing a much bigger problem.

He checked his phone and was surprised to find a voicemail from the detective asking him to call back.

He got back to him straight away.

"DI Garibaldi?"

"Speaking."

"It's Charlie Brougham here."

"Thanks for calling, Charlie. I shouldn't keep you long. I just have some information that you might like to hear."

Information? What had they discovered?

"We've identified the dead man."

"I see."

"The dead man is Frankie Dunne. Does that name mean anything to you?"

"Frankie Dunne, you say? No. I've never heard of him."

"He was twenty-six. Lived on the North Barnes estate with his mother."

"Well, as I said, I've never heard of anyone called Frankie Dunne. What about the others? Do any of them know him?"

"You're the first I've told. Dunne was a local man. Lived in Barnes and worked at the Marks and Spencers near the Bull's Head. Who knows? He might even have served you."

He could well have. Charlie wasn't a stranger to the food store at the end of the High Street.

"Well, Inspector," he said. "As I say, I've never heard of him, but if I can be of any further assistance, please—"

"I have no doubt we'll be speaking to you again, Charlie."

Charlie hung up and looked at the phone in his hand.

Frankie Dunne. The name meant nothing to him. But the North Barnes estate – that was a name that meant a little more.

Craig Francis was at his desk, writing – or, if he were to be brutally honest with himself, not writing. Sometimes it came and sometimes it didn't, and today it had so far shown no signs of putting in an appearance. When it came, it could be great. Ink flowed from his pen (he was old school in his preference for pen and paper) and sometimes he could write four or five poems a day. But when it didn't come it was tough. No matter how long he sat there, no matter how much he tried, nothing happened, and he was paralysed by the thought that he might never write a poem again.

His ringing phone offered the promise of distraction and, although he didn't recognise the number, he answered it immediately.

"Detective Inspector Garibaldi here. I'd like to ask you a few questions, if I may."

The detective with the Italian name. Craig regretted taking the call so quickly.

"Ah," he said, flustered. "Have you, er...has anything happened?"

"We have some information about the victim."

"I see. And—?"

"The victim is Frankie Dunne, twenty-six. Does that name mean anything to you?"

"Frankie Dunne?" Craig gave himself time to think. "No, I've never heard of him. Do we know anything about him?"

"He was local. Lived in Barnes."

"Really?"

"North Barnes. On the estate."

"I see. Well, I've never heard of him. Do we know anything more about what happened?"

"We're putting the picture together."

"Is there anything more I should know?"

"We'll be in touch again, Craig, if there is, but in the meantime do get in touch with us if anything else occurs to you."

"I've told you all I know," said Craig.

"I'm sure you have," said the detective, "but sometimes you think you've remembered everything and something else suddenly comes to you. Human memory's a strange thing. But, just to confirm, you didn't know Frankie Dunne?"

Craig paused again. "No, like I said, I don't recognise the name at all."

"OK. Thanks for your time."

Craig hung up and stared at the blank page of the notebook in front of him.

There was something about the name Frankie Dunne that had thrown him, and he couldn't work out what it was. He had met thousands of people over the years. Most names he forgot immediately and so he found it strange that the victim's name had made him hesitate in his responses to the detective's questions. Why had it struck a chord?

He picked up his pen and wrote the name in his notebook.

Frankie Dunne.

He narrowed his eyes as he looked at the page and as he did the two words became something else – no longer a name but a title.

He started to write.

The words came easily and with them came the realisation of why the name had meant something to him.

Soon he was looking at a poem – and, though he said so himself, a pretty good one. He picked up the notebook, leaned back in his chair and tried to think of a title.

'Injury Time'.

He wrote it above the poem, read through it once more, and then ripped the page out, shredding it into tiny pieces and reaching for the wastepaper bin below his desk.

Changing his mind, he got up and went into the kitchen. He put the shredded paper on a plate, reached for a box of matches, took out a match and lit it, then held the flame to the shreds of paper and watched them burn.

16

"And so," said Larry Benyon, looking up from his notes and turning to the man sitting next to him, "you, Adam Peacock, have done what no ex-professional footballer has ever done. You've written a novel."

He smiled at the camera and held up a book. "Here it is. *Kickback*." He put the book down and turned to his guest. "Footballers have gone on to do a lot of things, Adam. In the old days a lot used to run pubs. More recently, a lot have gone into management. Some have become TV pundits and broadcasters—" Larry broke off and knowingly raised his eyebrows to camera, "—some have become actors. Many have retrained and, given that most footballers' playing careers finish by their mid-thirties, this is all very achievable. But I can't think of any who have written a novel."

The guest beside him held up his hand. "If I could correct you, Larry. It has been done before. Remember Terry Venables?"

"Terry Venables? Of course I do. Sadly missed."

"I'm surprised you didn't know this then, Larry. In 1970 Venables published a novel that he wrote with Gordon Williams called *They Used to Play on Grass*. He was still playing at the time so you could be right about ex-players never having published a novel, but the thing about Venables is that he went on to write more books with Williams. The Hazell books. They were the basis of a TV series of the same name."

Larry had been looking down at his notes while Adam was speaking. How had his researchers missed this? He'd been told to spin it as a first, and here he was being lectured by Adam Peacock, a player he had never rated and whose wretched novel he had no doubt was as unreadable as his playing career had been unremarkable.

"I don't know if you've read it, Larry, *They Used to Play on Grass*, but the fascinating thing about it is that the novel predicted the end of grass as a football playing surface; Venables at the time was playing for Queens Park Rangers who, between the years 1981 and 1988, did actually play on an artificial surface at Loftus Road. So it's an interesting book in many ways and, as I say, it shows I'm not the first footballer, playing or retired, to have published a novel."

Larry looked up from his notes and forced a smile. He wasn't enjoying this. He didn't mind looking foolish on TV when it was something he chose to do himself, but when it was a result of someone else's cock-up he found it intolerable.

"That's very interesting, Adam. I must check it out."

"I'm surprised you haven't already, Larry. An intelligent man like you."

"It's on my list. So why don't you tell us about *Kickback*?" Larry picked up the book again, resisting the urge to hurl it to one side.

"Well, Larry, the first thing I'd like to say is that it isn't based on me or my experiences as a footballer. A lot of people make that mistake when they read a novel – they think it must be based on the author's own experiences. It's a work of fiction but it's rooted in something that I know *was* going on when I was playing and there's nothing to suggest that it isn't still going on now. And that's gambling. Players and those involved in the game, some at the highest level, betting on matches — and in some cases players betting on matches that they themselves play in. That's why the title is so good. *Kickback*. It suggests football and it also suggests illicit payments..."

Larry was looking at Adam Peacock but he wasn't taking much in. This couldn't be going any worse. Peacock had made him look like an idiot. OK, so he hadn't read the book. He didn't need to. That's what researchers were for. And he had been specifically told that this was a first. What's more, Terry Venables was the man who had beaten Peacock to it. Terry Venables! Not only had Larry played under him, he had known him well.

Someone would pay.

Peacock was drawing to a conclusion. "So it's about betting in football in the broadest sense. There are still a lot of clubs sponsored by gambling firms and a lot of betting around the game. But it's also a novel about people. You don't have to like football to like the book, and you don't need to know anything about gambling."

"Well, thank you, Adam. That's fascinating."

"Lovely to see you, Larry. I was worried I might not."

Larry raised his eyebrows. "Really?"

"Yeah. I thought you might be wearing a mask!"

"Not tonight. It's my night off."

"So it's just your Larry Benyon mask tonight, is it?"

"No mask, Adam."

"But we all wear masks, don't we? We all have something to hide."

Larry did his best to crack a smile as he turned to camera to round things off. "Well, on that note..."

As soon as they were off-air he hooked off his earpiece and turned to Adam. "What the fuck was all that about?"

"What was what about?"

"That stuff about masks."

"Just a little joke, Larry."

"Well it wasn't funny, OK? You weren't here to talk about any of that."

"I thought everyone would like it. I mean this band, celebrities in masks – everyone's talking about it."

"Someone's died, you know. It's not something to joke about."

"I thought—"

"You had no right. And what was all that shit about my Larry Benyon mask! We all wear masks! What the fuck are you talking about?"

"I thought it was a good point."

"Well it wasn't. It was totally out of order. Embarrassing."

Adam held up his hand. "OK. I'm sorry, I shouldn't have. But, tell me, Larry, did you *really* not know about Terry Venables's book?"

"Don't try and change the subject. I—"

"So you didn't then?"

"That's it! I've had enough of you." Larry stood up. "Where's Tom?"

As he stormed off set in search of his producer an assistant approached.

"Where the fuck is Tom?" Larry snapped at her.

"There's someone here for you, Larry."

"Fuck that, I need to see Tom. He made me look like a fucking idiot!"

"They say it's important."

"And so is this. Where is he? I'll fucking kill him!"

"It's the police, Larry."

97

"The police?"

The assistant looked at the note in her hand. "Detective Inspector Garibaldi and Detective Sergeant Gardner."

Larry looked round to see if he could catch sight of his producer. "OK," he said, following the assistant down a corridor. "But tell Tom I need to see him. And tell him he's in deep shit."

The detectives got to their feet as Larry entered the office. "Thank you for your time," said the short one with greying hair. "I know you're busy and I won't keep you long."

Larry looked from one to the other. "What's happened?"

"We now have the identity of the man found dead at Jimmy Clark's."

"I see. Who is it?"

"It's a man called Frankie Dunne. Does that name mean anything to you?"

Larry looked at the detective with a furrowed brow. "Frankie Dunne you say?"

The detective nodded and Larry gave a slow shake of his head.

"I'm sorry," said Larry. "I've never heard of him."

"He was twenty-six, lived in North Barnes. You've never heard of him?"

Larry gave another shake of his head.

"He played for your club."

"My club?"

"Barnes Athletic. You're honorary president."

Larry nodded but he wasn't taking in much of what the detective was saying. His mind was more on his researchers' failings, and what Adam Peacock had said about masks, than it was on the man found dead at Jimmy Clark's.

*

Hazel Bloom's phone had been ringing all morning, but she'd stopped taking calls some time ago and she now sat in the first-floor living room of her house on The Terrace, searching for mentions of her name in the newspapers spread out on the table in front of her.

She knew her thoughts should be with the dead man and his family, and for much of the morning they had been. But she was now thinking less about the damage done to them than the damage the whole affair was likely to do to her. All morning she'd been conscious of paparazzi on the other side of the road, leaning against the wall of the riverside walkway, cameras trained on her house. She knew that any publicity to do with the discovery of the body at Jimmy's and the unmasking of the band was unlikely to be good, so she had done her best to keep out of sight, taking the occasional peep through blinds and curtains to see if the photographers were still there, and ignoring the doorbell when it rang.

Whoever was ringing her bell now, though, was far more persistent than whoever had done it this morning, and when the ringing showed no sign of stopping, and was accompanied by loud knocks on the door, Hazel snuck another look through the blind to see if she could make out who it was.

Stepping back from the door on the pavement immediately below was the detective who had interviewed her. He looked up at her window and, catching sight of her through the blind, indicated with a wave of his hand that he wanted to come in. It seemed she had no choice, so she went downstairs, opened the door and ushered him in, quickly closing the door behind him as the cameras flashed.

"Quite a scrum," said the detective when he had climbed the stairs and sat down. "You're attracting a lot of interest."

"It seems so."

"I've been trying to call you."

"Ah, yes," said Hazel, "well the phone's been pretty busy and I haven't been answering."

"I see. Well, what I want to tell you is that we now have the identity of the dead man found at Jimmy Clark's."

"Who is it?"

"A man called Frankie Dunne."

"Frankie Dunne?"

"Does the name mean anything to you?"

"No," said Hazel. "I've never heard of him. What do you know about him?"

"We know that he was twenty-six and that he was a local. He lived in Barnes."

"Really?"

"North Barnes. On the estate."

"I see. And what was he doing at Jimmy's?"

"We don't know yet. But just to confirm – you didn't know Frankie Dunne?"

"No. I've no idea who he is."

"I expect you meet a lot of people in your line of business, don't you? Must be difficult to remember the names of everyone you've met."

"I have never met a Frankie Dunne."

"OK," said the detective, getting up from his chair. "Well, if the name suddenly strikes a chord or if there's anything else you think of that might be relevant do give me a call, won't you?"

"Of course."

The detective stood up. "I'll let myself out. Save you having to face that lot."

When he had gone Hazel sat down at the table, looking again at the news stories in front of her.

Frankie Dunne.

She kept running the name through her head to see if it jogged any memories.

Nothing came. She had no idea who he was or why he had been found dead at Jimmy Clark's wearing that Mick Jagger mask.

But then she thought of where he lived and a thought struck her.

For many years she had been a frequent visitor to the North Barnes Primary School – all part of her work for an education charity promoting literacy. It was work she enjoyed and work of which she was particularly proud. The kids responded well to her impressions and were always receptive to her talks about books and reading.

Frankie Dunne had been twenty six. If he had attended that school when he was young, could it be that he had been there for one of her talks? She had no idea, but the possibility that he might remember her, might have been one of those laughing faces in the school hall, made her reflect yet again on the bonds that connect us all and on the sadness of his death.

She hoped the police would get to the bottom of it soon. And she hoped they would do it without probing too deeply. Being questioned by those detectives had brought her out in a cold sweat – something about them had made her uncomfortable, heightening the sense of guilt she still carried with her every day.

She knew her fears were irrational. The chances of them unearthing anything were so remote that it seemed ludicrous to imagine it, but a tiny part of her still worried about exposure.

It had been a stupid thing to do and, even though it seemed she had got away with it and no-one would ever find out, she still carried with her the sense that, at heart, she was nothing other than a fraud.

Entirely appropriate for someone who had made their name as an impressionist.

Jimmy Clark ended the call on his mobile and sat down, looking around the hotel bedroom.

Sophie came out of the ensuite bathroom. "Who was that?"

"The police. They've identified the dead man."

"Who is he?"

"Frankie Dunne."

"Frankie Dunne? Do you know him?"

"Never heard of him. Twenty-six, lives in Barnes."

Sophie Clark raised her eyebrows. "Whereabouts?"

"On the estate," said Jimmy.

"I see."

"And what, exactly, do you see?"

Sophie sat at a dressing table and started to brush her hair. "I see that he lived on the estate. What I don't see is that if you don't know him, what was he doing at our house?"

"I have no idea. I—"

"And, more importantly, how did he end up dead in our garden?"

"If I knew that, I—"

"I don't believe it!" Sophie picked up a brush and started to run it through her hair. "I go away for a couple of nights and look what happens. Another ridiculous performance from you and your mates at the Bull's Head and then a murder in our fucking house!"

"We don't know it's a murder."

"OK then, a dead body in our fucking house. A suspicious death in our fucking house."

"I didn't ask for any of this to happen, you know."

"And, funnily enough, neither did I. And I'm not the one

who decided to put on silly masks and play in a band with a bunch of their celebrity chums! I told you no good would come of it. I hate to say I was right, but—"

"You love it."

"Love what?"

"Saying you were right." Jimmy moved to the window and looked out on the view from the hotel high on Richmond Hill: the Thames meandering through Petersham towards Twickenham. "It was harmless fun, my love, nothing more."

"Harmless? Really?"

Jimmy kept his back to Sophie. "You're assuming there's some link between what we were doing and this unfortunate death."

"Of course there's a link! You were all at our house the night before. He was wearing your fucking mask!"

"But that doesn't mean—"

"What else could it mean?"

"Look, love," said Jimmy, turning to face his wife, "until we know why this Frankie Dunne was at our house in the first place we can't make any judgements, can we?"

"Of course we can make judgements. And my judgement is that you were fucking fools to do this crazy thing in the first place and it's come back to bite you."

"Well, thanks, as ever, for your support."

"My support? You have, as always, my fullest support, but whatever happens this is not going to be easy. You do realise that, don't you?"

"Of course I do. Everyone's all over it. It's a feeding frenzy."

Sophie stood up and turned from the mirror. She stood in front of Jimmy, hands on hips. "And the others? Did any of them know Frankie Dunne?"

"None of them has a clue."

"Well, they would say that, wouldn't they?"

"So you don't believe them?"

Sophie walked past him to the window and looked out.

Jimmy moved towards her. "I thought you'd like a few nights in a hotel."

Sophie turned away from the window to face him. "Are you fucking joking?"

Of all his wife's characteristics, it was her inclination to excessive swearing that Jimmy found least attractive. Luckily it was something she indulged in only when the two of them were alone. In public she was a model of decorum, the perfect partner for a national treasure. It was only when they were out of the public, or any other, gaze that she let rip. Jimmy often wondered what would happen if the scale of her crudity were ever exposed, but not as often as he wondered about what would happen were aspects of his own life to suffer the same fate.

In that, he knew he wasn't alone. If his rich and varied life had taught him anything it was that everyone had something to hide.

17

Daily Mirror

MAN NAMED IN MASKED STARS MYSTERY DEATH

Yesterday, police revealed the identity of the man found dead on Monday morning at celebrity Jimmy Clark's Barnes mansion. He has been named as Frankie Dunne, twenty-six, of Barnes.

The discovery of Dunne's body has led to speculation about the circumstances of his death and attention has focused in particular on the group of celebrities who were at a party at Clark's house the night before Dunne's body was found. Presenter Larry Benyon, comedian Hazel Bloom, actor Charlie Brougham and poet Craig Francis were all at the house after playing in a band at the Bull's Head on Sunday afternoon. Calling themselves the Okay Boomers, the stars performed in masks and costumes to keep their identities a secret. It was the fifth performance by the band at the Barnes pub. Each time they have gone under a different name and each time they have worn masks relevant to that name. As the Okay Boomers their masks were the faces of Mick Jagger, Bob Dylan, David Bowie, Debbie Harry and Paul McCartney.

A police spokesperson said, "We are investigating the death of Frankie Dunne and are speaking to those who were at the house the night before his body was discovered. We have no reason to suspect that any of them are connected to his death."

The police were unable to confirm the rumour that Dunne was found in one of the masks worn by the band on Sunday, but said that the death was being considered as suspicious and they were conducting further investigations.

Turn to page 5 for the lowdown on the celebrity masked band, the names they played under and the masks they wore.

In one of Garibaldi's recurring dreams he was QPR's manager, addressing the team at half-time. The players sat on benches in their blue and white hooped shirts, heads turned towards him, listening attentively as he addressed them.

In these dreams QPR were always behind, usually trailing by two or three goals, and Garibaldi's role was to tell the team what needed to be done to turn things around in the second half. He was always calm and rational, a man the players listened to and respected. But what was strange about these team-talk dreams was that Garibaldi never got to see the second half performance. He always woke up or shifted into another dream – often one involving being on stage with famous country singers – and never discovered whether his words had worked.

The changing room he was in now may have been a far cry from Loftus Road and the players who sat on benches may have looked nothing like professional footballers, but they were listening to him with the same level of attention as the players in his dreams.

"I'm sure you know why I'm here." Garibaldi's gaze swept the room. "And I know you must have all been very shocked and saddened to hear about the death of Frankie Dunne."

He paused. Some players bowed their heads.

"I hear from your coach that you all had some moments together earlier to reflect on Frankie's passing . . ."

He stopped, hoping no-one thought he was referring to Frankie's prowess on the pitch.

"And I don't want to add to your pain or keep you long – I know you all want to get home – but I'm here to ask for your help. There are two things I want help with. The first is that one of the last things Frankie did was turn up here on Sunday afternoon to play with you for Barnes Athletic. What we don't know is where he went or what he did between leaving the clubhouse after the game and being found on Sunday morning. So if any of you spoke to Frankie on Sunday and he mentioned anything he was doing later that day we would like to know. And the second thing, more generally, is that if Frankie ever said anything to you – anything at all – that, given what's happened to him, strikes you as significant, we'd like to know that as well. I know what it's like in a football team. A lot of chat. A lot of banter. So if Frankie ever said anything, came out with anything you think might be relevant to our investigation into his death, then please tell us. I have some cards here—" Garibaldi reached into his pocket and took out a handful – "with my number and contact details, so think about it and if there's anything, anything at all, please do get in touch."

Garibaldi paused and looked at the players. They looked uncomfortable, as if he'd just asked them to play a formation they didn't understand.

"Any questions?" he said, casting his gaze round the room again.

One player put his hand up. "You're speaking as if Frankie was murdered or something. Do you know for sure?"

"Not yet," said Garibaldi, "but we're treating his death as suspicious."

Another player raised his hand. "This band. These stars who played in masks. Do you think they're involved?"

"All we know," said Garibaldi, "is that Frankie was found at the house of Jimmy Clark. I can't say any more than that. But the more we find out about Frankie and what he was up to, the easier we'll find it to get to the root of it all and find out how and why he died. That's why I'm here."

He paused. More heads were now bowed.

"So," said Garibaldi, putting the cards on a table. "I'll leave these here. Take one and get in touch if you think of anything that might be relevant."

He looked round the room, sensing an awkwardness in the silence, as if there were things some of the players wanted to say but were nervous about saying.

One of the players had his hand raised. "I'm Steve Palmer, the captain, and this may be nothing, but on Sunday we ...well, we were all teasing Frankie a bit. As you say, a bit of banter. We do it all the time – I mean to everyone, not just Frankie."

"So what were you teasing him about?"

"The girl he was going out with. We knew he'd been

with her on Saturday night so – yeah – there was a bit of mickey-taking. Nothing malicious or anything, just a laugh. Frankie was OK about it. He was used to it and just shrugged it off with a laugh."

"Do you know the name of this girl?" said Garibaldi.

"No. He didn't tell anyone, did he?"

The players nodded in agreement.

"All he said," said one of them, "was that she was a bit...special."

"Yeah," said another. "Said she was classy – you know, posh."

Garibaldi looked round the benches. "Did he say anything else to anyone about her?"

The players looked at each other, shaking heads and shrugging shoulders.

"The thing is," said Steve, pointing at the Barnes Athletic sports bags littering the changing room floor, "Frankie turned up without his kit. Said he'd left it somewhere. He had his boots in his boot bag, but not the rest. Typical Frankie, he could be a bit all over the place at times. Anyway, he had to borrow stuff and so we were all asking him where he'd left it, where he'd been last night, that kind of thing. And he said he was seeing her on Sunday after the match."

"Did he say where they were going?"

"He didn't say where," said Steve, "but he did say it was going to be special. He was really looking forward to it."

Garibaldi's eyes swept the room. "Did he tell anyone else about this? Did he tell anyone where he was going?"

More blank looks.

"And no-one here knows who she is?"

More shaking heads.

A player raised his hand. "I don't know if this is relevant," he said, "but I got a call from Frankie on Sunday evening."

"What time?" said Garibaldi.

"Can't remember exactly. Maybe around seven."

"What did he call about?"

"He said he'd remembered something."

Garibaldi raised his eyebrows.

"Yeah," said the player. "The thing is, we were having this chat after the game about music and bands and stuff." He turned to the others. "Frankie was mad on his music, wasn't he?" Players nodded and murmured agreement. "Especially old stuff. Sixties, seventies, that kind of thing. Anyway, he'd been trying to remember the name of a band. It was driving him mad – you know when something's on the tip of your tongue but you can't quite get it. So when it came to him he had to call me."

"What was the band?"

"Little Feet."

"Little Feat, eh?"

"I'd never heard of them."

Garibaldi nodded his approval. "Great band. And funny spelling, of course."

The player looked baffled.

"It's 'feat' with an 'a' not an 'e'. Always puzzled me, that. Could be a tribute to the Beatles, I suppose, but I like to think it's ironic self-deprecation."

The player turned to his teammates with a what's-he-on-about shrug.

"Feat as in achievement, "said Garibaldi. "So Little Feat ..."

The players looked none the wiser.

"Did he say anything else?"

"No," said the player. "That was it."

"No mention of where he was?"

The player shook his head.

Another player put up his hand. "Now I think about it," he said, "Frankie did say something to me about this girl."

Garibaldi raised his eyebrows.

"It was about music. He said she liked the same stuff. Said she was a real fan."

Garibaldi made a scribble in his notebook and snapped it shut. "OK," he said, his eyes sweeping the room to take in the whole team. "Well, please do get in touch if you think of anything else. Anything at all. Sometimes things that appear unimportant can turn out to be more significant than they seem."

Garibaldi closed the dressing room door behind him, regretting his inability to keep his obscure pop music trivia to himself, and wondering whether he had time to visit Barney, the Barn Elms plane tree.

18

Deighton, standing at the front of the room, put on her reading glasses and looked down at the paper she held in her hands.

"Frankie Dunne's death was the result of subarachnoid haemorrhage and subdural hematoma – a traumatic head injury caused by strike impact. Given that fragments of glass on Dunne's clothing match the glass from the broken vase in the bedroom directly above where his body was found and given that the balcony windows of that bedroom were wide open it's reasonable to assume that he fell from there. Some of the bruising on the face and upper body is more likely to have been caused by a physical struggle than by the fall so it could also be reasonable to assume that he was involved in a fight in the bedroom before falling or, indeed, being pushed. He had a high level of alcohol in his system. No traces of drugs but the level of alcohol would have made him unsteady on his feet. None of the DNA found on Dunne has a match on the national database, but we've taken samples from those who were at the party for purposes of elimination and there are matches for them, especially on the Mick Jagger mask, which we know they all tried on."

Deighton paused and looked round the room. "Any questions?"

Garibaldi looked towards Gardner, waiting for her hand to shoot up. It did.

"So," said Gardner, "do we have any evidence that it's actually murder?"

"Nothing conclusive, but the evidence that Dunne was in a fight, the evidence of a struggle in the bedroom and where he was found does seem to suggest that someone else was involved. Forensics found plenty of fingerprints in the house and we even have some on the broken vase. Not surprisingly, we have some matches with the Boomers for some of the prints in the house but none, alas, for the prints on the vase."

"These bruises on the body," said Gardner. "Do we know for sure that the fight and the fall are connected? He could have had the fight earlier and the fall from the window could be . . ."

She trailed off, as if she'd run out of conviction.

"It's possible," said Deighton. "You can't age a bruise precisely but the report refers to them as recent. What's clear is that we're dealing with a death that is, at the very least, suspicious, and could possibly be murder. Our problem is we have nothing on Frankie Dunne. None of those at the party claim to know who he was and why he might have been at Clark's house. We have no idea when he entered the house – all we know is when and where his body was found."

DC MacLean leaned forward in his chair. "It wasn't a big party, was it? How many were there? The five Okay Boomers and two of their partners. OK, so some of them were in masks for a bit and some might have been drunk but they'd surely have noticed Frankie Dunne if he turned up when the party was going on."

"What point are you making?" said DC Hodson.

"What I'm saying," said MacLean, "is if they all left before Dunne arrived, it can't have been any of them in the fight with him."

"That's making a big assumption," said Hodson.

"And what's that?" said MacLean.

"It's assuming that everyone's been telling the truth. This is a suspicious death, possibly murder, so we can't make the mistake of believing what anyone says."

"Okay," said Gardner, "but the cameras at the front of Clark's house show all those people leaving pretty much at the times they said."

"That doesn't mean they didn't come back," said Garibaldi.

"But the cameras don't show them coming back," said Gardner.

Garibaldi nodded. "Right. And they don't show Frankie Dunne coming in either, do they?"

"Have we checked on other ways of getting into Jimmy Clark's?" asked DC Hodson.

"There's a side gate," said Gardner, "but no cameras on it."

"What about at the back?" said Deighton. "It backs on to the Wetlands doesn't it?"

"Pretty much impossible to get from the Wetlands into the back garden," said Gardner, "even if you disguise yourself as an otter."

Deighton joined in with the laughter. She liked to show she had a sense of humour. "OK," she said. "So until we have more from the crime scene, we work on the assumption that even if Frankie Dunne wasn't murdered, there still seems no good reason for him being at Jimmy Clark's house in the first place and no explanation for why he was found dead on the gravel in a Mick Jagger mask."

"There's one other thing we need to consider," said Garibaldi.

Deighton raised her eyebrows. "What's that?"

"The masks. They're still missing. All except the Jagger one, of course, which was on Frankie Dunne's face. The band say they left them on a table in the hall."

"They could be lying," said Gardner.

"So could Jimmy Clark," said Garibaldi, "but if anyone's lying the big question is why."

The room fell silent for a few moments. No-one, it seemed, had anything to offer on the missing masks.

Deighton turned to the board behind her and pointed at the picture in the middle. "OK. Frank Dunne. Where are we?"

"The last thing we have on him," said Garibaldi, "is that he played football for Barnes Athletic at Barn Elms on Sunday afternoon. His teammates say he had a girlfriend. Posh apparently, and, like Frankie, a big music fan, particularly of old stuff. They think he was with her on the Saturday night and he told one of them he was seeing her later that Sunday after the match. We don't yet know who that girl is and we're still some way off knowing how he ended up at Jimmy Clark's."

"OK," said Deighton, "and what about the Okay Boomers?"

"Nothing again," said Garibaldi. "None of them claims to have known Frankie Dunne and none of them has any idea why he was found at Jimmy Clark's house. And when it comes to the Mick Jagger mask, again they have no idea."

"There must be a connection," said Deighton. "Something brought Dunne to Clark's house. We need to find out what it was and we need to find out why he was in that mask."

Deighton looked round the room. There was an embarrassed silence, a collective sense of bafflement.

Gardner spoke up. "Do we know where Jimmy Clark's wife was that night?"

"At a friend's in the country," said DC MacLean. "Gloucestershire. Didn't get back until Monday afternoon."

"OK," said DC Hodson. "So if Dunne got into Clark's house when the party was over and everyone had gone there was only one other person there. Jimmy Clark."

"Maybe Dunne wasn't alone," said MacLean. "Someone could have come in with him."

"But we can't know that for sure," said Gardner. "What we do know is that Jimmy Clark must have been there when Frankie Dunne, for whatever reason, was in his house."

"OK," said Deighton from the front. "But we have Clark's statement and he says he heard nothing at all and the first thing he knew about it was when he saw the body on the gravel."

"Is that likely?" said Gardner. "If there was a struggle, if Dunne fell from a bedroom window, wouldn't Clark have heard it?"

"He claims to sleep with earplugs," said Garibaldi. "And it's a big house. His bedroom's at the end of a hall on the other side of the house from the room Dunne fell from. If both doors were shut the chances are he wouldn't have heard it. The big question of course is ..." He stopped and looked round the room. "... whether we believe him. At the moment the only connection we have between Clark and Dunne is the Mick Jagger mask. And that mask also links him to the other Boomers who were all at the house that night. But if the Boomers are to be believed, none of them knows Dunne, none of them has any idea why he might be at Clark's house and they all claim to have left the house before Dunne arrived."

"So what are you saying?" said Deighton.

"I'm saying a mask tells us more than a face."

The room fell silent.

"Sorry?" said Deighton.

"A mask tells us more than a face," repeated Garibaldi. "Oscar Wilde."

"OK," said Deighton. "And where does this particular gem take us?"

"The Mick Jagger mask's telling us something," said Garibaldi.

Deighton raised her eyebrows, waiting for more.

"The trouble is," said Garibaldi, "we don't—"

"We don't know what it is?"

"Exactly."

Deighton fixed Garibaldi with a stare, saying nothing for several seconds, but keeping her eyes on him. Garibaldi gave a half-smile, but there was no hint of reciprocation.

"Well maybe when you do know what that mask is telling us, and you can give us more than smart-arse quotations, you'll let us know."

Garibaldi's half-smile shrank. He had never heard his boss's voice so loud and sharp – it was almost a shout – and he had never seen her look like this before. Her face often turned into a no-tolerance zone when he came up with left-field ideas and obscure references, but the moment always passed. Now, though, that moment was frozen and his boss wore the expression of someone whose tolerance tank had emptied.

She had genuinely lost her temper, and the room had fallen silent, unnerved by the showdown, feeling the awkwardness of a class rebuked by an angry teacher.

Garibaldi turned away.

"Giacomo!"

He turned back to the voice. It had come from Deighton but it wasn't Deighton's voice. It had come from different lips. Deighton still stood at the front of the room, but she was wearing his mother's mask again and talking to him in his mother's voice.

"You mustn't do that! Stay out of trouble, keep away from the bad people. Keep your head down, do well at school and then you can get on."

He had no idea what he'd done, but he knew it must be bad and he felt terrible.

"Be a good boy. Pray to God and ask for help."

It was the old story. Guilt wherever he turned. Feeling bad for letting down his mother and feeling bad for letting down God.

Garibaldi sensed the room's eyes were on him. He turned his head to see if anyone was looking at him, but no-one was.

He turned back to Deighton and the mask had gone.

"OK," she said in her own voice. "So we need to keep asking questions. Sensible questions." She paused and looked at Garibaldi. "We need to work out what Dunne was doing at Clark's house and we need to work out why he was in that mask." She looked at Garibaldi again. "With or without the help of Oscar Wilde."

She picked up her notes and walked purposefully back to her office, leaving the team to turn to one another with raised eyebrows and leaving Garibaldi to wonder whether it was time to do something about what kept happening to him.

19

"Marks and Spencers, Waitrose, Sainsbury's, Tesco, Lidl."

"Sorry?" Gardner's brow furrowed as she joined the traffic crossing Chiswick Bridge.

"Which are you?" said Garibaldi from the passenger seat.

"What is this? Some kind of test?"

"Just asking. Not that where you shop defines you or anything, but we're creatures of habit, aren't we, and we all have our loyalties."

"So you want to know where I do my shopping?"

"Yeah. I'm curious. I mean, I may have it wrong and you might not use a supermarket at all. You might, like many of the good people of Barnes, make a point of shopping locally, supporting all those independent stores and businesses, but my guess is that, like most of the world, you can't afford it."

"You've left out the Farmers' Market," said Gardner.

"Yeah, well no-one can afford the Farmers' Market, can they? What is it – ten quid for a bag of apples? So come on, which is it?"

"I've always been a Sainsbury's person myself but Chris, well, he likes Waitrose."

Garibaldi turned towards her. "Not a source of tension, I hope."

"We're coping, mainly because we vary it. Sometimes Waitrose for him, sometimes Sainsbury's for me. Marks and Spencers when I want a treat. And Lidl when I want a surprise in the middle aisle."

"Nothing quite like a surprise in the middle aisle," said Garibaldi.

"You go to Lidl then?" said Gardner.

"I pop in when I'm in Hammersmith, yeah, but I wouldn't say I'm a regular. In my married years it was a regular weekly Waitrose shop. Then in my single years it became anywhere, and since Rachel it's been a constant surprise. Variety. Spice of life. That kind of thing."

Gardner took a left at Chalkers Corner and headed through Mortlake. "So you're not a regular at the Barnes M&S, then?"

"Not a regular, no," said Garibaldi, "but I wouldn't mind picking up a pastry while we're there. What do you reckon?"

"I reckon picking up a pastry is always a good idea. Especially when you're in a state of shock."

"What's shocked you?"

"What do you think?"

"Deighton?"

"Yeah. Have you ever seen her like that? She's usually so calm whenever you ...you know ..."

Garibaldi turned to her. "Whenever I what?"

Gardner kept her eyes firmly on the road ahead. "Whenever you come up with ...ideas."

"You mean whenever I play the smart-arse?"

"No. I—"

"It's all right. You can say it. I know what I'm like."

"OK, well whenever you do it she usually manages to smile about it. She's never been like that with you before. I mean she was angry, right?"

Gardner gave Garibaldi a brief sideways glance.

"She was, wasn't she?" said Garibaldi.

"I hope she's all right."

Garibaldi looked out of the window as Gardner drove past the White Hart and went under Barnes Bridge.

"Yeah. So do I," he said, but he knew as he said the words that, shocked though he was by Deighton's reprimand, he was currently more concerned by his own state of mind than he was by his boss's.

Five minutes later they were in Marks and Spencers, sitting at a desk in an office at the back of the store opposite Kathy, the store manager.

"We're here to ask a few questions about Frankie," said Garibaldi.

"Such a terrible thing to happen," said Kathy, a middle-aged woman with tied-back hair and an air of efficiency. "It probably sounds silly, but we're a bit like a family here and to lose someone like that...it's shocked everyone."

"What was he like as an employee?"

"Lovely." Kathy reached for a tissue and dabbed at her eye. "Everyone liked Frankie. He always had a smile, always had a word for everybody."

"Was he reliable?"

"Reliable?" Kathy looked puzzled, as if the question had taken her by surprise "Well, yes, he was. I mean he had his moments, but most of the time he was fine. Like I say, everyone liked him. He was popular."

"When you say he had his moments...?"

Kathy laughed. "Nothing serious. He liked a laugh, that's all. Could be a bit of a joker and I'd have to have a word, but never anything serious. I think he really liked working here. It's difficult to think ...the whole thing's difficult to take in. We're all in a state of shock."

Kathy reached for a tissue and blew her nose. Garibaldi gave her time to compose yourself.

"Tell me, Kathy, had there been anything about his behaviour recently that struck you as unusual?"

"Unusual? No. He was the same as ever."

"Was he particularly close to anyone here?"

"He was good friends with Danny," said Kathy. "They were always chatting and larking about. Danny's in pieces. It's hit him really hard."

"Is Danny in today?"

"Yes. Would you like to talk to him?"

"If we could, please."

"I'll get him." Kathy got up and went to the door.

While he waited Garibaldi pondered his choice of pastry. He'd just settled on a pain au raisin when the door opened and a man wearing an M&S uniform and the frightened look of a schoolboy summoned to the headteacher's office came in.

"Thanks for talking to us, Danny," said Gardner, in her best friendly tones. "We know how shocked you must be about what's happened to Frankie."

"Do you know what happened?" Danny's face jumped from Gardner to Garibaldi.

"We're still investigating," said Garibaldi.

"To be found like that, at that bloke's house. I don't believe it."

"Did you know Frankie well?" said Gardner.

"What do you mean?"

Garibaldi leaned forward. "Did Frankie speak to you about what he was up to?"

122

"What he was up to? You mean you think he was doing something wrong?"

"No." Garibaldi shook his head and gave a reassuring smile. "No, we don't mean that at all. We mean did he talk to you about things."

"Things?" Danny's eyes darted between them again. "What kind of things?"

"Anything," said Garibaldi. "Football. Family. Music."

Danny smiled as if suddenly remembering all that his friend had spoken about. "He loved his football, did Frankie. He was Chelsea, like me."

Chelsea. Given the circumstances, Garibaldi would forgive them.

"So we spent a lot of time talking about them."

"He played a bit as well, didn't he?"

Danny smiled. "Yeah. He reckoned he could have made it if things had gone differently. I've no idea whether it's true but he liked to tell the story. How he was nearly scouted. He told that story quite a lot. And then there was his music. He talked about that a lot. He liked a lot of old stuff – not my kind of thing, but that didn't stop him talking about it."

"What about his family?" said Gardner. "Did he talk about them?"

"Not much. I remember when he moved back in with his mum, round about the time he started here, he spoke about that a bit, about what it was like living back where he grew up."

"Up on the estate?"

"Yeah. He said how much it was changing. But he didn't talk much about his mum. He did once say how tough it had been for her bringing him up by herself and trying to get by. He didn't say much about his brother and, as you know, his dad . . ."

Garibaldi nodded. "Tell me, Danny. Do you know if Frankie had been seeing anyone?"

"Seeing anyone?"

"His mates in the football team said he was going out with a girl. Saw her last Saturday night and apparently was going out with her again after the game on Sunday evening. Did he mention anything to you about her?"

"He did, yeah. Sorry, are you saying that it's got something to do with what happened?"

"We don't know. We're just trying to find out what he was up to that Sunday. What did he say to you about this girlfriend?"

"Just that he really liked her."

"When did it start?"

"A couple of months ago."

"Did he mention her name?"

"Cara."

"Surname?"

Danny shook his head.

"Did he say where she lived?"

"No. All he said was that he really liked her. Met her at a gig apparently."

"A gig?"

"Yeah. He was into his music was Frankie. He was mad about it."

"So he met this girl Cara at a gig. Did he say where it was?"

"I can't remember. May have been Hammersmith."

"Did he say who was playing?"

Danny laughed. "He may have done, but it wouldn't have meant anything. We were OK on Chelsea and football but when Frankie got onto music he lost me."

"So did he say anything else about this Cara?" said Gardner.

"Not much, but he was really excited about it, you could tell."

"How could you tell?"

"He had that look – you know, the one where you give this big smile when you're talking about something and you try to hide it but you can't. But I think he was worried as well."

"Worried?" said Garibaldi. "What was he worried about?"

"He said he really wanted it to work out. Nothing had worked out for him before and he really wanted this one to. I remember him saying he couldn't believe his luck and that compared to everything before she was different class."

"Different class?"

"You know, a bit special. I think that's why he was worried about it." Danny bit his lip. "Is it true that he was wearing a mask? I mean when he was found."

"We can't comment on that."

"So he was then? Bit odd, isn't it? And all those stars in masks as well. Pretty weird if you ask me."

"We're investigating it fully."

"You think he was murdered, right?"

"We're exploring all possibilities."

Danny bowed his head and shook it slowly. "So sad," he said. "So fucking sad."

Garibaldi stood up and held out a card. "If you think of anything, Danny, give us a call."

Danny lifted his head and reached for the card. "You'll find out what happened, won't you?" he said.

"We will," said Garibaldi, sounding as confident as he could.

20

Jimmy Clark paced up and down his hotel room, with the look of a man who had run out of patience. He paused in front of the window and turned to look out on the street below.

"What I would like to know, Inspector, is what progress you've made."

Garibaldi stood in the middle of the room, regretting his decision to respond to Jimmy's call by agreeing to see him. He could just as easily have dealt with his complaints on the phone. "It's still very early days," he said, addressing Clark's back.

"I'm aware of that," said Jimmy, "but it doesn't answer my question." He turned to Garibaldi, his face a combination of outrage and entitlement. "This whole thing is a nightmare, an absolute nightmare. I still can't believe it's happened."

"Nor can Frankie Dunne's mother," said Garibaldi.

"Of course." Jimmy looked momentarily abashed, but it didn't last for long. "Look, Inspector, I still have no idea why that man was in my house, or how he got in or even who the hell he is . . .was, but I hope you understand that we need to get this thing sorted as soon as we possibly can."

"The thought had occurred to me," said Garibaldi.

Clark held his gaze and the two stood opposite each other for a few moments saying nothing. Several times Clark seemed on the point of speaking but stopped himself.

Garibaldi walked to the window and looked out. If Clark had made him talk to his back he was determined to make Clark do the same. "Was there any other reason you wanted to see me?" he said. "Or was it simply to ask about what progress we've made?"

"No, that's it. I'm anxious to know."

"I'm sure you are, but as I say it's very early."

"And I'd like to know what you've found out about this Frankie Dunne."

"What we've found out, Jimmy, is for us to know. This is a police investigation and we'll tell you anything we think you need to know. At the moment nothing falls into that category."

"You mean you don't know anything?"

Garibaldi turned from the window. "I don't mean that at all. What I mean is—"

Jimmy held his hand up in apology, the first sign of contrition or humility he had shown since Garibaldi arrived. "I'm sorry. You're doing your job, of course you are. It's just that the whole thing is so traumatic. The body. The mask. Everything. I'm beginning to wish we'd never done it."

"Done what?"

"The band. It seemed a good idea at the time, a bit of harmless fun, but now ...everyone's talking about it, as if this murder—"

"We have no evidence that it was murder."

Jimmy waved his hands in frustration. "What do you mean?"

"We're treating the death as suspicious. It may be murder, but we don't—"

"Whatever it is, my point is that everyone seems to think it's linked to our band."

"Maybe that's because Frankie Dunne was found wearing one of the band's masks. To be more precise, your mask."

"But that isn't evidence of anything, is it? Just because it happened at my house and just because all the band had been there the night before doesn't mean we're ...connected. Somehow this Frankie Dunne got into the house when the party was over and ..."

Jimmy ground to a halt, faced with the difficulty of completing the story.

"And what, Jimmy? What do you think happened then?"

"What do I think happened then? I don't know, do I? The next thing I knew I was drawing back the curtains and seeing a dead body outside!"

"And you think he was murdered?"

"I don't know."

"But you just called it murder."

"Don't *you* think it's murder?"

"I don't know. That's what we're trying to find out. So tell me, Jimmy, you heard nothing at all during the night. Is that correct?"

"Nothing. Have you read my statement?"

"Strangely enough, yes. It's part of my job."

"Well, you'll see from that that I sleep with ear plugs, always have done. Means I can get to sleep anywhere. Planes, trains ..."

"And automobiles?"

"Sorry?"

"A film."

"Look, my bedroom's at the other end of the house from

the room where it happened and I had earplugs. I heard nothing. As I say the first I knew was when I saw the body. As for what happened when Frankie Dunne got into my house I have no idea. You're the detective. I was hoping that's what you might be able to tell me."

"We will, Jimmy, we will."

Garibaldi paused and reached into his jacket pocket for his notebook. He took it out and leafed through it. There was nothing he was looking for but he wanted to give the impression that there was. He liked the silence it produced, the unease it created in whoever he was interviewing.

"You're absolutely right," he said, snapping the book shut and looking up at Jimmy. "Everyone in the papers is keen to make the connection between what happened and the Okay Boomers. Or as they have been in previous incarnations, The Presidents, The Animals, The Players—"

"I know what we were called!"

Garibaldi smiled. "I'm sure you do. And as I say, they're keen to make a link and I suppose the reason they are is that it's such a strange thing to do. A bunch of celebrities forming a band and playing in masks. It takes some explaining, doesn't it? Maybe you could tell me how the whole thing came about?"

"Of course."

Jimmy walked to a chair and sat down. He pointed at another chair and gestured for Garibaldi to sit as well.

Garibaldi sat down and Jimmy cleared his throat and steadied himself, as if he were about to deliver a piece to camera.

"It all started with a charity event at The Olympic Cinema in Barnes. I'm a great supporter of local charities – in fact we all are, all of the band. We like to give back, particularly to the community we're part of. We may be celebrities but I'd like to think that we – and I know that I definitely do – realise not everyone has it quite as easy as we do. Anyway, this event was for a cause very dear to my heart. It was a fund raiser, an auction – you know the kind of thing, where items are offered and everyone gets pissed and pays ridiculous prices to secure them. Anyway, it was raising money for the community centre in North Barnes, the one that burned down. I'm sure you remember it."

Garibaldi nodded. He remembered it very well. He also remembered the investigation and the suspicion, never proved, that it may have been arson.

"Anyway, the organisers asked me to drum up support and we managed to get an excellent turnout, a lot of the local celebrities, and the five of us ended up at the same table. Hazel, Larry, Craig, Charlie and me. And the conversation turned to music. I can't remember what started it but it may have been one of the auction items – a rare pressing, maybe something to do with the Olympic Studios – because you know that's what the cinema used to be, don't you? A world-famous recording studio. If you know the area at all, you'll know about the Olympic."

"I'm a local," said Garibaldi. "I know it well."

"Well, as I say, we were at the same table at this charity auction and the conversation turned to music and someone asked whether any of us had ever been in a band. You know, at school, that sort of thing. And it transpired that we all had. I'd been a singer – a not very good singer it has to be said. Larry had played guitar. Charlie had played drums, Craig had played bass and Hazel keyboards. So there it was. We had a band, or at least the potential of a band sitting round the table and someone said we should give it a go. I can't remember who said it and I can't remember how it all happened but we ended up doing just that. Charlie booked us in for some sessions at a rehearsal studio and I have to say it was the most fun I'd had in ages. Everyone said how much they enjoyed it. We were all a bit rusty at first but we soon got the hang of it."

"So you decided to play some gigs?"

"It wasn't quite that simple. At some stage, someone suggested we should perform in public. Again, I can't remember who it was. It's funny, isn't it? Sometimes you can't be at all clear about who said what, whose idea was whose, how certain things have come about. Does that make sense?"

"I come across it all the time," said Garibaldi. "You'd be amazed at how faulty memories can be, especially when it comes to detail."

"Anyway, when it was first mooted it was greeted with ridicule. What a crazy idea!" Jimmy gave a laugh, the kind he delivered on TV, wide-eyed and full of mock self-deprecation. "I mean, where would we do it? The five of us playing together in a band would, we all agreed, attract a high level of interest. But the more significant question was *why* would we do it? Someone suggested a big charity event to raise some money or maybe getting involved in one of those Comic Relief type things, but that didn't go down well. And then someone – and, again, don't ask me who – suggested we avoid publicity by not letting anyone know we were doing it. We'd do it in disguise. In costumes and masks. You know that TV show *The Masked Singer*?"

"I've heard of it, yes," said Garibaldi, remembering Gardner's contribution to the team meeting.

"Well, the funny thing is, a couple of us had actually been asked to take part, myself included, but for different reasons none of us had been able to. Anyway, that idea of masks and disguise didn't go down too well either at first.

There was still this reluctance, but you could tell that the more people were thinking about it the more tempting the whole idea was becoming. Then someone suggested the Bull's Head, local for all of us, nice and small and low-key and then there was ...the bet."

Jimmy paused before the word to give it emphasis.

"The bet?"

"Well, not a bet as such, more a forfeit. The more I thought about it the more I realised it was something I'd love to do, a bit of harmless fun. So I suggested we do it as a one-off and I challenged them all. Let's do it, I said. Who's in? And I looked round the room and I could see that some were keener than others. Come on, I said. Who's brave enough? And everyone looked at each other and I could see they were still uncertain and so I said, 'You're not brave enough, are you?'. In fact, what I said was, 'Do you Dare?' which, if you remember, was the name of one of my quiz shows. Then slowly the hands went up, like some Hollywood movie.

But I could see some were still a bit uncertain, so I spiced up the dare. 'Okay' I said, 'we're all in, but to make sure we all stay in, how about this? First one to drop out pays a sum of money to a charity of their choice.'"

"A sum of money? How much?"

"I'd rather not specify, but it was substantial."

"Substantial enough to make everyone think twice before dropping out?"

Jimmy spread his hands. "Who knows? We're all pretty well off and I think I can speak for us all and say we're in the habit of giving to good causes when we can ..."

"So it was all your idea then?" said Garibaldi, writing in his notebook.

"The forfeit was, yes, but, as I say, the idea for the band

and the disguise, I can't be precise about who suggested them."

"So it was intended to be a one-off?"

Jimmy held up a restraining hand, as if to indicate he had his narrative under control.

"Once we were all in, we started to prepare. We'd play the Bull's Head and we'd wear masks to keep our identities hidden. Charlie, being an actor, and Hazel being an impressionist, well they had some good advice about how to disguise ourselves. We'd wear costumes appropriate to our masks, our characters. We'd change our voices and our accents if we spoke on stage. We'd even try to walk differently – apparently the easiest way to recognise somebody is by their walk. So yes, masks, costumes. And, as you know, we decided to theme each band. Give ourselves a name and then mask and dress up accordingly. Our first performance was as The Presidents. That was supposed to be it, but the funny thing was, having done it once and enjoyed it so much, we decided to do it again. We're all performers after all, maybe that's why we decided to carry on. I think everyone was enjoying it. I genuinely think everyone did it because it was fun, and that's why we carried on. Several incarnations, ending with the Okay Boomers. Good name, don't you think? Most of the stuff we play – or rather, played, as the game is most definitely up – was from the sixties and seventies. Baby Boomer stuff. And Okay Boomers, that's what they say, isn't it? All the youngsters."

Garibaldi reached for his notebook again and opened it. "So let's get this straight," he said, pretending to read but speaking from memory. "You were Mick Jagger, Larry was Bob Dylan, Hazel was Debbie Harry, Craig was Paul McCartney and Charlie was David Bowie."

"That's it. And I can tell you who was who in all the other bands if you like."

"That would be very helpful, Jimmy. You never know what might be handy."

"I'll send it through."

"And the other masks?" said Garibaldi. "Still no sign of them?"

"They've definitely gone. Somebody's taken them."

"Who would do a thing like that?"

"I have no idea."

"One of the band perhaps?"

Clark's eyes widened in exaggerated disbelief. "One of the band? Why would they do that?"

"I have no idea. But, tell me, why did you keep them all? Why didn't each band member keep their own?"

"Look, we wanted it all to stay a secret and the best way to do that was keep the masks and costumes together and out of sight. A stray sight of one of those masks and it could all unravel. So I kept them all safe. I guess now that the secret's out everyone can have their own – apart from the Boomer masks. that is. You know, I really can't understand who would have taken them. More importantly, I can't understand why."

"That Jagger mask is very lifelike," said Garibaldi. "Looks expensive too."

"We had them all made specially. Some film special effects person, a contact of Hazel's husband, Bill, did them. We all did this mould thing for him so he had our measurements, made sure we could breathe easily and sing through them. And, yes, they were great. We could wear them all night without a problem."

"You'd have thought you might have had enough of masks after the pandemic," said Garibaldi.

"Well, there's masks and there's masks," said Jimmy. "And these were very special ones."

"I see. Well, if anything else occurs to you . . ."

"Of course," said Jimmy. "And, look, I'm sorry if I've seemed a little tetchy. It's the pressure."

"I understand," said Garibaldi, turning the doorhandle. "Difficult times."

"These masks going," said Jimmy, "you don't think their disappearance is . . .relevant, do you?"

"I have no idea," said Garibaldi as he went through the door. "Tricky thing relevance isn't it? Sometimes you see it, sometimes you don't. It likes to keep itself hidden." He raised his hand in farewell. "A bit like a face behind a mask."

21

Garibaldi cycled through Richmond Park, thinking of the parts he visited with Alfie when he was a kid: King Henry's Mound, where you could look at St Paul's Cathedral in the distance through a gap in the trees; Pembroke Lodge, with its view over Petersham towards Twickenham; the Isabella Plantation, its colours changing with the seasons; Ian Dury's bench, the seat erected in the singer's honour where you could sit down and listen to 'Reasons to be Cheerful' through headphones. And, most special of all, the spot between Richmond and Sheen Gates, which provided a panoramic sweep of the city skyline: the London Eye, the Houses of Parliament, the city's domes and spires, the Gherkin. On a good day you could see it all from here: London spread out in its mesmerising mix of the old and new.

This was the spot Garibaldi had now reached, and he couldn't resist the temptation to stop and enjoy the view. He pulled up at a bench, propped his bike against it, sat down and looked into the distance.

The ringing of his phone snapped him out of his reverie. He checked the screen – not a number he recognised. He took the call. "DI Garibaldi."

"Sean Dunne here. I'm Frankie's brother."

"Sean, thanks for getting back to me. I was wondering if we could talk."

"Sure."

"Where are you?"

"I'm in Mortlake."

"When's a good time?"

"I'm free now."

"OK, Sean, where shall we meet?"

"Can you get to The Ship?"

"The Ship? Sure."

Garibaldi hung up. A bike ride through Richmond Park followed by the pub. The day was looking up.

When Garibaldi arrived at the riverside pub he approached the only man sitting by himself.

"Sean?"

The man put down his paper and got up. "That's me. Can I get you a drink?"

"Tempting," said Garibaldi, "and very kind of you, but duty and all that."

"OK." Sean sat down and Garibaldi pulled up a chair.

"I'm sorry for your loss. I—"

Sean held his hand up to cut short Garibaldi's condolences. "Thanks. I still can't believe it."

"We'll do all we can to find out what happened, Sean."

"You mean who murdered him?"

"We don't know at this stage whether—"

"I can't see any other explanation, can you? To be found like that at . . .at Jimmy Clark's house. Jimmy Clark! I mean, what the hell was he doing there? And what was he doing wearing a mask? This band, these celebrities, I mean what the fuck is that all about?" Sean gave a sad shake of his head.

"Such a good lad, Frankie. Always kept going, always had a smile, even when things weren't working out for him, which was most of the time."

"What didn't work out for him?"

"Where do you start? Maybe it began with the football. He thought at one stage he might make it but it wasn't to be. He was good, but not that good. There's thousands of kids like him who think it could be their future but how many actually make it? Hardly any. And then there was school. He did OK. Stayed on after his GCSEs. Did A Levels at sixth form college but the results weren't great so he didn't go to uni or anything. I went and I think Mum would have liked him to go as well. He had all kind of jobs after that, never really settled and then he started on the post, which seemed to suit him. Moved out of mum's but it all went wrong – I never understood how or why – and he moved back. That's when he started working at Marks. And everything seemed, you know, OK." Sean broke off and looked to one side. "I'm sorry," he said, turning back. "You probably don't need me to tell you all this —"

Garibaldi held up his hand. "No, please do."

"It's just – well, I need to talk about him."

"Of course you do. I understand."

Sean shook his head in disbelief. "The funny thing, though, is that for the past month or so he seemed in really good shape, better than he'd been for ages. I think it was this girl he'd started seeing. Frankie's love life had been like everything else. Things would look good and then they'd go wrong, but whenever he spoke about this girl there was something about him. That's what makes it all so sad. Everything seemed to be going right at last. Now this." Sean reached for his drink and took a couple of gulps.

"Did he mention this girl's name?"

"Yeah, he did. Cara."

"And did he say much about her?"

"Not really. He said he'd started going out with her but he didn't give much away. But I could tell just from looking at him that he was pleased. And then ..."

Sean looked away again. He bit his lip and said nothing for a few seconds.

"And then what, Sean?"

Sean turned back. "When I next spoke to him on the phone it all seemed much the same. We were chatting away about the usual stuff. Chelsea. Music. He was a big music fan, you know. When Dad died Frankie started listening to all the old sixties and seventies stuff Dad used to listen to. And that was the start of it, he became a big fan. Anyway, we were chatting away as usual and then at the end I asked how things were going with Cara and his voice changed, and I could tell something was up. First of all he said things were good, but I could tell he didn't mean it, and then he said, "I've screwed up, done some stupid things.""

"Did he say what they were?"

Sean shook his head. "That's the thing. I asked him what he'd done and he said he couldn't tell me. And then a couple of days later he's ...I know what you're thinking. You're thinking I should have told you this straight away, but to be honest I've been so ...it's been so difficult. I haven't been thinking straight."

"And you have no idea what he might have done?"

"Not a clue. I mean, it didn't come as a surprise, given what Frankie ...given what he was like, but then when he said it I didn't know he'd be found dead a couple of days later."

"So do you think whatever he did might be connected to his death?"

Sean spread his hands and laughed. "I have no idea! I've no idea what he did and no fucking clue how he ended up there, like that." He shook his head in disbelief, fighting tears. "Mum, God bless her, she did her best, she always did her best for us. It was tough when Dad went but she always did her best. And now she's lost a son as well as a husband. Heartbreaking, isn't it?"

Garibaldi gave him time to compose himself. "Just a few more questions, Sean. This Cara, do you have any idea where she lived?"

"He didn't say."

"And do you know if he saw her on Sunday after he played football?"

"I don't know, but if he went out with someone it was probably her. He said he was spending a lot of time with her."

"Is there anything else that you think we need to know?"

Sean took a deep breath and sighed. "No. I can't think of anything. It's just when he said that about having screwed up , I mean, I'd heard him say that so many times before, but when he said it this time it sounded different. Maybe I'm imagining it, but—"

"You've been very helpful Sean. I know how tough it must be."

"Do you?"

Garibaldi nodded, resisting the urge to tell him how much he did. "Well if anything occurs to you that you think might be relevant, don't hesitate to get in touch."

"Of course. And I'm sorry I didn't let you know earlier. To be honest I didn't really know what to do. Everything's so . . .it's so shit." Sean looked at his watch. "Oh, well. Guess I'd better be getting back to work."

"Where do you work?"

"In East Sheen."
"What do you do?"
"I'm an estate agent."
Garibaldi looked across the table at Frankie Dunne's brother and, having no idea how to respond, got to his feet, hoping that the look of sympathy he gave him was taken as a response to his loss rather than to his working as an estate agent.

22

Jimmy Clark was no stranger to the spotlight, but the one now shining on him was so bright it hurt his eyes and it was impossible to avoid its glare. As far as the media were concerned, Christmas had come early – the story was the gift that kept on giving. No-one could stop talking about it. No-one could stop speculating.

Never had he regretted anything more. He couldn't remember whether the band had been his idea or someone else's, but of one thing he was certain. Without the band Frankie Dunne would not have been found dead in the Mick Jagger mask and he wouldn't be going through so much shit.

The more Jimmy looked back on the masked band the more he realised he hadn't really enjoyed it. Yes, he'd got a thrill from the masks, the costumes and the secrecy. Yes, he'd derived a good deal of pleasure from performing – playing in a rock band was something he'd always wanted to do. And, yes, he'd relished the challenge of coming up with new identities.

But the truth was he hadn't greatly enjoyed the company. It was like so much of what he did in the business. On the surface it was all big smiles and best friends forever but he knew, as did everyone else, all kinds of bitterness lay just below the apparent bonhomie. And when it came to some of the players in the band he knew the exact shape of that bitterness.

Take Hazel Bloom, for example (a thought that had crossed his mind more than once). He knew what he had said about her on many occasions and he stood by every word he had uttered. He simply didn't rate her, and the only possible explanation he could find for her less than meteoric rise to something she would like to call the top, but he regarded as no more than the middle, was that she had slept her way there. She had the looks all right, but the unfortunate thing was that she thought she had the brains as well. OK, she may have been to Cambridge, but he knew many a dunderhead Cambridge graduate. Things may have tightened up now on the admissions front but back in the day, or at least back in Hazel's day, all kinds of inadequates could creep through the selection process, especially when, as he knew was the case with Hazel, they had applied to the only remaining single-sex women's college. What irritated Jimmy so much about Hazel was the way someone so obviously dumb made such a public effort to show herself otherwise.

And then there was Craig. Poor Craig. He may have had some cultural clout in those long-gone populist days of the sixties when his accessible (oh how very accessible) poetry marched to the beat of the populist drum; when the 'people' had the power and poetry could pander to them (to quote a neatly alliterative phrase he had once used in an anonymous column) but those days had long gone and Craig now cut a pathetic figure, penning the lightweight ditties that showcased his ineptitude. Quite how he had been seriously considered for a prestigious poetry prize Jimmy failed to understand and he was pleased he had managed to put a stop to it.

As for Charlie, there may have been moments when Jimmy regretted what he had done to him, but such moments didn't last long. One of his therapists had once told him the only thing you can change about your past is your attitude to it and that's what Jimmy had done, focusing on a future that was still his to shape and not wasting any time looking back. He may have been in his seventies but he was in no doubt that great things still lay ahead. Life really was too short and he intended to make the most of what was left of his.

"Are you working?"

The voice was Sophie's and it came from the other side of his study door. Long ago they had agreed she should ask the question before coming in. If Jimmy was working (or if he wasn't but didn't want to be interrupted) all he had to do was say 'yes' and Sophie would go away. If it was something urgent they had agreed that Sophie should simply say what had happened and why she needed to see him.

The system worked and Jimmy was in no doubt that it had been a way of avoiding a lot of rows over the years. Rows still happened, of course, but when he was at his study desk he knew there was a good chance of avoiding them.

"Yes, I'm working," he said, addressing the closed door. "Can you give me an hour?"

"OK."

Jimmy heard his wife's retreating steps, leaned back in his chair and sighed.

Their relationship, strained at the best of times, had, since the discovery of that body in the garden, got considerably worse. It might not have been quite so bad if Sophie had been at the Bull's Head gig and the party that followed – turning up the next day to find their house cordoned off by the police hadn't been the best way for her to find out. Jimmy had insisted he was on the point of ringing her to tell her the news but it wasn't the truth. The truth was that he thought Sophie wasn't coming back from her friend's in Gloucestershire until the evening and had decided to wait until he had a clearer picture of things before giving her a call.

After she had recovered from the surprise and as soon as they had a moment when they were alone together, she had let rip. It may have been the shock, but Jimmy knew it was more than that. Everything came out. All the old complaints were given a fresh airing – almost, Jimmy was impressed to see, delivered in chronological order right up to the present day. As was so often the case when presented with the wrongs Sophie felt he had done to her down the years, Jimmy was amazed that they had managed to stay married for so long.

He heard her steps approaching the door again, saw the handle turn, and before he had the chance to repeat that he was working, Sophie came into the study, slammed the door behind her and marched towards him.

"You know what, Jimmy?" she said, hands on hips, standing in front of his desk.

Jimmy looked up with an expectant smile.

"Fuck this 'are you working' shit!"

"I thought we agreed—"

"Fuck what we agreed! You're not working. You're just sitting here avoiding me."

"I'm actually quite busy—"

"Fuck off, you are! Look, ever since this thing happened I've been in a state, a real state. You might not have noticed because your head, as usual, has been so far up your fucking arse you can't see daylight."

"It's been a difficult time."

Sophie threw back her head and gave a loud guffaw.

"A difficult time! Tell me about it. I come back from Lucinda's to find our house is a fucking murder scene and—"

"It's not definitely murder."

"Whatever, there was a dead body in our fucking garden."

Along with her habitual swearing, his wife's use of 'whatever' ranked high in his list of things that irritated him about her.

"And that night," said Sophie, now wagging her finger at him like some irate headmistress, "I ended up having to sleep in a fucking hotel!"

Jimmy waited patiently. He had heard all this before, some of it three or four times. He was waiting for something he didn't already know, something big enough to justify her barging in like this.

"I know you've done a lot of stupid things in your career," said Sophie, "but this ridiculous masked fucking band has to be the most stupid by a very long way. This whole house feels ...violated. *I* feel violated. And I can't believe that ..." Sophie paused. "I can't believe you didn't know him! I can't believe you weren't ..."

Jimmy leaned forward and rested his arms on the desk. "How many times do I need to tell you? There was nothing like that going on. I have never seen this man, Frankie Dunne, before. I mean I *had* never seen him ..."

Sophie's laugh was full of disbelief. "I've heard that line before. And you know exactly where I heard it."

Jimmy knew all right. The spa break in New York when he thought Sophie was at dinner with friends and returned to the hotel unexpectedly early.

"Didn't know his name either, did you? Hadn't come

across him before, had you? Until that night when I'm sure that's exactly what you did!"

"I don't understand why you're going through all this old stuff, dear. We've been there before."

"There've been a lot of last straws over the years, haven't there? But I have the feeling this might prove to be the real one."

"What are you saying?"

"I'm saying..."

Sophie walked to a table and picked up a vase.

Jimmy liked to have flowers in his study – they had a calming effect and helped him concentrate.

But there was nothing calming about the roses that he now saw flying towards his head.

He ducked to his right to avoid them and the vase rushed past his left ear, smashing against the wall behind him, spraying water and shards of pottery into his hair.

Sophie turned and ran through the door.

Jimmy jumped up and followed her. He knew only too well what kind of mood had descended on his wife and how dangerous it could be.

He heard the front door slam and ran to it, rushing out onto the drive and through the gates. He stood on the pavement, looking up and down Castelnau, but there was no sight of her – she'd probably already crossed the road into one of the side roads that led down to Barnes village. He thought of following but decided against it. Experience had taught him that she needed time to cool down. It had also taught him to clear his head before he was tempted to do anything rash so, deciding that a walk towards the river might be what he needed, he set off in the direction of the Red Lion.

As he passed the pub and turned onto Queen Elizabeth

Walk, his phone rang. He checked the screen, thinking it might be Sophie calling to apologise, and saw Larry's name. He let the call ring out – whatever Larry wanted (and it was undoubtedly something about the Frankie Dunne affair) it could wait. Larry was difficult to take at the best of times, but at times like this – by anyone's definition a long way from the best – he was impossible. Who the hell did he think he was? Jimmy didn't know much about football but was prepared to take it on the authority of others that Larry had been a good player in his time. What he was not prepared to take, though, was the idea that it was acceptable for this footballer to become some kind of political commentator, some kind of liberal champion. What did Larry Benyon or all those like him – uneducated, illiterate, overpaid low-lifes – know about anything? Who were they trying to kid?

And yet, Larry Benyon, like the others, had played with him in the band. Anyone looking at the two of them together in rehearsal would think they were the best of friends. They would have no idea that Jimmy had written *The Crustie* article, nor that Larry Benyon might be aware of it – he'd heard from someone at the magazine that the identity of the article's author had been leaked, and the way Jimmy had caught Larry looking at him at times during band rehearsals left him thinking this could well be true.

No. Whatever Larry wanted, he would speak to him later. What he needed to do now was clear his head, and that's what he tried to do as he walked down Queen Elizabeth Walk towards the Thames. But, try as he might, he couldn't manage it. Nothing seemed able to stop him seeing images of the dead man lying on the gravel, and nothing could take his mind off what had happened the night before.

When he got home, there was still no sign of Sophie. Whenever she stormed out she had a habit of staying out for hours to drive home whatever pathetic point she was trying to make, so her absence was not a cause for concern, and he headed for his study to get on with some work. When the doorbell rang half an hour later he went to answer it, fully expecting it to be his wife, who also had a habit of storming out without her keys.

Jimmy opened the door, but it wasn't Sophie. It was someone in a hoodie, their head bowed to the ground.

"Yes?" said Jimmy.

They lifted their head, pulled down the hood, and there, staring at Jimmy, was a face he recognised.

Bob Dylan.

Jimmy looked down at his hand and saw something else he recognised.

A gun.

23

Garibaldi looked over his computer screen at Gardner walking towards him.

"We've got something," she said. "CCTV from the Bull's Head that shows Frankie Dunne going into the music room to see the Okay Boomers."

"So that's where he went," said Garibaldi.

"Yeah. Another link between him and the band."

"Is he with anyone?"

"A woman, but the camera doesn't get her face."

Garibaldi put his hands behind his head and leaned back in his chair. "And so this could be Cara."

"Looks like it. I've been through the list of those who bought tickets in advance and Frankie Dunne bought two. There are some names there we could chase but it seems unlikely that whoever that woman is would have bought tickets if Frankie had two."

"Chase them anyway. What about other cameras in and around the pub?"

"We're checking, but it looks like Frankie and this woman didn't go into the pub before the gig for a drink. They must have gone straight to the music room."

"What about cameras in the High Street?"

"A few shops. We're onto them."

"OK. And what time is this footage?"

"Seven thirty-one."

"So we know that Dunne left the clubhouse after the football on Sunday afternoon and we know that he went to the gig that evening but we don't know what he did between then."

"Maybe they went out for something to eat before the gig."

"Maybe, but nothing on Dunne's card."

"Cara could have paid."

Garibaldi looked at Gardner, considering possibilities, constructing narratives. If the girl Dunne was with was Cara, they needed to get hold of her quickly.

His phone rang. He checked the screen but didn't recognise the number.

"DI Garibaldi."

"Something terrible's happened," said a voice he immediately recognised.

Jimmy Clark sat in the chair of his living room, sipping a whisky.

"I could have been killed! And the mask! The bloody mask!"

"It must have been a terrible shock for you," said Gardner.

"Shock doesn't come close."

"Maybe you could take us through what happened," said Garibaldi.

"Of course." Jimmy cleared his throat as if, even under these extreme circumstances, he still needed to focus on the quality of his delivery. "I went for a stroll as I often do of an afternoon down Queen Elizabeth Walk towards the river. It's a route I'm very fond of; sometimes I even pop into the Wetlands, but I do like Barn Elms, the space, the trees ..."

Garibaldi wondered whether he knew about Barney.

"When I came back, I was heading for my study when I heard the doorbell. Sophie had gone out and I thought it might be her – she has a habit of forgetting her keys – so I went to answer it and got the shock of my life. There was a man in a hoodie standing there with his head bent towards the ground. He lifted his head, pulled back his hood and there it was. The Bob Dylan mask. Then he raised his hand and I saw what he was holding. I can't tell you, I've never been so frightened in my life. I thought my number was up."

"Did he say anything?" said Garibaldi.

"That's the thing. He said nothing. Nothing at all."

"I see," said Garibaldi. "And this gun. When did you realise—"

"Look, Inspector, I've never been shot before. I don't know what it feels like. All I saw was this gun and the next thing I know my face is soaked. I thought it was blood! I thought I was covered in blood! I didn't know it was a ..." Jimmy paused, as if uttering the next words was an affront to his dignity.

"You didn't know it was a water pistol?"

"No. And the mask! Bob Dylan! Larry's mask." Jimmy's eyes were wide with disbelief. He swivelled his gaze between Garibaldi and Gardner. "And before you ask – no, it wasn't Larry."

"How can you be so sure?" said Gardner.

Jimmy spluttered. "What do you mean? Of course it wasn't. I mean ..." He broke off, his certainty wavering. "Well, why on earth would he do that to me? And why would he do it in his mask? Bit of a giveaway, isn't it?"

"Are you absolutely convinced it was the same mask?" asked Garibaldi.

"Of course it was. How many Bob Dylan masks are there around?"

"I have no idea."

"Well, I'll tell you — there aren't any like that. It's no ordinary mask and I recognised it. Look, Inspector. A man was found dead at my house on Monday morning wearing my Mick Jagger mask. The other masks go missing and now I'm attacked and lucky to escape being killed by someone wearing one of them."

"When you say escape being killed . . ." said Garibaldi.

"It could have been acid, it could have been poison, it could have been anything! And it could so easily have been a gun. A real gun! I mean, what's going on?"

"Indeed," said Garibaldi, "what's going on?"

"It's all connected, surely? First that man found dead in my mask, then the masks go missing and now this!"

"We need to keep an open mind."

"An open mind! Any bloody mind, open or shut, can see that there's something very odd going on here. What am I going to do?"

"We'll need a statement."

"A statement's not a problem. The problem is what I'm going to do. What if this person tries it again?"

"I suggest you tread very carefully, Jimmy."

"Tread carefully? What the hell does that mean? I have important things to do, I have to get on with my work. How can I do that if I think that someone is going to do that again?"

"You just need to take sensible precautions."

"Sensible precautions! What are you talking about? Is there nothing you can do?"

"We're not in the business of providing personal protection, Jimmy. If you feel the need, I suggest you—"

"The others can't believe it and, I must add, they're all very worried. First the dead man and now this attack."

"Do they have any ideas about why it happened?"

"Why what happened? The dead man? The attack on me?"

"Either."

Jimmy threw his arms in the air in exasperation. "You're the bloody detective! Aren't you the one who's supposed to have the ideas?"

Garibaldi bit his tongue. If he hadn't liked Jimmy Clark before he had met him, he liked him much less now.

"As you say, the fact that your assailant was wearing a Bob Dylan mask might suggest some connection to the band and we'll be talking to them, but, as I said, we need to keep an—"

"An open mind, yes, you've said."

"Hello?"

The voice came from beyond the closed door. All three turned towards it.

The door opened and Sophie Clark put her head round. "Can I come in now?"

"Please do," said Garibaldi.

Sophie came in and stood with her arms folded. "What on earth is going on? And, more to the point, what are you doing about it?"

"We're pursuing several lines of investigation," said Garibaldi.

"And they're keeping an open mind," said Jimmy.

"What are we going to do?" said Sophie.

"We've advised your husband to take care," said Garibaldi.

"And I've asked them how I do that," said Jimmy.

"Maybe don't go anywhere by yourself for a while. Always have someone with you?"

"For how long?" said Jimmy. "I can't have a chaperone for the rest of my life."

"This whole thing's ridiculous!" said Sophie.

"Almost as ridiculous as a bunch of celebrities playing in a masked band," said Garibaldi.

It had slipped out. He knew he needed to stay calm and professional but couldn't resist it.

"Now look here, Inspector," said Jimmy, "what we did may have been unusual, but it didn't harm anyone, did it? It's not as though any of us has killed anybody, is it?"

"As I said, Jimmy, an open . . ."

"That's ridiculous!" said Sophie, leaping to her husband's defence, "none of the band killed Frankie Dunne and to think that any of the band would do this to Jimmy – it's preposterous!"

"I'm not suggesting anything," said Garibaldi. "I'm just asking questions."

"Look," said Jimmy, turning to Garibaldi, "I don't mean to be critical. I'm in a state of shock, that's all."

Garibaldi gave a slow, measured nod. "And just to confirm, Sophie, when this happened you were where?"

Sophie and Jimmy exchanged a fleeting glance, so quick that had Garibaldi not been looking for it he would have missed it.

"As I said, I was in Barnes doing some shopping."

"I see. And you walked there?"

"Yes, it's not far. As soon as I heard I came back immediately."

"Did you walk back?"

"More of a run than a walk."

"I see. So you run, do you?"

"I keep fit, yes—look, Inspector, what are you suggesting?"

"I'm suggesting nothing. Just trying to get a clear picture of what happened when." He turned to Gardner. "Well, we'll be on our way. But, as ever, if anything occurs to you ..."

"Of course," said Jimmy. "And likewise, if you ..."

Garibaldi's sharp glance cut him short. "We'll be in touch," he said as he walked with Gardner to the door.

Something about the way Jimmy and Sophie Clark had looked at each other in that brief moment had made him feel uneasy but, as with so many other things in this case, he couldn't work out why.

In the same way that he couldn't work out what kind of criminal offence it was to shoot someone with a water pistol, wearing a Bob Dylan mask.

24

"OK," said Deighton, looking round the room. "This bizarre assault on Jimmy Clark was carried out by someone wearing the Bob Dylan mask worn by Larry Benyon in the Okay Boomers gig on Sunday evening. We have no idea who it was. CCTV at the front of Clark's house shows someone in a hoodie walking towards his door. Their hood is up and their head's not visible. There are no distinguishing features in what they were wearing but we have pictures on file so take a look. As I say, it's a very strange incident but the fact that it involves one of the Boomer masks and the fact that it was an assault on Jimmy Clark, at whose house Frankie Dunne was found, very much connects it to the case." Deighton paused. "Any questions?"

Gardner raised her hand. "It's almost, I don't know, funny."

"I think it fair to say," said Deighton," that Jimmy Clark was far from amused."

Gardner looked puzzled. "But...a water pistol?"

"I know," said Deighton with a nod. "But the mask, the victim – we have to take it seriously."

"Can we assume," said DC MacLean, "that the water pistol man in the Dylan mask is the one who stole the masks?"

"As ever, we assume nothing, but it seems likely that it is."

"Did this man in the mask actually *say* anything?" said Gardner.

"Nothing," said Deighton. "Just raised his head, took down the hood, let Clark see his Dylan mask and then let him have it with the water pistol."

"OK," said Gardner, "so if he didn't say anything can we assume it's a man?"

Deighton nodded her agreement. "Good point. You can't tell for sure from the CCTV footage. The build might suggest a man, but we can't be definite. The problem we have is that this incident is clearly connected to what happened to Frankie Dunne but we have no idea how. We still can't be sure if Dunne was murdered, but signs of struggle in the bedroom and bruises on Dunne's body all suggest the involvement of an assailant. Whatever the intention of this water pistol incident was, it clearly wasn't to kill. So why did they do it?"

"To frighten Jimmy Clark?" said DC MacLean.

"Possibly," said Deighton. "But, again, why? The trouble with this case is there's too much speculation. We need facts. We need evidence."

The room fell silent, as if searching for facts. The length of the silence showed how few there were.

"These masks," said Gardner, breaking the silence. "There's only one set of them, right?"

"Only one set? Well, we ass—" Deighton paused, looking at Gardner with a mixture of confusion and admiration. "We assume nothing and you're right. We need to find out more about them. They were made by . . ." She looked down at her notes.

"By a contact of Bill Bloom's," said Gardner. "Hazel's husband."

"OK. Let's check it out." Deighton turned to the board behind her. "So we're looking for a connection between what happened to Frankie Dunne and what's happened to Jimmy Clark."

The room felt silent again. Garibaldi, who had said nothing so far, leaned back in his chair, arms folded. He sensed the tetchiness, the frustration at having nothing but a string of questions.

"OK," he said. "What we need to do is remind ourselves of what masks do. What do they do? They disguise you. They hide your face. So it's entirely possible someone pushed Dunne to his death thinking he was someone else."

He paused to let the room take it in.

"It could be a simple matter of mistaken identity," he continued, "a matter of thinking it was someone else behind that mask. And who might they think that someone was? Well, there was one person particularly associated with that mask and that person was Jimmy Clark. He'd been wearing it that evening in the Bull's Head."

"But surely," said DC MacLean, "you couldn't mistake Frankie Dunne for Jimmy Clark? I mean, Dunne's young and fit and Clark, well he's not is he? Surely you'd tell from their bodies, from their shape."

"You're right," said Garibaldi, "but when you're looking at someone in a mask where do your eyes go? They go to the mask. That's where they're drawn."

"OK," said Gardner, "but if someone thought it was Clark behind that mask, doesn't that narrow it down to the other Boomers? They were the only ones who knew Clark was wearing the Jagger mask."

Garibaldi shrugged and spread his hands. "Do we know that for sure?"

"Not for sure, no. But the whole thing was secret, wasn't it?"

"We need to find out," said Garibaldi. "Because if Frankie Dunne was killed because someone thought he was Jimmy Clark we have a connection between his death and Dylan with the water pistol. In both cases someone was out to get Jimmy Clark."

"But hang on," said Gardner. "Dunne ended up dead and Clark ended up wet. It doesn't add up."

"Sure," said Garibaldi. "Dunne ended up dead, but we don't know for sure that he was *killed*. Bruises, signs of a struggle. It's not definitive evidence."

"But a water pistol?" said Gardner. "What kind of act is that? How does that 'get' Jimmy Clark?"

"Right," said Deighton from the front. "We need to consider everything. It could well be that Clark was the target in both cases. And if someone was out to get him we need to ask who and why. But even if this theory's right we're still left with the problem of working out what Frankie Dunne was doing at Jimmy Clark's house. It's his death that we're investigating and we can't abandon that investigation because we're blinded by some theory of mistaken identity."

She threw a glance in Garibaldi's direction. Garibaldi felt reprimanded even though the more he thought about his theory the more convincing it seemed.

"So," said Deighton. "Let's get back to Frankie Dunne. We know that he was at the Okay Boomers gig at the Bull's Head. We have camera footage of him going into the music room on Sunday afternoon. And he was with a woman."

Deighton nodded towards Garibaldi.

"Yeah," said Garibaldi. "Her head's turned away from the camera so we don't have much to go on but the chances are this woman is his girlfriend, Cara. At the moment all we have is her name, but we need to find her. Dunne's mates at the football knew he was going out with her but say he didn't give much away. His mate at M&S, Danny, says Dunne was really happy with her. But that's all we've got. There's one other thing we need to remember, though, and that's what his brother Sean told us. Frankie spoke to his brother on the phone a couple of weeks before he died and said that he'd screwed up and was in trouble. He didn't say anything more than that, and according to Sean Frankie often said it, but it could be significant."

"It could be," said Deighton. "And we need to keep our focus on Frankie Dunne. It's possible that Clark could have been the target, we can't rule anything out, but we need to remember it's Dunne's death we're investigating. We need to find out more about him. By all means—" she cast another glance towards Garibaldi, "—find out more about Jimmy Clark but let's not be too smart-arse about things and keep our focus on the facts. Mask or no mask, it was Frankie Dunne who died."

Deighton had done it again. There was no disguising the hostility in her voice. She had lived with Garibaldi's theories for a long time and was more than familiar with his desire to see things outside the box (sometimes in a different box entirely) and his fondness for the obscure reference or quotation. And she was practised at, if not tolerating them, then giving the appearance that she did.

So why did she keep turning on him?

Gardner fell in beside him as they walked back to their desks. "Someone got out the wrong side of bed again this morning."

"It's probably the investigation," said Garibaldi, momentarily thrown by an image of Deighton and Abigail in bed. "When you don't seem to be getting anywhere it gets to you."

"Still. I'm surprised she's done it again. And I thought that theory of yours was a pretty good one. That the killer thought he was getting Jimmy Clark and not Frankie Dunne? Do you think it's likely?"

"I've no idea," said Garibaldi. "It just came to me so I thought I'd throw it out there."

"Makes sense, though, doesn't it?" said Gardner. "I mean it's a neat connection to the Bob Dylan water pistol thing, but do you really think someone would want to kill Jimmy Clark?"

"It's more than possible," said Garibaldi, sitting down at his desk. "Whenever I've spoken to him I've felt like doing it myself."

www.bbc.co.uk/news

TV STAR IN BIZARRE MASK ATTACK?

Days after a dead man was found at his house, Jimmy Clark has been involved in a bizarre incident. Sources have informed the BBC that yesterday the TV star was assaulted on the doorstep of his Barnes home by a masked man. The attacker, who sprayed Clark with a water pistol, is said to have been wearing one of the masks worn by the celebrity masked band, the Okay Boomers, in their performance at the Bull's Head on Sunday.

Police have yet to confirm details of the incident and its possible connection to the discovery of Frankie Dunne's body at Clark's house. DCI Karen Deighton said, "We are exploring all possible lines of enquiry in our investigation into the death of Frankie Dunne."

Frankie Dunne's body was discovered the morning after a party at Clark's house attended by members of a band of celebrities who have been performing under a range of names and in a variety of masks and costumes to preserve their identity.

The celebrities – Jimmy Clark, Larry Benyon, Hazel Bloom, Craig Francis and Charlie Brougham – were unavailable for comment.

25

"Cheers!"

Craig clinked his glass against Hazel's.

"Cheers!" Hazel met his eye and then glanced round the bar of the Red Lion – not so much, Craig thought, to see who was there as to see who'd noticed that she was. She turned back. "Though I can't find much to be cheerful about at the moment, can you? I can't stop thinking about it. First that poor man and now this thing with Jimmy. I couldn't believe it when I heard it. The Dylan mask! And a water pistol for fuck's sake! I mean what's going on?"

Craig had no idea what to say. Like Hazel, he was completely baffled.

"Jimmy's totally shaken up," said Hazel. "And who can blame him? I mean it sounds harmless enough – a water pistol and a mask – it even sounds childish, but it's kind of freaky as well, isn't it?"

"It is. And I guess it's connected in some way."

"Has to be. The mask. Jimmy's house. But as for why . . . I tell you, Craig, this whole thing is awful. I don't know about you, but I'm not getting much sleep. I feel like Lady Macbeth."

"You mean—?"

Hazel laughed. "Not the blood on the hands bit, just the disturbed sleep."

"What? Sleepwalking?"

Hazel laughed again. "Not as far as I know. Or if I have been, Bill hasn't mentioned it. No, this whole thing's got to me. I'm finding it difficult to focus."

"Yeah. Me too."

Hazel leaned back, ran her hands through her hair and sighed. "Look, Craig, I wanted to talk to you because...well, because I wanted to talk to the most sensible of all of us."

"But he wasn't free so you chose me."

Hazel gave a brittle laugh. "I'm serious. You are. Larry, Charlie, they're OK and as for Jimmy – no, I've always thought you're the least, how shall I put it, touched by fame?"

"You mean the least famous?"

"Not at all. I mean touched as in affected by."

Craig had never been able to work out whether or not he actually liked Hazel. It was a problem he had with many people he met through his work, but with Hazel it seemed particularly acute. What she did was good, especially her impressions, and he enjoyed her company. She'd made band rehearsals fun and brought a welcome energy to their performances, but something about her irritated him in a way he couldn't pin down. Maybe it was her insecurity. All showbiz people, no matter how confident their public personae, were insecure, but there was something unnerving about the way Hazel showed it. Whereas he had made a career out of playing down his education and intelligence, Hazel had done the opposite. She always seemed to be trying to show how clever she was.

Hazel leaned across the table. "I can't stop thinking about that poor man. So young, not much more than a boy, lying there, dead, in that mask. And I keep wondering...look, we're not *involved* are we? We don't know Frankie Dunne and the fact that he was found at Jimmy's after our party, that doesn't connect us, does it?"

"Not necessarily, no. But I can understand why the police think it might."

"Those detectives made me feel so guilty! I mean I'm *not* guilty, obviously, and I can't believe any of us is, though..." Hazel screwed up her eyes and turned her head to one side, as if weighing something up.

"Though...?" prompted Craig.

Hazel turned back. "I'll be honest with you Craig, when it comes to Jimmy I have my doubts."

Craig gave a knowing laugh. "Well, we all have our doubts when it comes to Jimmy, don't we?" He knew the rumours. Jimmy Clark's infidelities. Jimmy Clark's sexual tastes. The real Jimmy Clark that lurked behind Mr Nice Guy. "Are you saying he's not telling the truth?"

"I'm saying I have my doubts. We all say we have no idea who this Frankie Dunne is and my question is, what was he doing in Jimmy's house after we'd all left? Why was he there when Jimmy's wife was away?"

"So you think it's something sexual?"

"It's possible, isn't it?"

"It's possible, but there's nothing criminal about that, is there?"

"But there is something criminal about pushing someone out of a window."

"We don't know that's what happened."

Hazel shook her head dismissively. "And the mask. What are we supposed to make of the mask?"

Craig spread his arms wide. "I know as much, or as little, as you do."

"The thing is," said Hazel, "the mask points the finger even more firmly at Jimmy, doesn't it? It was his mask after all."

"But we were all fooling around with it. I'd been wearing it. So had you."

"We weren't found dead in it, though, were we?"

Hazel sipped her drink and took another look round the bar. "OK, I'll be absolutely straight with you here, Craig. The thing is, I've never really liked Jimmy. Something happened some time ago. I've never told anyone about it but now that this has happened I just feel the need to unload it and, as I say, you're . . ."

"I'm the one least touched by fame."

Hazel held up her hands. "I really didn't mean it that way. Look, I'm really not sure I should tell you this—"

"Please do. You can trust me."

Hazel braced herself. "OK, well a few years ago someone was planning a new quiz show, a comedy quiz show. I can't even remember what it was going to be about or what it was going to be called, all I know is that it never got made but at the planning stage someone suggested that I should be a permanent team captain and Jimmy was dead against it. I have it on good authority that he dismissed me as – and I can give you the exact words – a 'jumped up, talentless bitch who's not as clever as she thinks she is and who's slept her way to success'."

Hazel paused, waiting for a reaction.

"Are you *sure* he said that?" said Craig.

"I have it on excellent authority. And I know what you're going to say. That's what the business is like. You've got to be tough-skinned if you want to succeed, don't think you're not going to make enemies. Et cetera. I know all that, and I've had bad things said about me by many people, but the thing is I've been able to keep out of those people's way. Then the band thing happened and I ended up spending more time in Jimmy's company than was good for me. I couldn't get it out of my head — that that was what he really thought of me."

"I'm sorry," said Craig. "Maybe you shouldn't have—"

"Shouldn't have joined the band? Right now, I'm wishing I never went anywhere near the bloody thing. I'll be honest with you, I enjoyed getting together to give it a go. It was a laugh, a real laugh. But when it was suggested we perform in public, that's when I should have said 'enough'. And when masks were mentioned . . ." Hazel threw back her head with an exaggerated laugh. "I don't have a problem with masks. After all, I spend much of my working life putting them on when I do impressions—- not real ones, you understand, but imagined ones — but I should have realised the whole thing was a potential minefield."

Craig nodded. He couldn't agree more. "I felt the same, but if I'm honest, I didn't want to be the first to say no. And then there was the forfeit—"

He shook his head at the memory. It may have been pocket money to other band members but it wasn't to him, and it certainly wasn't to his wife.

"I know," said Hazel, "it wasn't the money so much as the thought of being the first to go, of letting the others down. And the truth is, once it had started I quite enjoyed it. The costumes, the music, the secrecy, the performances. It was fun, wasn't it?"

"I thought it was," said Craig, "but now it's over I think maybe I was kidding myself."

"Really?" said Hazel. "Well, maybe I was too, thinking

I was OK spending so much time with Jimmy. I've been around too long – we've both been around too long – to believe that you can trust those who claim to be your friends. Neither of us is a starry-eyed youngster dreaming of fame and desperate for success. But there's something about Jimmy, something about what he said. I find it very difficult to forgive him."

"Who told you he said it?"

"My husband. A good friend of his was at the meeting when he said it. And the friend thought I should know."

"OK," said Craig, "so is this why you think Jimmy's not telling the truth about Frankie Dunne?"

"All I'm saying is I don't trust him. We all know he's not what he seems. All that public school, old fogey charm. It's a complete front. Underneath there's someone else entirely."

"Are you suggesting he's . . ."

"There's a Hyde to his Jekyll. We all have our dark sides. It's just a matter of how dark it is and how often we give in to it."

"So you think Jimmy's involved in what happened to Frankie Dunne?"

"I think he has to be. His house. His mask. He finds the body."

"What do you mean, he finds the body?"

"He was the one who found it. He called the police. Perfect cover."

"No, I don't see it."

"Look, I'm not saying for sure, I'm just throwing it out there. And as for this water pistol thing, that really points the finger at him doesn't it? I mean I don't know for the life of me who's done it or why but it's . . ."

Craig nodded as Hazel gave further consideration to the implications of the assault, but he was no longer taking in anything she was saying. His mind was somewhere else entirely, thinking of the time when he himself had been on the wrong end of Jimmy Clark's sharp tongue.

Quite how Jimmy Clark had ended up on the judging panel of the Stanza Poetry Prize he had no idea – like everything in Jimmy's career it was something he had slipped into, his charm smoothing his passage into so many areas of the nation's cultural life. And what it was that had provoked his blistering dismissal of Craig's nominated volume (reported to him in confidence by a fellow judge) he still could not fathom. He liked to think it no longer rankled but he knew, deep down, that it did. "Not so much Wordsworth as Woolworths. A cut-price poet and a cut-price intellect – a travesty of the art and a lightweight contender". The words were engraved in his memory like a line from one of his own poems.

So why, when he knew what Jimmy had said about him, had he agreed to play in the band? Why had he chosen to spend so much time with someone for whom, if he were honest, he had nothing but contempt? Was it the forfeit and the fear of being the first to bale, or was it something more, that old feeling of needing to be part of the gang, to keep in with those who mattered? Was it the fear of the outsider who wanted to belong, the fear that had accompanied him through his whole career?

If he'd been strong enough to say no, things might have turned out differently. Frankie Dunne may still have died, but at least he himself would have been nowhere near the scene and he would have been spared the police questioning that had brought him back to his one dealing with the dead man.

Yes, it had been a very long time ago. And, yes, Dunne had been no more than a kid, but the memory had rushed back with frightening clarity – the training session at Barnes Lions when Dunne's ferocious, two-footed, studs-up, leg-breaking tackle on his son had triggered protective parental instincts in a way that had frightened him and provoked his threat to Dunne after the session.

"Do anything like that again to my son and I'll break your legs and then I'll fucking kill you!"

That's what he'd told him when he took him aside after the session. The loss of control, the murderous rage, was familiar to him – he'd lived with it for most of his adult life – but whenever it surfaced it always shocked him. For many years he had lived in fear that it might have terrible consequences, and he had also lived in fear that his secret, known only by his wife and the few others who had been on its receiving end, might become more widely known.

That the nation's favourite poet should be exposed as the perpetrator of so many far from poetic acts remained his greatest fear.

"And then I'll fucking kill you!" He could still hear himself delivering the threat to the young Frankie Dunne.

He'd made it the final line of 'Injury Time', one of the few poems in his illustrious career that he had chosen to burn.

26

Doreen Amos opened the door of her house on the North Barnes estate, and looked surprised when Garibaldi and Gardner showed their warrant cards and introduced themselves.

"I've already told the police everything I know," she said.

"I'm sure you have," said Garibaldi, "but I hope you don't mind answering a few more questions."

Doreen looked at Garibaldi and Gardner suspiciously before slowly pulling the door wider, stepping back and closing the door behind them.

"We have your statement," said Garibaldi, sitting down in the living room, "but wondered if you could tell us a little more."

"As I said, I've already ..." Doreen stopped herself and looked from one to the other, her eyes wide with disbelief. "I still can't take it in, you know. To see him lying there like that. In that mask! And then that thing with Jimmy. Another mask! Is that what you're here about?"

"Part of it yes," said Garibaldi.

"Well I really can't help you there. It's horrible. The whole thing is horrible and goodness knows what Jimmy must be feeling. What a dreadful thing to happen. I tell you, he was in a terrible state when I saw him in the garden that morning, and so was I. To see the body lying there like that in that mask. And then to discover that it was Frankie—"

Garibaldi shot Gardner a glance.

"You knew Frankie Dunne?"

"Yes. I mean, when I turned up that morning and saw Jimmy out there with the body I had no idea who it was and I never got to see his face. It was only when I read it in the news that I realised." Doreen clasped her hands tightly in her lap. "Everyone round here's devastated. Lovely lad." She shook her head slowly. "His poor mother. As soon as I heard who it was behind that mask I went round there. "

"You went round to Eileen Dunne's?" said Garibaldi.

"I've known her for years. Our boys were at school together."

Garibaldi took out his notebook. "Can we go back for a moment? When you saw Jimmy Clark standing over the body on Monday morning, you had no idea who was behind the mask?"

Doreen shook her head. "No idea at all."

"The Mick Jagger mask was still on?"

"Jimmy – Mr Clark – said he'd called the police and they'd said not to touch him, not to touch anything. He told me to stay inside until the police came and that's what I did. So I had no idea it was Frankie. And, as I say, as soon as I found out I went round to Eileen's. I had to."

"Does Eileen know that you clean for Jimmy Clark?" said Gardner.

"She does, yes."

"And does she know you were there shortly after Jimmy Clark discovered the body?" said Garibaldi.

"That's what I told her when I went round. And I told her I didn't know it was Frankie because of the mask."

"When we spoke to Eileen," said Garibaldi, "she didn't mention any of this."

Doreen's eyes widened. "If she was anything like she was when I saw her she wouldn't have been making much sense. She was in a state of shock. Couldn't take anything in."

"And you've known Eileen for a long time?"

"We go back years. As I said, Frankie was at school with Mark. That's my son. Him and Mark, they grew up together. Primary school. Secondary school. And they stayed close since they left. They still saw each other, still played football together."

"For Barnes Athletic?" said Garibaldi.

"That's right." Doreen looked surprised that he knew.

Garibaldi looked at the photographs on the mantelpiece and pointed at one of a young boy crouching with a football at his feet. "Is that him?"

Doreen turned. "Yeah, that's him. And in that one—" she pointed at a picture of a team, "—he's with Frankie. They were nine or ten I guess. I still can't . . ."

Doreen reached for a tissue. "Poor Eileen. I can't imagine what she's going through, and to think that when I turned up that morning and saw the body lying there – to think it was Frankie . . ."

"Where does Mark live, Doreen?" said Gardner.

"Just over the bridge in Hammersmith. The Queen Caroline estate."

"Do you have his phone number?"

Doreen looked taken aback. "Why do you need that? You don't think he's involved in any way, do you?"

"Not at all," said Garibaldi. "We just need to speak to Frankie's friends, people who knew him."

"Mark's taken it very badly. I mean, we're all upset but Mark, it's like he's lost a brother. He's gutted. Can't take it in at all. Couldn't believe it when I told him and now that he's back—"

"Has he been away?"

Doreen nodded. "He was away when it happened. Took his wife to the coast for a few days. Nothing fancy, but they had the chance to stay in a mate's place in Brighton. They'd had it booked for ages and they hadn't been away anywhere for a long time. You know the way things have been, tough times for everybody, cost of living and all that. I didn't tell him until he came back. I mean, I didn't want to ruin it for them. And when I told him he was furious, really angry."

"Angry?"

"Yeah. He thought I should have told him about Frankie. But I didn't want to ruin their break. I mean, what if I'd told him and he'd wanted to come back. Did I do the right thing?"

"I'm sure you did," said Garibaldi. "What does Mark do, Doreen?"

Doreen sighed. "What does he do?" She furrowed her brow, as if she found it a difficult question. "A bit of this, a bit of that. A few driving jobs here and there and he does some delivery thing, you know takeaways on his bike and stuff, what's it called Deliveroo or something, or is it Uber Eats, I can't remember. His wife hasn't got anything regular either. Like me, she does some cleaning but you know how it is, it's tough. Frankie, he was lucky to end up at M&S, he loved it there."

"Tell me, Doreen," said Gardner. "When did you last speak to or have contact with Frankie?"

"You don't think I—?"

Gardner held up a reassuring hand. "We don't think anything, Doreen. We're just trying to find out as much as we can."

"I hadn't seen Frankie for a while, but I did speak to him recently." Doreen looked puzzled. "When did I speak to him?" She nodded as the memory clarified. "That's it. Of course. I spoke to him last Thursday; I remember now because Mark was going off to Brighton that night after training and that's when Frankie gave me a call."

"What did he call you about?"

"He said Mark had picked his football kit up by mistake and he needed to get it back. I told him Mark was away and he seemed pretty fed up. Said he needed it and asked if I had a key to Mark's place. Well, I don't have one so I told him and that was it. As I say he was annoyed at first, I could tell, but then he was OK about it and that...well, that was the last time I spoke to him. Next time I saw him he was...well, you know where he was. Lying there...that mask..."

"How long have you been cleaning for Jimmy Clark, Doreen?" said Gardner. Her voice was always soft and gentle, unlike Garibaldi's.

"About five years now."

"Five years? You must know him pretty well."

Doreen shrugged. "Not really. I'm just his cleaner. I mean, he speaks to me and we have a little chat so I sort of know him a bit, but not very well."

"How often do you clean for him?"

"Once a week. Monday mornings usually, unless he tells me otherwise."

"And what's he like to work for?"

Doreen's smile suggested she was privy to a side of the celebrity few got to see. "I know not everyone likes him and they find him a bit stuck-up, but he's never been like that with me at all. He's always been OK. I was worried at first, because I'd never cleaned for a famous person before and when the agency suggested it they made a big thing about how I needed to be careful and not tell people things."

"What kind of things might you tell them?" said Garibaldi.

"I don't know. Things about his personal life, I suppose. They probably thought I might find out something and, I don't know, sell it to the newspapers."

"And did you find out anything?"

Doreen looked shocked. "Like what?"

"Anything."

"Well, I wouldn't tell you if I did, would I?"

"Really?" Garibaldi put on his best stern teacher face. "I think you would if you were being asked questions as part of a police investigation into a murder."

"Yes, of course, I mean . . .you don't think Jimmy Clark's involved, do you?"

"All we know is that Frankie Dunne was found dead at his house and Jimmy Clark found him. Tell me, Doreen, had you ever seen Frankie Dunne at Jimmy's house before?"

"Frankie? No, never."

"And had Jimmy ever mentioned him at all?"

"Why would he? We didn't talk about stuff like that."

"Stuff like what?"

Doreen looked startled, as if she'd walked into the path of blinding headlights. "I don't know what you mean."

"What I mean," said Garibaldi, "is we are trying to work out what Frankie was doing at Jimmy's house late on Sunday night and what he was doing in that mask. If they knew each other . . ."

"I don't know what you're suggesting."

"I'm not suggesting anything. I'm just asking if they knew each other."

"I have no idea, but I don't think so. I still can't believe it.

All I did was turn up on Monday and there was Jimmy out there in the garden standing over a body. I had no idea it was Frankie. That mask ..." Doreen gave her head a shake, as if trying to rid herself of the memory. "I've had nightmares about it, I really have. I've woken up in the middle of the night seeing Mick Jagger's face!"

"It must have been awful for you," said Gardner, leaning forward. "We appreciate the trauma you've been through."

"And I've given a statement," said Doreen. "I've told the police everything."

"What do you talk about, when you have a little chat with Jimmy?"

"We don't have long conversations or anything but he sometimes asks after the family and things like that. Wants to know what they're up to."

"And what about Jimmy's wife?"

"Sophie? She's OK."

"You don't sound convinced."

"She's OK. They both are. I probably get on better with Jimmy, but maybe that's because I see more of him and he tends to talk to me more than Sophie. Look, I know a lot of people think he's a bit la-di-da and snooty, but I think he's OK and I can't tell you how upset he was when he found that body."

"You weren't with him when he found it, were you?"

"No, but I could tell he was shocked. I mean, who wouldn't be?"

Garibaldi took out his notebook and leafed through it. He stopped at a page. "So Jimmy Clark called it in at 8.15 and you arrived at 8.30. So there was fifteen minutes between him calling the police and you turning up?"

"He said he'd called the police and they said not to touch anything and to wait for them."

Garibaldi nodded to Gardner and they both stood up.

"Thanks for your time, Doreen," he said as he walked towards the door. "We'll be in touch with your son."

"I'll let him know, but I can't think he's...I still see it, you know, that mask. There's something about a mask."

Garibaldi followed Gardner to the car, nodding inwardly at Doreen Amos's words.

There was, indeed, something about a mask.

27

Charlie Brougham sat in The Olympic Cinema members' room, conscious that eyes kept turning towards him. Or, to be more painfully accurate, towards Larry Benyon. When it came to fame, Larry was in a different league. Charlie may have once been in that league himself, but it was now long ago, a fading distant memory of a time when the lights shone on him brightly. Being with Larry, though, brought it all back to him. The way he managed to give the impression he had no idea anyone was looking at him while conveying enough discomfort to give the simultaneous impression that he knew everyone was — at the height of his own fame Charlie had carried himself in exactly in the same manner.

"Thanks for coming out," said Larry.

"No problem." Charlie took a sip of his cappuccino. It was mid-morning, too early for a drink.

Larry leaned across the table and lowered his voice. "Tell me, what do you make of it all?"

The question puzzled Charlie. The truth was he didn't have a clue what he made of it all, but the way Larry had asked the question made him think there was something he'd missed, as if Larry knew things of which he was unaware.

"When you say 'it all'?"

Larry spread his arms, palms up. "The whole thing. The body at Jimmy's and now this thing on Jimmy with the mask and water pistol."

"The honest truth is I have no idea. Shocked and horrified by the dead man, obviously, but when I first heard about what happened to Jimmy I have to admit I thought it was quite funny."

"Yeah, me too."

"But then when I thought about it, it's not funny at all. In fact, it's pretty frightening. OK, it was only a water pistol, but it could have been anything. And that mask ..."

"Do you think it's got anything to do with the dead man?"

Charlie stroked his chin. "Difficult to think otherwise, isn't it? Why else would they wear one of the masks?"

"Exactly. And then there's also the question of where they got it. We know they disappeared, so the chances are whoever took them—"

"We can't know for sure."

"We can't know anything for sure, and that includes why whoever it is did the fucking thing in the first place. I can only think it was to frighten him, to warn him."

"Warn him of what?"

"Search me."

"But there's another question, isn't there, Charlie?"

"What's that?"

"The question of whether we're safe. Could the same thing happen to us?"

"But we're ...I mean I haven't done anything."

"And you think Jimmy has?"

"I'm not saying that."

Larry sat back in his chair, his raised eyebrows suggesting

that he wasn't convinced. "Look," he said, leaning forward again. "Can I be honest with you?"

"Sure."

What was coming? Charlie braced himself.

"I don't think we've all been telling the truth."

"What do you mean?"

"This man, Frankie Dunne. I don't believe none of us knew him."

"You think we've been lying?"

"Not all of us, no."

"Well I haven't been."

"I'm sure *you* didn't know him, and I'm sure most of the others didn't either. I believe Hazel and I believe Craig, but . . ."

"But Jimmy?"

Larry shrugged. "All I'm saying is it's a bit unlikely he could end up in his house like that, wearing that mask, unless . . ."

"Unless what?"

"Look, if he wasn't there when we left he must have got into that house some time after the last of us left. When was that? One o'clock? So how did he get in?"

"He could have broken in."

"The police say there was no sign of breaking in, so my guess is that . . ."

"You think . . . ?"

Larry gave a slow nod. "Jimmy let him in."

"Why?"

"Young man. Fit. Handsome."

"I don't see it."

"His wife was away."

"Look," said Charlie, "if anything like that had gone on the police would have told us, wouldn't they?"

"I don't know. But we've all heard things about Jimmy." Larry leaned back in his chair, adopting the expectant interviewer look he wore on TV. "Tell me, Charlie, what do you make of him? I mean, really make of him."

Charlie hesitated. What game was Larry playing? "He has his faults," he said, "but then who doesn't?"

He wasn't ready to give Larry his true opinion. Not yet.

"But do you trust him?" said Larry, "because I'll be honest with you. I don't. I don't trust him one bit. He—" Larry stopped and looked anxiously round the room, as if trying to decide whether or not to continue. "He did something to me once."

"Did something?" said Charlie.

"Look, I don't know whether to tell you this but given...everything, I think maybe I should. The thing is, Jimmy wrote something about me once. Something pretty nasty."

"Really? I don't remember seeing it."

"You wouldn't have. It was in that ridiculous old fogey magazine *The Crustie*."

"I know the one," said Charlie, deciding not to add that he was a regular reader.

"I shouldn't imagine for one moment that you read it, but even if you did you wouldn't have noticed it because it was all anonymous. Or rather, it was under the name of a columnist who goes by an alias. My guess is there's a whole load of them taking it in turns. 'The Grumbler', that's what it's called. Every month a different grumble from him, or at least I assume it's a him. It really is Grumpy Old Man territory. Anyway, one of these articles was all about me and I have it on very good authority that said article was written by none other than Jimmy Clark."

"Really? What did—?"

Charlie stopped himself. He didn't want to seem too keen to know the details.

"What did he write?" said Larry. "I'd like to say I can't remember but the truth is I can remember every word. I could probably quote you the whole thing if you want, that's how much it hurt."

"I know what you mean," said Charlie, still keen to hear the details. "I can quote you chapter and verse of all the bad reviews I've had. The real stinkers. They're the ones you remember, aren't they? The ones that stay with you and follow you around, whispering in your ear."

Larry's smile was one of weary acknowledgement. "I'm used to criticism. I've been on the end of it ever since I started out as a footballer all those years ago. Benyon's overrated. Benyon can't pass, can't head. God knows why he's worth that much. But that was nothing to when I started in broadcasting. And, to be fair, I expected it. If you're known as a footballer, people find it difficult when you try to reinvent yourself as something else. But there was something about this Jimmy Clark – sorry, this 'Grumbler' article – that set it apart. "Who is this man?" That's how it began. "Liberals are bad enough, but when the one spouting liberal platitudes is best known for having been a footballer, the whole thing becomes more laughable than usual."

Larry chuckled. "And you thought I was joking when I said I'd remembered the whole thing. But that's not the worst. Do you want to hear the rest?"

Charlie couldn't wait. His nod tried to disguise his enthusiasm.

"He said, 'The problem with Larry Benyon is that he expects us to take him seriously. He knows he can only afford to parade his left-of-centre views because of the massive wealth he acquired from his footballing career and we all know what professional footballers are like. Low-born high-achievers untouched by charm or culture. Larry Benyon addresses the nation like a player abusing the referee. His platitudes, unlike the player's, may not be foul-mouthed but any sensible person knows he, and his bleeding-heart sentiments, deserve only one thing – a red card."

"Wow!" said Charlie. "Didn't hold back, did he? And, if I may say so, quite a feat of memory on your part."

"As you said, these things stick."

"And you're absolutely sure that this was Jimmy. He was 'The Grumbler'?"

"Absolutely convinced."

"But then why . . .?" Charlie furrowed his brow, puzzled. "Why, if you knew he had written this about you, if you knew that was what he really thought of you, why did you agree to be part of the band?"

Larry threw his head back and looked up at the chandeliered ceiling. "Exactly," he said. "Why? I've asked myself that question so many times. Every time I've been with him, spoken to him, that article has run across my mind, so why did I choose to do something that meant I'd be seeing even more of him? And the only answer I can think of is that it seemed a good idea at the time. You know the score, Charlie. You know that half, even more, of the people you work with are slagging you off behind your back, that's just how it is. If you decided not to work with anyone you think, or know, has done it you'd probably stop working. That, unfortunately, is the way the world goes round."

"I know that," said Charlie, "but this wasn't work, was it? It was a joke, a private joke, a bit of fun. You didn't need to do it, did you?"

"I know, but . . ." Larry put his elbows on the table and

leaned forward. "I suppose I didn't want to be the one to say no. And then, there was the forfeit. Money wasn't the issue, of course it wasn't, but I've always been competitive: you have to be to play at the top for so many years and I hate to back down from a challenge. Looking back on it, maybe it was a mistake but...but once it got going, well I have to say I quite enjoyed it. Didn't you?"

Charlie laughed. "Enjoy it? Yeah, I suppose I did."

"Maybe that's why I didn't stop. But, yeah, when it comes to Jimmy, you know how it is. It can be difficult, but you just get on with it, don't you? Trust no-one, but make it look like you do."

Charlie nodded vaguely, but he wasn't really taking anything in. His mind had turned to other matters and he was thinking not so much about what Jimmy had done to Larry as about what Jimmy had done to him. The marriage may now have been well and truly over, but some things, like bad reviews, had a habit of sticking and Charlie knew he would never forget how he felt when he discovered Jimmy Clark had been having an affair with his first wife.

But that wasn't all that was troubling him – he was also thinking about Frankie Dunne.

When he first heard the name of the dead man it meant nothing to him at all. Then, when he heard where he lived, he had a different reaction – not a feeling that he might, after all, know who the dead man was, but memories of a time when he was a frequent visitor to the North Barnes estate.

He wondered whether there might still be people up there who remembered him.

People who might also have known Frankie Dunne.

28

Garibaldi hadn't meant to tell Deighton. It had just come out, and as soon as it had he'd immediately regretted it. Not because it would make her wonder about his state of mind and whether he was fit for work, but because he had yet to tell Rachel.

Now, looking at his boss sitting at her office desk, he remembered that evening when he had told her. Things since then had not improved. If anything, they had got worse. How else could he explain that weird experience in the meeting when Deighton had lost her temper with him and he had seen her, fleetingly, in his mother's mask? It had been bad enough seeing her lose her temper, but that was nothing compared to the shock of seeing his mother's face, of hearing his mother's voice reminding him to be a good Catholic boy.

He had no idea what to make of it. Deighton. His mother. God. Was it all some weird kind of Freudian psychodrama?

"So, Frankie Dunne," said Deighton. "Where are we?"

Garibaldi was so lost in thought that he didn't respond.

"Jim? Are you OK?"

He came to. "Sure, yes. Miles away."

"Where are we with Frankie Dunne?"

"OK, right. Well, we know he had a girlfriend called Cara and it seems likely he was with her on Sunday after he played football. We also know that he told his brother Sean that he'd screwed up and thought he was in trouble."

"And does Sean have any idea what this trouble might be?"

"No. But he said it didn't surprise him. Apparently things had a habit of going wrong for Frankie."

"OK," said Deighton, "and this Cara, do we know anything about her? Her surname for example?"

"Nothing. That's all we've got."

"What about Dunne's phone records? Any calls to someone called Cara?"

"We can't find any."

"How about camera footage from near Jimmy Clark's?"

Garibaldi shook his head. "Nothing yet."

"Anything more from the crime scene?"

"As you know, we've got fingerprint and DNA matches for the Okay Boomers and partners – pretty much as you'd expect given that they were all there partying. But all of these were downstairs, not in the room from which it seems Frankie Dunne fell, and none of them match what was found on the broken glass vase."

"Anything on Dunne's car?"

"ANPR hasn't shown any movement worth following. Seems he didn't use it too much. He didn't take it anywhere at all that weekend."

"And what about the cleaner?"

"Doreen Amos? We've spoken to her. What we didn't know was that she knew Frankie Dunne. He was good mates with her son and she was close to the family, good friends with Frankie's mum. We're talking to her son later.

We're also looking at the Bull's Head – who bought tickets for the concert and what they've got on their cameras. There's no evidence of a link between the concert and what happened to Dunne but . . ."

"But check everything," said Deighton, nodding her approval and putting on her reading glasses as Garibaldi got up and headed for the door.

He turned before he reached it. "Look," he said, "I hope I'm not out of order asking this but we have, you know, exchanged a few confidences in the past . . ."

Deighton looked at him over her glasses. "If you're going to ask if I'm OK, please don't. I'm fine."

Garibaldi hesitated. Should he push it? Should he tell Deighton that he thought she'd seemed out of sorts recently and that her loss of temper had shocked not only him but the rest of the team?

Or should he leave it? His own problems were enough to deal with.

He said nothing for a few moments, trying to hold Deighton's gaze, but she looked down at the papers on her desk as if to say the conversation was over.

Garibaldi opened the door. "Take care," he said as he walked out and closed the door behind him.

Take care? He hadn't meant to say it. It just came out, the way it had just come out when he'd told her that stuff about his mum. He'd meant to say 'thanks' or 'see you later, boss' but, instead, he'd told her to take care – further proof that his relationship with her might be more complex than he liked to think.

Garibaldi locked his bike to the railings outside the entrance to a block of flats on the Queen Caroline Estate and waited for Gardner.

"You took your time," he said when he saw her hurrying towards him.

"Quicker by bike," said Gardner, "I know. You've told me before."

She was right on both counts. Short journeys in London were often easier on two wheels and he reminded his sergeant of this on a regular basis.

They climbed the stairs, went along the first-floor walkway and paused outside a door. Garibaldi rang the bell.

The man who came to the door was in his twenties, slim and bearded.

"Mark Amos?" said Garibaldi.

The man nodded.

"We spoke on the phone earlier," said Garibaldi, as he and Gardner showed their warrant cards.

"Sure." Mark Amos stepped back and showed them in.

Garibaldi took a quick look round the living room as he sat down. It was sparsely furnished and dominated by a large-screened TV.

"I can't take it in," said Mark.

"It must be very upsetting," said Gardner.

"Upsetting? That doesn't come close. Have you found who killed him yet?"

"We don't yet know that it's murder," said Garibaldi.

"What else can it be? What other reason is there for him being found dead in that mask at that tosser's house?"

"You mean Jimmy Clark's?" said Gardner.

"Yeah, that tosser."

"Your mum's Jimmy Clark's cleaner, right?" said Garibaldi.

"Yeah, but that doesn't mean he's not a tosser. Doesn't mean we're best mates. Him, and the rest of them in that fucking band, they've obviously got something to do with it."

Despite the intensity of his feelings, Mark spoke softly. His voice was high-pitched, close to a woman's, and it made his anger more powerful.

He gave an incredulous laugh. "I mean, look at where he was found and look at what he was wearing. One of the masks that they'd been wearing in their stupid fucking band!" He shook his head as if words couldn't express his bewilderment. "Frankie and me, we go way back. We've known each other since we were kids . . ."

Garibaldi pointed at a photo of a football team on the mantelpiece. "Are you with him in that picture?"

"That's right," said Mark, getting up to look at it. "Barnes Lions. Guess we must have been nine or ten. He was good, Frankie. Could have made it maybe, if things had gone differently."

"And you both still play?" said Garibaldi.

"Yeah, we do . . . I mean did."

"For Barnes Athletic?"

Mark nodded.

"Were you there when I came down to speak to the team?"

"I was in Brighton. Took my girlfriend on a short break. We needed it. Things have been tough."

"I'm sorry."

"Nothing particular just, you know, work, money. It's not easy." Mark shook his head as if to clear it. "Anyway, about Frankie—"

Garibaldi took out his notebook and opened it. "Tell me, Mark, when did you last see him?"

"At training on Thursday. I left for Brighton after it that night. So yeah that was when I last saw him – the last I ever saw him."

Garibaldi consulted his notebook. "When we spoke to your mum she said that Frankie gave her a call while you were in Brighton."

Mark looked surprised. "Did she? She didn't mention it."

"Maybe she didn't think it was important."

"What was it about?"

"Let's see." Garibaldi leafed through the notebook. "Ah, yes. He said you'd picked up his bag by mistake. He had yours and you had his and he needed it. I guess they must be identical. Club bags maybe. Anyway, he wanted to know if your mum had a key."

"Did he? My mum didn't say anything."

"Maybe she forgot. She had other things on her mind."

Mark paused for a few moments. "Yeah, we'd picked up each other's bags. I didn't realise until I got back from Brighton. We've got the same bags. Barnes Athletic crest on the sides. Surprised it's never happened before. But look, we should be talking about those celebrity wankers, not our fucking sports bags!"

Garibaldi gave an understanding smile. "I take it you don't think very highly of them."

"What they did to Frankie? No, I don't."

"There's no evidence that they did anything to Frankie," said Gardner.

Mark turned to her. "He was found at Clark's house in one of their masks and they'd all been there the night before! Do I need to do your job for you?"

"We appreciate that you're very distressed," said Garibaldi.

Mark threw his hands up in despair, his lips tightened in a frown. "I told him no good would come of it."

Garibaldi exchanged a glance with Gardner. "Come of what?"

"I told him to stay away but he wouldn't listen. He thought it was great. He thought she was great."

"What do you mean?" said Garibaldi.

"This girl he'd started seeing."

"Cara?"

"That's it. Cara. He was really excited about going out with her, but I did warn him. I don't know how they got together – he said something about them meeting at some gig – but from everything Frankie said she was ...different. Posh. I know some say it can work but as far as I'm concerned you can't trust them. Believe me, I've seen them close up. You try delivering meals to them ..." Mark paused and ran his hands over his eyes. "As soon as I heard where Frankie was found I knew I was right."

Garibaldi waited. Mark looked as though he couldn't bring himself to say what he needed to.

"The thing is, this girl Cara told Frankie that she was good friends with Jimmy Clark's daughter. Really good friends."

"She said she was good friends with Clark's daughter?"

"Yeah, and when I found out where he was found—"

"You think that's how Frankie ended up at Jimmy Clark's house?"

"I'm not saying that. I've no idea how he ended up there. It's just that I remembered the connection. I was going to get in touch to tell you, but when you rang and said you were coming round ...I mean, it has to be important, doesn't it?"

"I don't know," said Garibaldi, "but it's good to know. Every detail helps. You never know what might be relevant. Did Frankie say anything more about Cara's friendship with Jimmy Clark's daughter?"

"Just that she knew her. He said the first time he met

Cara at this music thing she asked where he lived and when he said Barnes the first thing she said was, 'Oh Barnes, do you know Jimmy Clark?' Like everyone in Barnes knows each other and that someone like Frankie would know the likes of Jimmy Clark. I remember we had a laugh about it because we're both used to what happens when you tell someone you live in Barnes – they automatically think you live in some massive house and you're rolling in money."

Garibaldi gave an understanding smile. The same thing happened to him. When he told people where he lived he knew their first thought wasn't of a modest ex-council flat tucked behind the shops near the river.

"Anyway, Frankie was laughing about it because when Cara asked him whether he knew Jimmy Clark he didn't know what to say because he didn't know him, but his mate's mum was Jimmy's cleaner."

"Did he tell her that?"

"He did, yeah. He was worried at first that it might put her off him but he told her. And Frankie said Cara thought it was brilliant. She said she couldn't wait to tell Jimmy Clark's daughter."

"Did Frankie mention Cara's surname?" asked Gardner.

"No. Cara. That's all he said."

"Did he say where she lived?"

"He mentioned Fulham but he didn't say where."

"And did he say what Cara did?"

Mark shook his head. "That's another thing I need to tell you. Frankie said he hadn't told Cara the truth about his own job. Frankie worked at Marks and Spencers, right? Well, that's not what he told Cara."

"What did he tell her?"

"He told her he worked in IT."

"Why did he do that?"

"That was Frankie all over. A bit of a chancer. I guess he was worried that if he told Cara the truth she might think he wasn't good enough for her. As I say, I did warn him, but he didn't listen."

"When you say warn him, what exactly did you warn him about?"

Mark looked irritated at having to explain the obvious. "I warned him to keep away from that lot."

"That lot?"

"People like that, they've never done us any favours. Anyway, that was Frankie for you. Always close to trouble." Mark stopped and smiled, as if struck by a memory. "That's how he played football as well. Lucky not to get sent off on Sunday apparently."

"What did he do?"

"Bit of a scuffle with one of their players. The ref didn't see half of it apparently."

Garibaldi looked at Gardner and shut his notebook. "Well, that's been very helpful, Mark. Thanks for your time."

"You'll get them, won't you?"

"When you say 'them' ...?"

"Whoever did it."

"We don't know that he was—"

"What was Frankie doing at that fucking house? Why did my mum have to go into clean and see him lying there like that?"

Mark's eyes were wide with bewilderment. He was close to tears.

"We'll do everything we can to find out," said Garibaldi, getting up to leave. "And if you think of anything else—"

"It's one of them," said Mark. "It has to be. The mask, the place. It's obvious, isn't it?"

Garibaldi nodded and headed for the door, wishing everything in the case was as straightforward as Mark Amos seemed to think.

29

When Alfie moved in with Alicia the pre-match ritual changed from a coffee in the Bush Theatre bar to a pint in the Crown and Sceptre. Garibaldi wasn't sure what brought about the change but, on the whole, thought it a good thing. It may have meant more trips to the loo once they got to the ground but it also meant a less inhibited experience – at recent matches he'd found himself not only shouting out thoughts he would usually keep to himself in language he would normally avoid but also, much to the annoyance of those who sat behind him, standing up to deliver them.

Garibaldi took Alfie's preference for a pre-match pint as another indication that, despite his ex-wife's reservations, his son was doing fine. Kay may have thought Alicia not good enough (or, influenced by her appalling partner, too woke) and may have considered Alfie's job in the Camden bookshop beneath the expectations of an Oxford graduate, but Garibaldi thought Alfie was in a good place – even if, given his own antipathy to North London (too high, too hilly, too far from the river), he had to see the place metaphorically rather than literally.

Over the years, and especially since he split with Kay,

Garibaldi's trips with Alfie to Loftus Road had assumed a disproportionate significance in his life. He often wondered whether the old cliché that football was like religion was in his case particularly true – that it had replaced the faith in which his parents had brought him up and which he had publicly disowned shortly before they died. Sometimes he wished he had restrained his adolescent impulses and kept his doubts to himself, but he knew such regrets were futile. Like so many other things, there was nothing he could do about it now.

The QPR home games were his way of bonding with Alfie. There were moments when that bond had weakened (he remembered with pain the days when Alfie had been at Oxford and stopped coming) but it had always been there and Garibaldi guessed it always would be – a bit like the 'twitch on the thread' he remembered reading about in an Evelyn Waugh novel, something that could always pull you back.

Today, finding it difficult to stop thinking about masks and struggling to block the recurring image of Deighton momentarily turning into his mother, he was particularly glad to have a game to go to and as they checked their watches, finished their pints and left the pub, Garibaldi felt his mood lighten.

As they pushed through the turnstiles, he relaxed even more.

Soon they would be in their seats behind the goal, immersed in this brief respite from their lives outside, believing that what was happening on the Loftus Road pitch was the most important thing in the world.

Later, Garibaldi lay on the sofa next to Rachel, trying to call out the answers to *Only Connect*. They were on the missing vowels round, the one in which they both did best, shouting their answers at the screen in quick succession. On one occasion, Garibaldi had accused Rachel of equating the loudness of her answers with their speed, and of claiming points when all she had done was repeat his own correct answers a fraction of a second after he had given them. It had led to one of their most serious rows and a night on the sofa. One of the things he had learned since Rachel had moved in was that quizzing for Rachel was a serious business.

Tonight, Rachel was romping away with it. Garibaldi was doing his best, but he felt out of sorts, and he sensed this was down to more than the afternoon's disappointing home defeat. Even the prospect of his favourite Saturday night activities – takeaway curry, *Match of the Day* and sex – couldn't lift his spirits, and he found himself thinking more and more about masks. He kept imagining performing as an Okay Boomer, looking at the Bull's Head audience through eye slits and singing through a mouth opening. The idea filled him with a terrible claustrophobia.

The quiz was over. Rachel zapped Richard Osman off and turned to Garibaldi.

"You OK?"

"Yeah, I'm fine."

"Really? You weren't getting many tonight."

"Well, you know how it is. Win some, lose some."

"Just like QPR, eh?"

"Exactly."

Rachel hauled herself up off the sofa. "Oh well, keep the faith."

Garibaldi looked at Rachel. Her words sounded strange, as if someone else had spoken them.

Rachel started to walk towards the bedroom and turned.

Garibaldi's hands went to his mouth. There it was again. That mask.

"You've got to believe, Giacomo." His mother's voice.

"But what if you don't, Mum?"

"You pray."

"But if you don't believe—"

"Sorry?" Rachel's voice now. "Jim. Are you all right?"

He was still looking at his mother's face. He got up from the sofa and stretched his hands towards it.

"Who are you talking to?"

The mask had gone. Rachel stood in front of him.

"What's going on Jim? What the hell's going on?"

She took his hands in hers and drew her face close, looking deep into his eyes. "Jim?"

Garibaldi took a breath and steadied himself. Was this the time? Yes, it was.

"There's something I need to tell you," he said.

"Why didn't you tell me earlier?" said Rachel when he had finished.

"I didn't want to worry you."

"You should have told me."

Garibaldi, remembering the evening when he'd chosen to tell Deighton, felt a stab of guilt. "I thought it might go away."

"Well, it hasn't, has it? This is serious, Jim. I mean, don't you think you should see someone?"

"I already am seeing someone. That's the problem."

"This is no time for jokes."

"But what can anyone do? What is there to say? It's not as though it happens all the time and when it does . . . well, when it does I get through it."

"But that was weird. I mean, really weird. What if it

happens at work or when you're doing something important? What if you're interviewing someone, for example, and it happens then?"

"Look," he said, "I can't explain it, but all I know is I think about it nearly every day. No, not nearly. Every day. It may have been a long time ago, but losing both parents like that. In an instant. In one car-crash instant. It's with me the whole time and I'm reminded of it every time I get on my bike or climb into a passenger seat."

No-one at work knew the reason for his inability to drive and it was still a source of humour at the station, where the DS 'Uber' Gardner jokes and the cries of 'on your bike' when he left to go anywhere had worn thin some time ago.

No-one, that is, apart from Deighton. It was another thing he'd told her.

"Look," he said, "I'm sure I'm not the only person in the world who imagines people are with him."

"Imagining's one thing. Speaking to them's another. Are you sure you don't need . . ."

Garibaldi raised his hand. "I'm OK."

"Well, you're not, are you?"

"I'll deal with it. Look, if it happens again with you, just say 'I'm not your mum, I'm Rachel'."

"Fine. And what if it happens again with someone else?"

Garibaldi shrugged.

"How often *has* this happened?"

"A few times. Look, I didn't want this, not tonight. We were talking about you, not me and it just . . .happened. Can we leave it?"

"Leave it?"

"I should have told you earlier. I'm sorry."

Rachel said nothing.

"Look, why don't we go out tomorrow night? I'll try to get away. Maybe we could go and see some . . .some jazz."

Things were so bad that he was even prepared to go to some jazz in the hope of making them better.

30

"Funny things masks, aren't they?" said Gardner as she drove Garibaldi to Bill Bloom's Soho office. "I think it's the way they don't move. They hide the face but it's not like it's a face itself. It's still, it doesn't give anything away. Strange, isn't it? Could be frightening to some people, I guess."

"Yeah. Could be."

"I hadn't really thought much about them before all this. I mean, we put masks on all the time in the pandemic but they were different. I didn't really think about them at all. Everyone did it and it became, I don't know, normal. But these masks are something else. The more I think about the whole mask thing the more interesting I find it. "

"Yeah," said Garibaldi. "Me too. In fact, I've been looking into them. I've been doing a bit of research."

"Research? Don't tell me. Wikipedia."

"I may have started there, yes, but—"

Gardner turned to him. "So what have you found?"

"Well the first thing I found was that the Okay Boomers aren't the first band to have performed in masks. Far from it. There's this heavy metal band, Slipknot, who've been doing it for some time. Then there's an art rock band called

The Residents and the Russian protest band Pussy Riot. And then there's this band called Los Straitjackets, a surfing guitar band who perform in Mexican wrestling masks."

"Mexican wrestling masks? Sounds creepy."

"Totally."

Los Straitjackets. It may have been many years ago, but as soon as Garibaldi had seen the name it had all come back to him and he'd remembered how strange he'd felt the night he saw them play with Nick Lowe at Shepherd's Bush Empire. At the time he'd thought it was simply too many beers, but looking back on it now, it occurred to him that it might, in fact, have been something else.

It might have been the Mexican wrestling masks.

"And I also found that masks have a lot of functions. We know they protect because, as you say, we wore so many of the bloody things during Covid, but down the years they've been used in all kinds of ways. Think ritual, ceremony, performance. Think Bacchanalia, Noh Theatre, Commedia del Arte, Venetian Carnival."

Garibaldi paused, giving Gardner time to think.

"Think Hallowe'en."

Gardner nodded, as if this was an easier think.

"And let's not forget," said Garibaldi, "that the mask's a crucial form of disguise in the perpetration of criminal acts. Not to mention its popularity with those of particular sexual tastes . . ."

"Yeah, about that—"

"About what?"

"Sexual tastes."

"I said not to mention it."

"I know, but do you think . . . ?"

"What I think is that, as you say, there's something about a mask."

"You're fascinated, aren't you?"

Garibaldi laughed gently. "Fascinated? Yeah, maybe that's the word."

If the posters on the wall of the Soho office were anything to go by, Bill Bloom's film production company was hugely successful. It was only when Garibaldi sat down with Gardner and had a chance to look at them more closely that he realised many of them advertised films that had nothing to do with Bill Bloom at all.

"We won't keep you long," said Garibaldi, "but we'd like to ask you a few questions with regard to the death of Frankie Dunne."

Bill Bloom, tall and slight with a long mane of obviously dyed dark hair, dressed in a black suit and white shirt, had the air of someone keen to impress with their creative credentials. He reminded Garibaldi a little of Nick Cave – it was as though he had deliberately cultivated the similarity.

"I'm shocked," he said from behind a large glass table, impressively free of paper. "We both are. Hazel was completely distraught when she heard about it. To happen at Jimmy's house after their gig, after their party – she couldn't believe it."

"I understand," said Garibaldi, "that you were one of the few people outside the band who knew about their activities."

"That's right, yes. I was in on it right from the beginning, mainly because I had contacts who could help with the masks and the costumes. The masks!" Bloom spread his arms wide to show the extent of his amazement. "What can I say?"

"You arranged for them to be made?"

"That's right. You can do extraordinary things

nowadays. Special effects. Make up. CGI. And they wanted good masks."

"So," said Garibaldi, "you made, or rather you arranged to have made, the masks for all the band's performances?"

"That's right."

"And their most recent appearance was as the Okay Boomers."

"Yeah. Dylan, Bowie, Jagger et cetera. I think they were probably my favourites. They were good, probably the best."

"How good they were isn't our concern. What concerns us is that Frankie Dunne was found dead wearing one of them."

"I know. It's crazy, and now this thing on Jimmy by someone in the Dylan mask."

"Exactly," said Garibaldi. "But let's start with the dead man. Tell me, Bill, were you at the Okay Boomers concert at the Bull's Head?"

"No, I wasn't. I didn't go to any of them. I let Hazel do her thing with the others. I knew they wanted to keep their identity secret so I made a point of keeping it quiet. I arranged the masks and costumes by myself and I didn't tell anyone here about the band. Absolutely no-one. I kept details of the masks and costumes entirely to myself. In my own diary."

"In your diary?" said Garibaldi with raised eyebrows. "Could I have a look?"

Bill looked defensive. "At my diary? There's nothing there that . . ." He gave an if-you-must shrug, opened a desk drawer, took out a large red Moleskine diary and handed it to Garibaldi. "It's mainly lists. Masks to be made. Costumes. Band names."

Garibaldi flicked through the diary, stopping at a page

where 'The Comedians' was written at the top. Below that was a list of the band members and the masks and costumes to be made for each. Below that was the venue – the Bull's Head.

"As I said, I kept it very much to myself, but obviously, given what's happened and Hazel's involvement in it, everyone here now knows all about it."

"OK," said Garibaldi, "so, to clarify, you didn't go to the gig on Sunday and you weren't at the party at Jimmy Clark's afterwards?"

Bloom shook his head. "No, as I said, I let Hazel get on with it. It was her thing."

"Where were you on that evening, then, Bill?"

Bloom looked puzzled, as if someone had just called him by the wrong name. "Where was I? You don't for one moment think that I—"

"I'm not thinking anything. I'm just asking where you were."

"It sounded like you wanted an alibi. Anyway, I was at a film. At the Riverside as it happens. A Woody Allen retrospective."

"Woody Allen, eh?" said Garibaldi. "I thought he'd been, what's the word, 'cancelled'."

"Some of his films are magnificent," said Bloom, "and will remain so, regardless of what Allen may or may not have done in his personal life."

"Never trust the teller, trust the tale, eh?"

Bloom gave Garibaldi a quizzical look.

"D H Lawrence."

"Of course."

Garibaldi leaned forward in his chair.

"Did you know, or have any connection with the man found dead at Jimmy Clark's?"

"Frankie Dunne? None at all. If I had done, I'm sure Hazel would have told you."

"That's assuming that Hazel would have known of any such connection, isn't it?"

"Look, detective, I have no idea who Frankie Dunne was, no idea what he was doing at Jimmy Clark's house and no idea how he ended up dead. Is that clear enough?"

Garibaldi sensed Bloom's temper fraying. "Very clear, thank you." He looked round the room, taking in the posters on the walls. "Looks like you've been involved in some interesting films."

"I have," said Bloom. "I've been very lucky."

Garibaldi pointed at one poster in particular. "Though I guess not all of these are yours."

Bloom's eyes followed the direction of Garibaldi's finger. "Not all of them, no."

"If I'm not mistaken, that one was produced in Canada, wasn't it?"

"*The Lost Clause*? Yes, it was. I'm good friends with the producer."

"I liked it," said Garibaldi. "Nothing like a literary thriller, is there?"

Bloom looked puzzled again, as if he found Garibaldi difficult to fathom.

"But that one's definitely yours, isn't it?" said Garibaldi, pointing at another poster.

Bloom looked where he was pointing. "Ah yes! *The Neighbourhood*."

"Those were the days, eh? When Britannia was cool and we all loved romcoms. And starring none other than Charlie Brougham, of course."

"Charlie and I go back a long way."

"I see."

"So all the Boomers know each other quite well," said Garibaldi, his eyes on the poster.

"Not all of us, but we – Hazel and I – we've known Charlie for a long time and we've known Craig for a fair bit as well. Larry Benyon and Jimmy Clark we don't know quite so well."

"This whole masked band thing," said Garibaldi, turning back to Bloom. "All a bit strange, isn't it? I mean, when Hazel told you about it and spoke about the masks, didn't you find it all a bit . . .odd?"

Bloom laughed. "Odd? When you've been in the business as long as I have your concept of 'odd' becomes pretty elastic. I thought it was a bit . . .misjudged perhaps but on the other hand I could see why they wanted to do it. It was a laugh, I guess, and once it was suggested maybe it was difficult to say no. I mean, no-one wants to be the killjoy, do they?"

Garibaldi took out his notebook and flicked through a few pages. "This assault on Jimmy Clark."

"Pretty bizarre, isn't it? I mean, a water pistol?"

"Given that whoever did it was wearing the band's Bob Dylan mask, we're taking it very seriously. It forms part of our investigation. Do you have any idea who might have done it?"

"I have no idea who and I've less idea why. As I understand it, the masks were taken from Jimmy Clark's after the party. My guess, and I'm sure it's your guess as well, is that whoever took those masks is the person who attacked Jimmy Clark. And it wouldn't be ridiculous to think it's the same person who murdered that poor man."

"We don't know that it is murder."

"Really? Looks like it to me."

"The thing that puzzles me, Bill, is the way it all comes

back to Jimmy Clark. The body was found at his house and he's the one who was on the wrong end of the masked man's water pistol."

"Look, I don't know Jimmy well but from what I've heard about him I'm sure he's made some enemies."

"Enemies who might want to kill him?"

"No-one's tried to kill him, have they? It was only a...look I have no idea. What drives anyone to kill?"

Garibaldi nodded his agreement. "A question I've been forced to contemplate far too often."

Bill's lips tightened and he leaned forward, resting his elbows on the table and clasping his hands in front of him.

"Look," he said, "I'm telling you this because it's the kind of thing you need to know, not because I think that...anyway, the thing is Jimmy Clark can be mean, spiteful and vindictive. That doesn't make him unique in our line of work but, as I said, he's made himself many enemies in his time. It's all smiles on the surface, it's all darling this and darling that but beneath that it's something else entirely. I mean, there he is suggesting this band to Hazel and playing in it with her and yet I have it on good authority that he has said some very nasty things about her. A friend of mine was in a meeting when he let rip on his real feelings about Hazel."

"What did he say?"

"It wasn't pleasant. He was dead against her being given some role in a new quiz show. Accused her of being talentless and having slept her way to the top. Or it may have been slept her way to the bottom. That's the kind of joke he'd make."

"I see," said Garibaldi, flicking back through his notebook, "and did you tell Hazel what you were told?"

"I did, yes —" Bloom spread his arms, threw back his

head and looked up at the ceiling. "Hang on! Look, I haven't told you that because I think Hazel would want to . . . I mean she'd never do anything because of that . . . If I thought that I'd never have told you."

"One more thing, Bill, before we let you get back to work. Do you have the contact details of the man who was in charge of making the masks?"

"Guy? Yeah, sure."

Bill reached for a sheet of paper and scribbled down a name and number.

"When it comes to masks and stuff like that," he said, handing the paper to Garibaldi, "Guy Armstrong's your man."

"OK" said Garibaldi, taking the sheet and putting it in his pocket. "Thanks for your time, and if anything else occurs to you—"

"Of course."

Outside the office Garibaldi gave Gardner the sheet with Guy Armstrong's contact details. "One for you, Milly," he said. "I think I've had enough of masks for today."

31

Sophie Clark sat on the edge of her chair, cradling a mug of tea and looking from one detective to the other. The woman detective seemed straightforward enough, her every utterance betraying the lack of intelligence Sophie's previous dealings with the police had led her to expect from them. But the one called Garibaldi was a different thing entirely. Something about his whole manner unnerved her and she couldn't pin it down. It could be the habit he had of looking at her for a few seconds before asking a question, or it could be the way he kept flicking through his notebook as if there were things in there of huge significance. Or maybe it was the way he kept coming up with references that surprised her. There was nothing that said a Metropolitan Police detective couldn't come out with literary quotations but the way this one had just quoted Oscar Wilde – 'give a man a mask and he will tell you the truth' – had thrown her entirely. That's why she was choosing her words carefully, wary of revealing more than she should.

"It must have been a great shock," said Garibaldi, "to learn that a body had been found in your garden."

"It was," said Sophie. "First that and then the ridiculous – I don't even know what to call it. Was it an assault?"

"We're treating it as that, yes. And it's forming part of our investigation."

"This whole thing is awful. Absolutely awful."

"Remind me, Sophie, where were you when Jimmy discovered Frankie Dunne's body?"

"I've told you this already. I went away on the Saturday to stay with a friend in Gloucestershire and I came back Monday afternoon. Look, Inspector, you can't possibly think that—"

He held up his hand, whether to apologise or whether to stop her she couldn't tell.

"I'm just trying to establish the facts, Sophie. Who were you staying with in Gloucestershire?"

"Lucinda Critchley, an old school friend. I can't believe it! You're actually asking for an alibi! As if I could possibly...look, I'll give you her number. Give her a call."

"So you weren't at the Okay Boomers concert at the Bull's Head?"

"I've told you. No."

"Have you been to any other performances by the...masked band?"

"I've been to a couple, yes, but I really let Jimmy and the others get on with it. It was their thing."

"You sound as though you don't approve?"

"Given what's happened, it's difficult to think it was a good idea, isn't it?"

"I don't know. It depends on whether you think the death and assault are directly related to it, doesn't it?"

"They have to be, don't they?"

Garibaldi nodded and consulted his notebook. "So you went to some of their concerts. Which ones were they?" He flicked over some pages. "The Presidents, The Animals, The Players or The Comedians?"

Sophie felt her anger rise. "Does it matter?"

"I don't know. I'd just like you to tell me."

"I went to The Presidents. I remember because Jimmy was Trump."

"I see. Any others?"

"Is this relevant?"

"I don't know."

Sophie spluttered. "The Players. I was there for that one. And The Animals. I think that's it."

"And what animal was Jimmy?"

"He was a cow."

"I see." Garibaldi consulted his notebook again. "Can we get back to Frankie Dunne, Sophie? You have absolutely no idea who he was?"

"None at all."

"You'd never seen him before? You didn't recognise him, maybe from seeing him around Barnes?"

"Our paths never crossed."

She hadn't meant it to come out like that. It made it sound as though she would have nothing to do with someone from the estate.

"And your husband Jimmy?"

Why was he asking this? Jimmy had already told them he didn't know Frankie Dunne. What were they expecting her to say?

"He didn't know him either."

The man paused again and gave her the look.

"And you believe him?"

"What are you suggesting, Inspector?"

"I'm suggesting nothing, merely trying to establish the facts."

"Well the facts are that a man has been found dead and my husband has been assaulted and I think your time would be better spent trying to track down who's behind it rather than asking these ridiculous questions!"

She knew, as soon as she said the words, that she should have kept quiet. She could see Garibaldi's irritation.

The woman detective leaned forward. "We can see you're upset," she said. "It must have all been very distressing."

"It has been. It is. Look, I'm sorry, I shouldn't have lost my temper. I know you're doing your job."

"Tell me, Sophie," said Garibaldi, "did Jimmy have any enemies?"

"What do you mean? Anyone who might want to ...to do something to him?"

"Not necessarily, just people he'd crossed."

What should she say? Where should she start? Even the most cursory glance over her husband's past threw up so many things. She thought of his affairs. She thought of his appetites. She thought of how so many people would find it difficult to believe that someone so apparently civilised, polite and charming could have kept another side of himself so well hidden for so long.

"Jimmy's a good man," she said. "I can't think of anyone who might want to attack him like that. And as for Frankie Dunne I can't begin to explain it. The whole thing has me baffled, especially the masks."

"Has it occurred to you, Sophie, that if someone killed Frankie Dunne they might have been intending to kill someone else?"

"You mean ...?"

"It could be that someone thought it was your husband behind that mask. After all, it was the one he was wearing at the Bull's Head concert, wasn't it?"

"And then the attack ...so you're saying Jimmy was the target?"

"I'm suggesting it as a possibility."

"No, I don't see it. I mean who ...?"

She shook her head. The whole interview had unnerved her and she was keen for it to end before she revealed anything.

"I don't understand," she said. "I'm terrified. Do you think Jimmy's safe? Do you think *I'm* safe?"

"I'm sure if you're both sensible ..."

"Sensible? I'm not sure I'm making myself clear here, Inspector. A man has been found dead in this very house, my husband has been assaulted on the doorstep by someone in a Bob Dylan mask. And you say we need to be sensible!"

Garibaldi nodded, as if he understood the dilemma. "Just be careful," he said. "There's no more we can say or do."

"Apart from find out who's behind it all."

"Of course."

"And as for what the press are going to make of this ..."

"There will, I should think, be quite a bit of coverage."

"I can imagine it already!" said Sophie, keen for the detectives to go. She needed time by herself to think things through.

32

Cassie Clark's confidence smacked of money and breeding, and it irritated Garibaldi enormously.

"I presume this is about these dreadful things that have happened," she said in the living room of her Chiswick home. "I can't tell you how awful it is to think of a man found dead like that in that house. It's the family home, it's where I grew up. And as for the attack on my father, I really don't know what to say, apart from thank God he's OK. I mean, it may only have been a water pistol this time but who knows what might happen next. I sincerely hope you get whoever is responsible."

"That is part of why we want to see you, Cassie, we—"

"I'll help in any way, though I don't know if I can shed any light on what's been going on. I had no idea about this ridiculous masked band, none at all—"

"Maybe you could—"

"And as for this...this assailant, I don't know where to start. I mean, the mask!"

Cassie had inherited her father's love of talking. This, combined with her fondness for interruption, was adding to Garibaldi's irritation.

"Have you any idea why Frankie Dunne might have been at your parents' house that—"

"That night? None at all. When I first heard it I thought he might have been a burglar but then when I heard about the mask and the whole thing with the band it all seemed a bit more complicated than that."

"And you didn't know—"

"Didn't know Frankie Dunne? Never heard of him. No idea who he was."

"And with regard to the other incident—"

"The attack on Dad? Not a clue, though the mask seems to link it to the murder, doesn't it? Maybe it's the same person, I don't know."

"OK," said Garibaldi. "As I said, there is another reason why we need to speak to you. It appears that Frankie Dunne had recently started going out with a girl and this girl said she was a very good friend of Jimmy Clark's daughter, and that—"

"She said she was a good friend of mine? Who is she?"

"We only have her first name. Cara."

Cassie Clark looked blank. The blankness looked genuine, though, given that she was making her name as an actress, with several widely praised TV and stage performances to her name, Garibaldi wasn't entirely convinced.

"Cara, you say?" said Cassie, her brow furrowed in puzzlement. "I have to say that I really do not have a close friend called Cara. To tell you the truth I'm not sure I know *anyone* called Cara. Did this person say *how* this Cara knew me?"

"No. Just said she was very good friends with you. Had been for a long time."

Cassie continued to look puzzled. "And who was it who told you this?"

"A friend of Frankie's. Frankie told him all about it. Said he'd started going out with this girl Cara some months ago."

"Look, Inspector," said Cassie, "I really don't know anyone called Cara. Either Cara herself or this friend of Frankie can't be telling the truth."

"We have no reason to think that they aren't," said Garibaldi.

Cassie's look proclaimed her innocence. If anyone was at fault it clearly wasn't her.

"What's important," she said, "is finding out who's behind these things. And I don't see how my supposed friendship with Dunne's girlfriend is at all relevant."

"It's relevant," said Garibaldi, straining to stay patient, "because it's a connection between Dunne and your father. It might explain—"

"It might explain why he was found dead in Dad's Mick Jagger mask? Are you sure?"

"We can't be certain, but—"

"If by some extraordinary miracle I remember that I am, and have been, a very close friend of someone called Cara I will, of course, let you know."

"That's very good of you," said Garibaldi, unable to keep his tone irony-free.

"But I wouldn't hold your breath."

Garibaldi got up to leave, keen to be out of Cassie Clark's company.

"Is that Mark?"

"Speaking."

Garibaldi, phone to his ear, leaned back in his chair and put his feet on the desk. "I'm following up about Frankie's girlfriend, Cara. You said she was good friends with Jimmy Clark's daughter."

"That's right. I thought it might be important."

"You were right, Mark, and thanks for mentioning it.

But the thing is we've spoken to Jimmy Clark's daughter, Cassie, and she claims not to be friends, let alone good friends, with anyone called Cara."

"Really? That's odd."

"It is, and I just wanted to check that you've remembered the details correctly."

"It's definitely what he said. He was full of it."

"And she was definitely called Cara?"

"Yeah. Cara. I can't have misheard it. I mean Cara doesn't sound like anything else, does it? Zara, maybe, but no, it was definitely Cara. Don't you believe me?"

"I'm not saying that. I'm just checking."

"Have you found out who did it yet?"

"We're getting there."

"That lot," said Mark. "They deserve everything coming their way. It's one of them that killed Frankie, it has to be."

"There's no evidence that it's—"

"And what about that thing with Jimmy Clark? The masked bloke with the water pistol. Shows he must be in it right up to his neck, doesn't it?"

"As I say, we're looking—"

"This Cara was definitely friends with Jimmy Clark's daughter. That's what Frankie said. You know what? She's probably covering up for something. That's what they're like, that lot. I still can't believe it, you know. Those arseholes prancing about in masks, trying to keep it a big secret and Frankie lying there in that garden."

"Well, thanks for your time, Mark."

"You will get them, won't you?"

Garibaldi hung up, and waved at Gardner, beckoning her over. She walked to his desk and stood on the other side of it, eyebrows raised.

"This Cara thing, all a bit puzzling, isn't it?"

"Yeah," said Gardner, "I mean why would she say she was a good friend of Jimmy Clark's daughter when his daughter claims not to know her?"

"Can you think of any likely explanations?"

Gardner's face tightened into the defensive look she wore when she thought she was being tested.

"It could be . . ." she said. "No, maybe not."

"Go on," said Garibaldi. "Say it."

"Well, there are two possibilities I can think of. The first is that this girl Cara was lying when she said she was friends with Cassie Clark."

"OK. And the second?"

"And the second is that Cassie Clark's lying when she says she doesn't know her."

"Right. It could be that as well. But there's a third possibility."

Gardner looked as though she couldn't tell whether or not she was expected to have a guess.

"The third possibility is that Frankie Dunne was lying when he told Mark Amos."

"Of course," said Gardner in a way that suggested she thought the idea too obvious to have mentioned.

"The problem with all these possibilities," said Garibaldi, "is we have no idea why, if any of them lied, they would choose to do so. Why would they need to?"

Gardner bit her lip. "I suppose Jimmy Clark's daughter might lie if she was involved in some way . . ." She shook her head. "No, that doesn't make any sense, does it?"

"It could. She could be lying because she doesn't want to admit to a connection with the man found dead at her father's. But why would she do that?"

"And Frankie may have lied because . . .?"

"Maybe because he was trying to impress his mates – you know, bragging about his new girlfriend."

"Could be," said Gardner.

"As for Cara," said Garibaldi. He sat up, as if struck by a sudden thought. "Do we *really* have no idea who she is? Do we really know nothing at all about her?"

"A bit difficult when all you've got is her first name."

"It's not that usual a name is it?"

"But even so."

"What about the electoral roll?"

"We don't know where she lives."

"Somewhere in Fulham. Doesn't that narrow it down enough? How many Caras do you think there are in Fulham?"

"I have no idea."

"But you're about to find out, aren't you?"

Gardner gave a resigned nod. Garibaldi got up from his seat and hooked his jacket off the back of the chair.

"And while you're doing that," he said, "I think I'll pop down to Marks and Spencers."

Danny looked at Garibaldi across the office table. "Have you found out what happened?"

"We're getting close," said Garibaldi. "The reason I want to speak to you again, Danny, is to ask you a bit more about Frankie's girlfriend, Cara. I remember you saying..." Garibaldi got out his notebook and leafed through it. "I remember you saying that he'd met this girl called Cara and really liked her. They shared a love of music and Frankie said she was a different class."

Danny nodded. "Yeah, that's right."

"Do you remember him saying anything else about her?"

His shrug tried to suggest he didn't but the way he shifted in his seat hinted that he did.

"What kind of thing?"

"Anything. For example, did he say anything about Cara's friends?"

Danny shook his head. "Not that I remember."

"Nothing about one of them being Jimmy Clark's daughter?"

"Jimmy Clark's daughter? No—" Danny's attempt at a double take was unconvincing. He'd clearly never practised them. "Hang on. Now you mention it he did say that. I remember now because Frankie thought it was funny that he should be going out with a good friend of Jimmy Clark's daughter."

"I see," said Garibaldi. "Strange that that should have slipped your mind, isn't it, Danny? Given that Frankie was found dead at his house, you'd have thought your memory might have been jogged ..."

"Yeah," said Danny, a blush flooding his cheeks. "I was, you know, nervous. Bad enough to hear he was dead but then to have you turn up here to question me, it freaked me out."

"Well, now that you're not quite so freaked out, is there anything else you can remember?"

"Yeah." Danny looked sheepish. "Frankie said he hadn't told this girl Cara he worked here. Said he'd made up some story about working in IT."

"I see. Did he say why he'd done this?"

"Yeah, that thing he said about her being different class, I think he meant it. Not just special but actually different class. He thought if he told her he worked here she might think he wasn't good enough for her. He said she wasn't a snob or anything, but he didn't want to risk it."

"I see," said Garibaldi. "Well, it would have been very helpful if you'd told us all this when we first spoke to you."

"I know. I'm sorry."

"So is there anything else?"

There was another pause, the longest so far.

"OK, there is something," he said eventually. "I don't know if it's important but a few weeks ago Frankie got a call here at work. He didn't say who it was from or what it was about but he said he had to disappear for a bit and could I cover for him. You know, if anyone asked where he was, make up some excuse, that kind of thing. Difficult to do but we've managed it for each other on the odd occasion. Anyway, he came back a couple of hours later and when I asked him if everything was OK he said it was fine."

"Do you have any idea who the call was from?"

"No, but the way he acted made me pretty sure it was Cara."

"How did he act?"

"It wasn't anything he did. I could just tell from his face. He looked like he did whenever he spoke about her."

"And you've no idea where he went?"

Danny shook his head.

"And no idea what he did?"

Another shake.

"You say a couple of weeks ago. Can you be more precise?"

"Not really, no. But hang on—" Danny looked down to the floor and crinkled his face as he tried to remember. "I'm pretty sure it was the day of the Chelsea–Man United game. Yeah, it was, because I remember when Frankie asked if I could cover I was worried he wanted me to do it later and I needed to get away early to go to the match."

"Are you sure?"

"Pretty sure."

Garibaldi gave a slow nod and fixed his eyes on Danny,

trying to see if there was anything else he'd been keeping to himself. He sensed there wasn't but decided to ask anyway.

"Before I go, Danny, I'll give you one last chance to try to remember anything else that either slipped your mind or you were too traumatised to tell us."

"That's it."

"Withholding information's a serious offence, you know, and I'd hate to think . . ."

"That's it. I know I should have told you about Cara's friend before. I mean anything to find out who did this. It was just – this will sound silly – I thought telling you about Frankie would be like betraying him. I mean, I can't believe he's done anything wrong, but—"

"Why can't you believe he did anything wrong?"

"Because he . . . he just wouldn't. I mean, I know he wasn't perfect, but . . ."

"No-one's ever quite what they seem, are they, Danny? They can always surprise us."

Garibaldi snapped his notebook shut and thought of treating Danny to a philosophical insight into the masks we all wear.

He decided against it, heading out into the store to pick up a cinnamon bun.

"We nearly had a breakthrough," said Garibaldi, standing at the door of Deighton's office.

Deighton looked up from her screen and hooked off her reading glasses. "Nearly?"

"Yeah. I thought we'd found a connection between Frankie Dunne and Jimmy Clark."

"But we haven't?"

"No. Mark Amos told us that the girl Frankie was going out with—"

"Cara?"

"That's the one. He told us that Cara told Frankie she was very good friends with Jimmy Clark's daughter. So it looked like we had something linking Dunne and Clark. But I've just got back from speaking to Clark's daughter and she claims not to know anyone called Cara."

"She could be lying."

"I got the impression she wasn't. And, anyway, why would she?"

"Maybe Dunne was lying."

"I don't see it," said Garibaldi. "Why would he lie about that?"

"I don't know, but then I don't seem to know much when it comes to this case." Deighton shook her head, picked up a pile of papers and jabbed a finger at them. "And they're loving it. Absolutely loving it. Not just celebrities playing in a masked band, not just a murder at a celebrity's house. And not just the masked man at Jimmy Clark's with a water pistol. What they really love is the fact that we seem to have no bloody clue what's going on. It would be nice to think they're wrong, but I'm afraid they're not."

Deighton put the papers down with a sigh. "It all comes back to that band, doesn't it?" she said. "The band and the masks."

The masks.

Garibaldi thought again of Nick Lowe and Los Straitjackets.

A knock on the door made them both turn.

Gardner was standing in the doorway. "I've got something," she said.

Deighton ushered her in and Gardner stood there looking from one to the other, slightly out of breath, her eyes wide with excitement.

"I've just got back from Guy Armstrong, the man who made all the masks. Anyway, I was checking the details with him, going over what masks were made when and he said something that took me by surprise. We were talking about the Okay Boomers and he mentioned a second set."

Gardner paused, allowing the revelation to sink in.

"That's right. Apparently they made a second set of Okay Boomer masks."

"Who ordered them?" said Deighton.

"He says the order came from Bill Bloom."

"He didn't say anything about that to me," said Garibaldi. "Let's get onto him."

"But wait." Gardner held up her hand. "That's not all. I asked him to check the details of the order and guess where the masks were sent?"

Another pause. Gardner looked like she was enjoying it.

"They were sent to Frankie Dunne."

33

Larry Benyon couldn't understand why Jimmy thought it was a good idea. Sure, there were things to talk about but did they need to do it together?

The phone in his hand rang. He checked the screen. Hazel.

"Hi, Hazel."

"Larry, has Jimmy been in touch?"

"Yeah. I've just spoken to him."

"What do you think?"

"I don't see the point, not while the investigation's still going on."

"It sounds to me like he's got something big to tell us, like some confession."

Larry paused. It had never occurred to him that Jimmy might want to make some big announcement, but it didn't seem such a ridiculous idea now that Hazel mentioned it.

"Are you going?" said Hazel.

"I think so," said Larry. "Not turning up would seem like an admission of – well, I was going to say guilt but I can't believe any of us are guilty of anything."

He walked over to the table and picked up a newspaper.

On the front page was the headline 'Masked Stars Death Still a Mystery'.

"You've seen all the papers?" he said.

"Most of them," said Hazel.

"They been giving you hassle?"

"A fair bit. To be honest, I've been trying to keep my head down. How about you?"

"No worse than usual."

Larry did his best to sound unconcerned but the truth was that ever since Frankie Dunne's body had been found and the band had been unmasked his anxiety about the press had rocketed. They'd always been after him, keen to expose some dirt that would bring him down, but he'd learned to deal with it over the years and had so far escaped significant damage. But that wasn't to say that mud hadn't been flung in his direction. Quite the reverse – plenty had come his way, but none of it had stuck, not even when the #metoo movement was at its height and prominent men were being brought down on what seemed an almost daily basis. That was when his fear had been at its most acute, and he took the fact that he had come through unscathed as proof that certain things were safely buried. The money he had paid, and continued to pay, had been enough to buy the silence of the women concerned.

"Have you spoken to the others?" said Hazel.

"About the invitation? No, you're the first."

A silence followed. Hazel was the first to break it. "You know when you said you can't believe one of us is guilty, do you really believe that?"

"I'm not sure what I believe at the moment."

"The thing is," said Hazel, "there's this one thought I keep coming back to. One idea."

"What's that?"

"That if Frankie Dunne was murdered it might have been a mistake. Whoever did it might have wanted to kill someone else."

Larry paused, thinking it through.

"And," said Hazel, "whoever did it would have thought it was Jimmy because they knew the Mick Jagger mask was his."

"So you're talking about—"

"Us. The band. The Boomers."

"But we'd all been wearing the mask that night. We'd been playing round with all of them."

"I'm just saying—"

"I don't get it. Dunne didn't look a bit like Jimmy. One of us wouldn't have made that mistake. And what about their voices? Whoever it was would have known it wasn't Jimmy. No-one speaks like him."

"Maybe he didn't say anything. You don't strike up a conversation in a fight, do you?"

Another silence.

This time Larry broke it. "So do you really think it could be one of us behind the attack on Jimmy?"

"As you say, difficult to believe, but—"

"If it *is* one of us, the next question you have to ask is why. *Why* would any of us want to do it?"

The *Crustie* article scrolled in front of Larry's eyes like an autocue.

"The thing is," said Hazel, "we all know that Jimmy in his time has said things and done things . . ."

"Has he done them to us, though?"

"I've heard things."

Larry paused. Did Hazel know about the article?

"What have you heard?"

"Look, I shouldn't say this, but I've heard that he was

incredibly rude about Craig when he was on the panel of some poetry prize. And I've also heard that he had an affair with Charlie's first wife."

Larry took it in. Craig and Charlie. He couldn't imagine either of them pushing Jimmy to his death. Nor could he see them in the Bob Dylan mask with a water pistol.

"You must have heard things about Jimmy," said Hazel.

"Sure, I've heard things." Larry had heard many things about Jimmy, and one of them was what Jimmy had said about Hazel. "But I still can't see how anyone would want to kill him because of something he said about them. I mean, sticks and stones and everything . . ."

"Murder's not like that. Not that I know or anything, but it's not always rational. I mean, how can it be? As I said, I – anyway, will I see you at Jimmy's later?"

"Yeah, I'll be there."

Larry hung up. Of course he'd be there. If Hazel was right and Jimmy had something to reveal, he didn't want to miss it.

Ever since Craig had come in on the end of Gina's conversation with the detectives he'd wondered what she had told them. He could understand that they needed to talk to her – she had, after all, been at the concert and the party – but he hadn't liked the way they had engineered it so that they spoke to her while he wasn't there.

He knew she wouldn't have told them the whole truth. She'd have kept quiet about the problems they'd had in their marriage over the years, the way her insecurity and jealousy had threatened to destroy their relationship. He could easily imagine what she might have said about his work as a poet because he'd heard her say it so many times before – that she went to his readings because she was being supportive, that she tried to accompany him everywhere because she felt it was an important thing to do. Doubtless she had said the same about the band. She wanted to be supportive. That's why she'd been to every gig and that's why she had come back to Jimmy's after the Bull's Head. Nothing about her neurotic suspicion and paranoid jealousy.

The trouble with Gina was you never could tell what she was likely to do or say. He'd asked her what she had told the police and she'd given an account of the interview, but Craig couldn't be certain that her account was complete. Nor could he be certain that, despite her comments, Gina had said nothing about Jimmy Clark's Woolworths comment.

And now he'd received the invitation. He knew he had to tell her.

"He's asked us round," he said.

"Who?"

"Jimmy. He wants us all to get together."

"What about partners?"

"He didn't say, but I assume it's just us."

"Bit strange, isn't it?" said Gina, the edge in her voice painfully familiar.

"Yeah, I mean what's there to talk about? We're in the middle of a police investigation. Why doesn't he just let them get on with it?"

"Maybe he's got something he needs to tell you."

"Like what?"

"You're going, are you?"

Craig gave the look he was practised at giving – critical, but tolerant. "Looks like I have no choice, doesn't it?"

"What do you mean?"

"Well, it'll look odd if I don't turn up, like I'm guilty or something."

"You're not, are you?"

Craig gave the look again. "I'm not going to dignify that question by giving it an answer."

Gina turned her back and walked away.

Craig, still unsure how much his wife had told the detectives, went into his study to start another poem.

Charlie Brougham leaned on a wall outside the studio. *Coming to Terms* was not getting any better – if anything, it was getting considerably worse and he was seriously considering whether he might be better off ditching the whole thing. He knew such an action would bring with it problems. There were contractual considerations he would need to discuss with his agent, but it had come to the point where he feared that his reputation, already in need of repair, would be beyond any kind of resuscitation if the film ever saw the light of day with him in its starring role.

Yet again he felt the urge for a cigarette.

His phone rang. Jimmy Clark.

"Jimmy, how are you?"

"I'm well. How are you, my boy?"

"Fine. You find me in a much-needed break from filming."

"In something new are you? You must tell me about it."

"I will. You're OK, I hope, after that incident?"

Jimmy laughed. "I'm fine. Lucky it was just a water pistol."

"But even so. What if it had been a real gun? And that mask. The Bob Dylan mask. I don't believe it."

"It gave me a considerable shock, I have to say, but here I am, alive to tell the tale."

Charlie paused, waiting for the real reason for the call.

He couldn't believe Jimmy was ringing merely to check on his well-being.

"Do the police think it's linked to the . . .?"

"To the death? It's difficult not to link it, isn't it? I mean, the mask's a bit of a giveaway, isn't it?"

Charlie paused again.

"Look, Charlie, the reason I'm ringing is to ask whether you're free tonight?"

"Tonight?" Charlie hesitated. "I'll have to check."

"I hope you are, because I'm getting the band together."

Getting the band together? What was he up to?

"We must all be worried sick. I know I am, so I thought maybe we should get together to just, you know, be there for each other."

What a ridiculous idea. Charlie couldn't think of anything worse.

"Everyone else is coming," said Jimmy. "So I really hope—"

That was it. He had no choice.

"I'm sure I'm free. I'll check but assume I can make it unless I let you know otherwise."

"That's great, Charlie. My place at eight. I think it would be really good for us. We need to support each other."

Charlie hung up. He tried to think of supporting the others but all he could think of was what Jimmy Clark had done with his first wife.

Bill Bloom sat at his desk leafing through his Moleskine diary. He hadn't liked the way the detective had looked at it. His brow had furrowed and his eyes narrowed as he had turned the pages and it had made Bill feel strangely guilty. As he came to the page that listed the Okay Boomer masks and costumes – who would be wearing what and the specifications he should send to the mask makers – that feeling of guilt had intensified.

His phone rang. He looked at the screen. Hazel.

"Hi," said Hazel. "Look, sorry about this but there's a change of plan tonight. I know we were going out, but Jimmy's asked us all round."

"Us?"

"The band."

"What's he done that for?"

"He thinks it would be a good idea."

"Seems like a terrible idea to me."

"I know, but—"

"So you're going, then?"

"Don't think I have much choice. If I didn't show it would look like . . ."

"Look like what? That you're guilty?"

Hazel fell silent.

"You still there?" said Bill.

"I'm here. Look, I'm going to have to go. I just wanted to let you know. He wants us there at eight, so . . ."

"OK."

"Will you be home before then?"

"I'm not sure."

"Well, see you when I do, then."

"Sure."

Bill hung up.

He felt uneasy. Not just about the get-together at Jimmy Clark's but about the whole thing. Whenever he thought of the Jagger mask on the dead man at Jimmy Clark's or the Dylan mask on Clark's attacker he felt strangely implicated. He may have only arranged the making of the masks and costumes but he now regretted getting involved at all.

And he regretted his wife's involvement even more.

He shook his head in an effort to clear it.

As he did, his phone rang again. A number he didn't recognise.

"Bill Bloom."

"Bill, it's Detective Inspector Garibaldi here."

34

Garibaldi sat at his desk, phone to his ear, his eyes scanning the notes in front of him.

"Thanks for your time earlier, Bill. There are a few things I'd like to follow up."

"Of course."

"We've spoken to Guy about the masks and discovered something interesting."

"Really? What's that?"

"You told us that you ordered only one set of masks for each of the band's performances. Is that right?"

"Absolutely. We only needed one set. They were one-off things."

Garibaldi leaned forward and put his elbows on the desk. "That's interesting, because Guy told us that you did order more than one set."

"Well, he's got it wrong. I definitely didn't."

"He says you ordered an extra set of the Okay Boomer masks."

"The Okay Boomers? Really? He's wrong. I didn't. I mean, why would I?"

The confusion in his voice sounded genuine.

"And that's not all," said Garibaldi. "These masks that you ordered—"

"I'm telling you, I didn't order them."

"OK, but whoever ordered them had them delivered to somewhere, to someone, very interesting."

"Look. I really have no idea what you're talking about."

"This extra set of masks, Bill, were delivered to Frankie Dunne."

"Frankie Dunne?"

The line fell silent. Garibaldi said nothing for a few seconds.

"Are you serious?" said Bill. "Frankie Dunne? But he's the one – he's . . ."

"Exactly. He's the man found dead at Jimmy Clark's. Found dead in a Mick Jagger mask."

Another silence.

"I really don't know what to say. I have absolutely no idea about any of this. I can't—"

"Tell me, Bill, were you ordering these masks yourself, you weren't getting anyone else to do it for you?"

"I dealt directly with Guy."

"Did Guy know what they were for?"

"I didn't tell him, no. I mean he knows now, obviously, but that's because everyone knows."

"So it was only you dealing with him?"

"That's right. Did Guy say *I* ordered the extra set?"

"That's what he said, yes."

"But that's absurd."

"Did anyone else have access to the details?"

"No. I kept it to myself, in my diary, my personal one. I showed it to you. It wasn't in the work one I share with my assistant."

"So your assistant couldn't have had access to it?"

"Cara? No, she wouldn't. She doesn't—"
"Did you just say Cara?"
"Yes. Cara. My assistant."
Garibaldi's mind jolted. "Your assistant's called Cara?"
"That's right, yes. Why?"
"Did she by any chance know Frankie Dunne?"
"I have no idea."
"Do you think I could have a word with her?"
"I'm sorry, no. She's not in. She's been off work for a few days."
"Do you have her number?"
"Sure. Hang on a minute."
Garibaldi waited while Bill found the number.
Cara. Could it be coincidence? It could be, but as he scribbled down the details, ended the call, got up from his desk and walked to Deighton's office, his instincts were telling him it wasn't.

35

Jimmy tapped his glass with a spoon and waited for the chat to die down.

"No speech or anything. I just want to say a few words."

He looked round the room and took in the faces – Hazel looking as though she was doing an impression of herself, Charlie looking like the ageing wreck he had become, Craig looking as if he were searching for a rhyme he couldn't find, Larry looking as if he were too famous to be there.

How he loved them all.

"First of all," said Jimmy, "I—"

"This sounds like a speech," said Charlie.

"It's not," said Jimmy. "I just want to thank you all for your wishes and your kindness after I was involved in that unsavoury incident."

"You're OK, though, aren't you?" said Hazel, her stress on 'OK' suggesting she thought he wasn't.

"I'm fine. That doesn't mean it wasn't a huge shock, of course. And it could have been so much worse.

"And the police," said Craig, "do they have any idea?"

"My question exactly," said Jimmy with a derisive snort. "A dead body in my garden and an attack on me and I think it's fair to say the police have no idea at all."

"I'm not impressed," said Larry. "Those detectives, especially the short-arsed one with the Italian name."

"Garibaldi," said Craig. "And the way he looked at you. It made you feel guilty."

"Me too," said Charlie.

"Look," said Jimmy, raising his hands in a calming fashion. "Like you, I do not believe for one second that any of us is involved in the death of Frankie Dunne. Nor do I for one moment believe any of you came to my door in the Bob Dylan mask with a water pistol. I'm just sorry that these unfortunate events mean the end of our band, because I can't tell you how much I enjoyed it."

"Hear hear!" said Hazel, raising her glass.

The others raised their glasses as well. Someone said, 'the band!', and they all repeated it.

Jimmy looked round the room. He was pretty sure noone believed him when he said he didn't suspect any of them. They must, like him, have harboured suspicions that if Frankie Dunne had been attacked it was meant to be an attack on him, a case of mistaken identity caused by the Jagger mask, and they must have suspected that the bizarre water pistol incident, while not physically harmful, was another attempt to get him in some way.

It was easy enough to think of motives. Take Charlie Brougham. It may have been a long time ago and with an ex-wife, but even so. Then there was Larry Benyon. What if he'd found out who really wrote that *Crustie* article? And as for Craig and Hazel, what if they'd found out what he had said about them? The real question, though, was whether any of them would feel so strongly that they would want to attack him and possibly kill him. First of all, would they have the nerve? Secondly, would they take the risk? Why would people in their position do anything like that?

As he asked himself the question another thought occurred to him, one so obvious that he was amazed it hadn't crossed his mind before. Of course they wouldn't do something like that. Not themselves. They'd do what all rich people do – they'd get someone else to do their dirty work for them.

Suddenly everything took on a different complexion and, as Jimmy listened to the conversation around him, he saw each of the band members in a different light, imagining them slipping fat envelopes of cash into the hands of hired criminals.

"Anything on the masks?"

Larry's question brought Jimmy out of his thoughts.

"Nothing," he said with a shake of his head. "But it seems pretty clear that whoever took those masks wore one of them when they attacked me."

"You say 'they'," said Craig. "Do we have any idea whether it was a man or a woman?"

"I didn't see enough to make a call," said Jimmy. "My eyes were on the mask and they didn't say anything."

"I know this is going to sound very neurotic," said Hazel, "but are we *safe*? I mean a murder and an assault. Is this whole thing to do with us, the band?"

The room fell silent. Jimmy sensed each of them weighing up their own safety.

"The only link," said Larry, "is those masks."

Jimmy looked from face to face, wondering whether to voice his suspicions. He'd intended to keep them to himself but having everyone together like this seemed too good an opportunity to miss. What harm could it do?

He cleared his throat. "There is actually one other link, and I'm sure it's one that's occurred to each of you?"

He saw eyebrows raised, and sensed curiosity.

"That link is, of course, me."

He paused and grinned, waiting for a response.

"Explain," said Charlie.

"Frankie Dunne was found dead here at my house and he was found wearing the Mick Jagger mask I had been wearing on Sunday afternoon at the Bull's Head."

"So someone thought it was . . ." Hazel stopped and looked at the others.

"Thought it was me. Exactly. I didn't think so at the time but the assault has made me think it's a serious possibility."

"But," said Larry, "who would want to kill you?"

A silence fell on the room. The longer it went on the greater was the sense that each of them was drawing up a list.

"Quite so," said Jimmy. "Well, there may be some who've had the thought cross their mind, but I never, until now, thought there might be anyone who'd actually *do* it."

He meant it as a joke, but no-one laughed.

"What I don't understand," said Charlie, "is what this Frankie Dunne was doing here in the first place. The police say he didn't break in, you say you didn't know him—" Charlie paused briefly but long enough for Jimmy to sense he wasn't convinced. "None of us knew him. I mean, that's right, isn't it?"

Everyone turned to each other and nodded.

"Look," said Jimmy, "I didn't get us all together to do what the detectives can't. I just wanted us to be here to, you know, support each other because God knows this whole thing has been awful."

"The trouble is," said Craig, "we have no idea whether it's over. Hazel's right, we don't know what's going on in the mind of whoever's done these things." He held his arm out towards Jimmy. "You think you might have been the target in both, but can we know that for sure?"

"Craig's right," said Larry. "There's still a chance that for some crazy reason it's the band that's the target. It could be that someone's got ... I don't know, got a *thing* about us. They discovered our secret and ..." He looked as though his idea was running out of steam. "Look, if someone had a thing about us and they got into this house that night, late at night and saw someone in a Mick Jagger mask they'd definitely think it was one of us."

"Exactly," said Jimmy. "And they'd very likely think it was me."

"When you say a *thing* about us," said Craig, "what do you mean exactly?"

Larry threw his arms wide. "I have no idea, but then I have no idea why anyone would want to attack anyone at all. People who attack and kill and murder – they're not entirely logical, are they? They're driven by some kind of passion, one that's gone too far, that they can't control."

"So," said Hazel, "you think it's someone who knew all about our secret band."

Larry nodded. "It could be."

"Well, if it was, that narrows it down a bit doesn't it?" said Jimmy. "We kept it all pretty secret, didn't we? Look – we're doing what I didn't want us to do. I didn't get everyone here to go over everything. I just—"

"Difficult not to, though," said Hazel. "It's a bit like one of those murder mysteries when you get all the suspects together in a room and ..."

"I see," said Craig, "so we're suspects, are we?"

"No. I didn't mean that. I meant it's *like* that."

"Look," said Jimmy, reaching for a bottle and going to each glass to fill it up. "Why don't we have a drink and try to forget it? Difficult I know but I didn't get everyone here to make us more worried. As I said, I wanted to make us feel better, to feel ...supported."

As Jimmy filled each glass he looked each of them in the eye. Had he ever trusted any of them? He suppressed the thought and turned his attention to making the rest of the evening pass amicably. There was no further mention of masks and no-one returned to amateur attempts at detection. Wine was drunk, takeaway food was eaten and the conversation focused on showbiz gossip.

It wasn't a late night, and when the last of the band had left Jimmy decided to go to bed to read rather than wait up for Sophie's return from the theatre.

As so often happened when he read in bed, he fell asleep after ten minutes or so, and woke up with a start to find the book on his chest and with no idea how long he'd been sleeping.

Given the size of the house, it was difficult to hear anything when he was in the bedroom, especially when he was wearing earplugs and the door was shut. But tonight he'd fallen asleep before putting them in and with the door open (he always kept it open when Sophie was out) he was convinced he'd been woken by a noise from downstairs. It had to be Sophie, back from her night out. She'd be upstairs soon – she always came to bed quickly when she got in. No drinks or winding down. It was a case of straight in and straight up – so much so that if she ever chose to stay downstairs for any length of time Jimmy knew something was up.

As he picked up his book and started to read again, Jimmy wondered whether that might be the case tonight, and the longer she failed to appear the more he started to think that something, indeed, might be up.

Who had she been to the theatre with? All kind of things came Sophie's way when she went out with friends and often they were things about him. He could remember clearly the times when she'd discovered them, the way she'd stayed downstairs and he'd gone down to find her sitting at the kitchen table or in front of the TV, whisky in hand, looking at him in a way that left him in no doubt that he would have some explaining to do.

The thought of Sophie discovering things triggered memories of the email.

He felt again the shock he'd experienced when he first read it; when, totally freaked out by its contents, he'd almost been panicked into confession. Other emails, phone calls and a long letter had followed, but he'd kept his head and he was glad he had. The thing may not have gone away entirely, but he felt he had weathered the worst of the storm.

But what if, by some chance – and he couldn't fathom how – Sophie had found out? There was no logical reason to believe she had, but once the thought was in his head it refused to leave and he kept imagining her brooding downstairs, waiting to confront him.

What should he do?

Part of him wanted to do nothing, to stay in bed and wait for Sophie to come up. He could always pretend to be asleep and leave the tricky conversation until tomorrow.

But another part wanted to know, and it was that part that pulled him out of bed to the door.

He opened it and called out.

"Sophie?"

There was no answer.

He walked along the landing and went down the stairs, calling out as he neared the bottom.

Still no response.

He stood in the middle of the hall and called in both directions.

Silence.

He went into the kitchen and peered round.

Empty.

"Sophie?"

He walked across the hall to the living room.

Nothing.

He turned back for the kitchen.

Then he heard the door open and saw his wife walk in.

Whatever he had heard that had made him come downstairs, it hadn't been Sophie.

36

Deighton stood at the front of the room, swinging her reading glasses in her hand and waiting for quiet.

"Right," she said. The chat subsided and she turned to the screen behind her. On it were photos of the five Okay Boomer masks. "These—" she pointed with her finger, "are photos of the masks worn by the band at the Bull's Head. The Jagger one we've seen because it was on Frankie Dunne when he was found, but, given that the masks disappeared from Jimmy Clark's, this is the first time we've seen the others. We got the pictures from Guy Armstrong, who's the man who made them. But he's given us more than that. He's given us some very interesting information. It appears that an order was made for an extra set of these masks and these masks were delivered to the home address of Frankie Dunne."

She paused to let the room take it in.

"Armstrong says the order came from Bill Bloom but Bloom denies any knowledge. So, if Bloom is to be believed and he didn't order the extra masks, the question we need to ask is who did, and why did they have them delivered to Frankie Dunne." She paused again. "Any thoughts?"

Garibaldi looked at Gardner as her arm shot up. "If

Dunne had the masks, could that explain why he was found in the Jagger mask? He was wearing the mask that was delivered to him with the others."

"It could be," said Deighton, "but as ever, we can assume nothing. At the moment we simply don't know."

"It may explain how he got the mask," said Garibaldi, "but it doesn't explain why he was wearing it that night at Jimmy Clark's."

DC MacLean raised his hand. "So if the masks were taken from Jimmy Clark's that night and if Dunne had his own set, that means there are two lots of masks out there, which means —"

"Not quite two full sets," cut in DC Hodson. "We've got the Jagger mask that was on Dunne's body."

"OK," said MacLean. "But two of all the others. So Dunne might have had one set, but who's got the others?"

"But hang on," said Gardner, "if Dunne had that set of masks delivered to him, the question is where are they? They weren't found in the search of his house, were they? So what did he do with them?"

"The question that remains," said Deighton, "regardless of how Dunne got hold of the masks, is why was he wearing one of them when he was found."

"Maybe he wasn't wearing it," said Garibaldi.

"Wasn't wearing it?" Deighton's look suggested she wasn't ready for another of his left-field theories. "He was found in it. It was on his face."

"OK," said Garibaldi, "but that doesn't mean he put it on himself. It doesn't necessarily mean he was wearing that mask when he fell – or when he was pushed – from that window. What we haven't considered is whether the mask could have been put on *after* he fell to his death."

There was a short silence.

"Hang on," said Deighton, "so you're suggesting that someone killed Frankie Dunne and put the mask on him to...to what, exactly?"

"I don't know," said Garibaldi. "Maybe to make it look like it was all to do with Jimmy Clark's band, to link it to them. Or maybe..."

Garibaldi was struggling. The idea had just come to him and he hadn't thought it through.

"Or maybe they wanted us to think it *was* a case of mistaken identity, that they thought it was Jimmy Clark under the mask and that's why they killed him."

Deighton gave out a heavy sigh. "We're going round and round." She put on her glasses and consulted the papers in her hand. "But we may have a possible lead. Cara. Frankie's girlfriend. Bill Bloom's assistant is called Cara and if it's the same one we have an important link. We're talking to her when?"

"Straight after this," said Garibaldi. "She lives in Fulham, which tallies with what one of Dunne's friends said about her. So fingers crossed."

"OK," said Deighton. "And where are we on Dunne's phone records? Any calls to or from a Cara?"

"None," said DC MacLean. "Not a Cara amongst them."

"I've checked the electoral roll," said Gardner, "and guess how many Caras there are in Fulham?"

Gardner raised her head and looked round, as if she expected everyone to hazard a guess.

Garibaldi was about to offer one. He liked the question – very House of Games.

"I'll tell you," said Gardner. "There are thirty-nine and I've telephoned them all. None of them claims to have known Frankie Dunne and none of them claims to be friends with Jimmy Clark's daughter."

"Why would they?" said DC MacLean, "if they did know them they'd have been in touch."

"Would they?" said Gardner. "I'm not sure."

"But if they'd been with Frankie the night before he was found dead at the house of one of her best friends—"

"There could be all kind of explanations," said Garibaldi. "They could be frightened. They might not be registered to vote—"

"Isn't everyone registered to vote?"

"Among young people it's about one in five unregistered," said Garibaldi, pleased to have retrieved the figure. "And there's one other possible explanation and that's that this Cara doesn't live in Fulham."

"Okay," said Gardner. "So maybe—"

"One other thing about this Cara," said Garibaldi. "Danny, Frankie's mate at M&S, says Frankie got a call at work one day and asked him to cover for him while he went off to do something. Danny's pretty sure the call was from Cara."

"But he doesn't know for sure?" said Deighton.

"Not for sure, but he thinks he knows the day it happened so we can go through his phone records. I know we haven't been able to trace a Cara on them, but we might need to look again." Garibaldi paused. "Hang on," he said. "There are no Caras on Dunne's phone records, right? And we've been told that Cara was friends with Jimmy Clark's daughter but Clark's daughter claims not to know her. So could it be that there's no Cara at all?"

"What do you mean?" said Deighton.

"Frankie Dunne could have made her up. Could Dunne be some kind of fantasist spinning a tale about a girl that doesn't exist?"

Another silence. It felt as if everyone was considering the possibility.

Deighton looked like she couldn't work out whether it was a good idea or another Garibaldi curveball. "Unlikely," she said, "but we can't rule it out. We need to explore every possibility while never losing sight of the basics: ABC."

Assume nothing. Believe nobody. Check everything.

No-one in the room needed it spelled out.

37

It had always struck Hazel Bloom as ironically appropriate that she should have made her name as an impressionist. What was an impressionist, after all, if not someone pretending to be someone else? And wasn't that what she had spent her whole life doing? She sometimes tried to reassure herself that this kind of simulation was no more than what everyone else did to some extent, but she knew that in her case the fraudulence ran deeper.

She had no idea where her talent for mimicry had come from but she sensed it may have had its roots in a deep discomfort about who she actually was. It had first manifested itself at school, where her pin-point imitations of teachers greatly amused classmates and it had accompanied her through her entire academic career.

She still had no idea how she had managed to fluke her way into Cambridge, still less how she had managed to stay there, but she had a very clear sense of how, after three years of spending most of her time performing in Footlights and narrowly avoiding getting sent down for failing to meet academic standards, she had managed to emerge with a degree.

The memory still haunted her, as did the prospect of

retrospective exposure. She could still see the girl at the next desk in the exam hall, the raised eyebrows and accusatory glance when she saw what Hazel was up to. She knew she wouldn't get away with it now – things were much tighter by all accounts, but back then such cheating was not unknown and she knew that without it she wouldn't have scraped the Third which she had ever since tried to hide or pass off as the result of her Footlighting. Her degree, she insisted, didn't mean she wasn't clever and she liked to take every opportunity to show that the opposite was the case.

Recent events had affected her in all kinds of ways, but the way they had made her more than usually conscious of what she had done disturbed her. She knew exposure was no more likely now than it had ever been but the dead body, the questioning by the police, the masks – it had all made her very anxious. Especially the masks. She may have worn them metaphorically all her life but wearing real ones in the band and their centrality in the police investigation had made her think about them in a very different light.

And now there were two sets. Bill had told her about the extra set of Okay Boomer masks delivered to Frankie Dunne, the man found dead at Jimmy's. What did this mean? Did it help explain anything?

As far as she could see, it explained nothing – simply added to her acute anxiety.

Hazel was so anxious that she kept practising her impressions. It was her way of dealing with nerves and anxiety. Others turned to drink or drugs, but whenever Hazel felt stressed or unable to relax she turned to her work, developing new material and polishing her repertoire of impersonations. In this respect, she knew she was lucky. Whenever she felt under pressure she responded by working harder (a bit like Boxer in 'Animal Farm' she often thought, though she kept the unflattering comparison to herself) and, as a consequence, the more uptight she felt the better her work became. But that didn't mean she enjoyed it. Far from it – given a choice, she would rather work less and feel more relaxed. In recent days relaxation had been particularly hard to come by. Ever since the discovery of that body at Jimmy's and the disturbing assault on him by the masked man with the water pistol, her nerves had been in a terrible state and she drew scant consolation from the fact that at least she'd been working hard.

Today, after a morning of practice in front of the camera, she had tried to unwind by going for a run by the river. She took her favourite route, crossing Barnes Bridge to the north side, heading up to Hammersmith through Chiswick, crossing the bridge and coming back along the towpath. It may not have cleared her mind but by the time she came off the towpath in Lonsdale Road and neared her home on The Terrace she felt like doing something that afternoon other than work, a sure sign that the run had in some way helped.

Thankfully, the gaggle of paparazzi on the other side of the road had disappeared and she was able to relax as she slowed down and came to a halt at the front door. She reached for her key and was about to put it in the lock when she was conscious of someone standing behind her. She turned and saw a face she recognised.

Debbie Harry.

38

Gardner glanced sideways at Garibaldi as she drove down the Fulham Palace Road. "This thing about Frankie Dunne being killed in a case of mistaken identity."

"What about it?"

"Do you really believe someone thought they were killing Clark?"

"I'm not sure what I think," said Garibaldi, "but the more I find out about Jimmy Clark, the more I realise how many people dislike him."

"Enough to want to kill him?"

"Who knows? I do know one thing, though."

"What's that?"

Garibaldi reached down to his feet and held up a Gail's bag. "I know that sometimes," he said, lifting out a cinnamon bun and an almond croissant and holding them towards her, "we all need a little boost."

"Yeah, that's what Chris says. I'm not sure he means a sugar boost, though."

Garibaldi broke the pastries in half. "Things OK?"

Things. They both knew the shorthand.

"Things are good," said Gardner. "I mean this investigation's pissing me off, mainly because, like you, I can't get my head round it, but when I manage to get home and when I see Chris . . .yeah things are good. How about you?"

Garibaldi didn't know where to start. "Things are OK," he said, deciding on the simplest option.

Gardner reached for her half of the cinnamon bun and put it in her lap. "These masks," she said, "they remind me of something Chris likes to say."

Garibaldi's heart sank. Another self-improvement mantra was coming his way.

"What's that?"

"'Be the best version of yourself'. A version of yourself. I mean, a bit like a mask, isn't it? We don't always wear the best one, but we all wear one, don't we? A version, I mean. It's like we have these different selves. Makes you wonder whether you ever really know anyone."

Garibaldi nodded, impressed that, despite her exposure on a daily basis to Chris's half-baked nonsense , Gardner was still capable of talking sense.

Gardner took a quick bite of her croissant. "I mean take Deighton, for example. How often have I watched her and listened to her when she's taking a meeting and wondered whether I really know her?"

Garibaldi nodded in agreement. Deighton could still surprise him – he was still trying to work out the best way to respond to the way she'd snapped at him in those meetings.

"You know what?" he said, finishing off the cinnamon bun, "if this job has taught me anything over the years it's what William Goldman once said."

"William Goldman?"

"The screenwriter."

"Right. What did he say?"

"He said, 'nobody knows anything'."

Gardner nodded, turning down the corners of her mouth

and raising her eyebrows. Goldman's philosophy clearly didn't form part of Chris's positive thinking programme.

"He was talking about the movies," said Garibaldi, "but it's a great line, isn't it? Up there with Einstein."

"Einstein?"

"Yeah. Know what he said? He said, 'the more I learn, the more I realise I don't know.'"

"OK. Well, you could take either line and apply it to this case, couldn't you?"

"You could," said Garibaldi, "but there are a couple of things we know for sure."

"Yeah? What are they, then?"

"The first is that we eat too many Gail's pastries."

Gardner laughed. "Right. And the second?"

"The second is that Cara Ferdinand is one of the thirty-nine."

"The thirty-nine?"

"One of the thirty-nine Caras in the electoral roll in Fulham."

"And she's off work with vomiting and diarrhoea, right?"

"Poor thing. Let's give her another call, shall we?" Garibaldi took out his phone. He dialled but there was still no answer. "Maybe she's in bed."

"Or on the loo."

Garibaldi took a bite of his cinnamon bun. "Yeah. Maybe we should pick up some Lucozade on the way."

Cara's address was off Munster Road, in a street of small, terraced houses and large, pavement-parked SUVs.

There was no answer when Gardner rang on the doorbell.

"Like you said," said Garibaldi. "Probably on the loo."

Gardner rang again. This time they heard footsteps.

The man who opened the door was dressed in cords and

a cardigan. His heavy-framed glasses and shock of grey hair gave him the air of an academic.

Garibaldi and Gardner introduced themselves and showed their warrant cards.

"Sorry to bother you," said Garibaldi, "but we'd like to have a word with Cara."

"Cara?" said the man. "What's happened?"

"Nothing's happened," said Garibaldi, "we'd just like to ask her a few questions."

"I'm afraid you can't," said the man.

"We understand she's not feeling well," said Gardner, "but if she's well enough to spare us a few minutes that would be great."

"Not feeling well? What do you mean?"

"We tried to contact her at Bloom Productions," said Garibaldi, "but they said she's off sick."

"Off sick?" said the man. "She's not off sick, she's on holiday."

"On holiday?" said Gardner. "So she's not at home, then?"

"No, she's gone to stay with an old friend in Brighton. She's there for a week."

Garibaldi exchanged a look with Gardner. "Do you think we could come in for a second?"

The man stood back from the door, holding it wide, and ushered them into the living room.

"Please," he said, clearing papers off two of the chairs, "have a seat."

Garibaldi glanced round the room. Books were everywhere – not only on shelves but piled high on a table and around the computer on the desk by the window.

"We were led to believe that Cara was at home because she was ill."

"I see," said the man. "Well, that's definitely not the case."

Garibaldi tried to work out the man's likely relationship with Cara. He was old, in his sixties perhaps, but not so old that a relationship between them was unthinkable.

"Tell me," he said, "you're Cara's ...?"

"I'm Cara's father."

"I see."

"Frank Ferdinand." He gave a smile. "I know. Almost the Archduke. And almost the Scottish band of the same name."

Garibaldi laughed. He had taken to him.

"Cara's been living here since her mother died."

"I'm sorry."

Frank gave a resigned shrug. "Cancer. What can you say? Terribly sad. And Cara, well she's struggled. She was living in a shared flat in Dalston but she wanted to move back here for a while."

"I see," said Garibaldi. "Well, I'm sorry Cara's not here but I'm a little puzzled as to why she's lied to work about her whereabouts."

Frank scratched his head. "Yes, I find that very strange myself."

"Do you know who she's staying with?" said Gardner.

"Yes, I do. Yasmin, an old school friend."

"Do you have her number?" said Garibaldi.

"I don't think so," said Frank.

"Do you know Yasmin's second name?"

Frank screwed up his eyes in an effort to remember. "I think I do. When they were at school Cara used to call her by a nickname that was based on her surname. Now what was it ...?" Frank gave a tortured smile. "Marshy. That was it. Yasmin Marsh. She called her Marshy."

"Do you have her address?"

"Afraid not. I'd offer to go and have a look in Cara's address book but to my knowledge she doesn't have one. Youngsters don't, do they. It's all on phones."

"Does she have a laptop here?"

"She took it with her I think. I can go upstairs and have a look if you want."

"No need at the moment, Frank. We tried to call Cara before we came here but got no answer. When did you last speak to her?"

"I can't remember. I don't think I've spoken to her since she left. Let's see, that was a couple of nights ago. So, no, I haven't spoken to her since she went to Brighton, no." Frank looked at them, his eyes full of fearful possibility. "You don't think anything's *happened* to her, do you? I mean, why would she tell work she was ill and tell me she was on holiday?"

"Tell me," said Garibaldi. "How long has Cara been living here with you?"

"Let's see, Maria died just over a year ago. It was her first anniversary last month. So, yes, Cara's been here for about a year. She moved back soon after to help with the arrangements and said she needed to be here to help me, but I'm afraid it's been more a case of me looking after her. These things are never easy, but Cara's found it all very difficult. I've struggled as well, of course I have. It's…difficult. Cara's found work challenging over the last year. So have I." Frank pointed at the computer on the desk. "I do some teaching but used to be – no, still am – a playwright. Maria was an actress."

Frank looked around the room as if his wife might be lurking in a corner. "Can you tell me why you need to speak to her?"

"We have no reason to believe she's in trouble," said

Garibaldi, "but we do need to speak to her with regard to a recent suspicious death."

"Suspicious death?"

"You may have read in the papers about the man found at Jimmy Clark's house."

Frank's face froze. "Are you saying that Cara—"

Garibaldi held up his hand. "We're not saying anything. We just need to speak to her."

"I've read about it, of course, and seen it on the news. It seems completely bizarre. A bunch of celebrities playing in a masked band, wasn't it?"

"It was, yes."

"And Jimmy Clark's house, you say?" Frank shook his head, his expression a mixture of disbelief and disapproval. "Hang on, are you saying Cara's connected to this?"

"We have reason to believe that Cara might have been going out with the man who was found dead."

"What? She can't have been!"

"Why not?"

"I'd have known. She'd have told me what had happened." Frank swivelled his gaze between Garibaldi and Gardner. "Wouldn't she? I mean—"

"The man was called Frankie Dunne. Did Cara ever mention him?"

"Frankie Dunne? I'd remember if she did. Frankie. That's my name – without the 'ie' bit, that is."

"Do you know whether she has a boyfriend?" asked Gardner.

"Well, no. I don't. We've been trying to get on with our lives. I haven't really asked Cara too much about what she's been up to. I don't want to put too much pressure on her or anything. She's vulnerable. We both are. My main concern is that she's OK."

"So she's never mentioned a boyfriend called Frankie," said Gardner, "and to your knowledge you don't even know if she has a boyfriend?"

"That's right. But if you're saying it's her boyfriend who was found dead—"

"Those who knew Frankie say he'd started going out with a girl called Cara."

"It could be her," said Frank. "I really don't know."

"One other question, Frank. Apparently Cara said she was very good friends with Jimmy Clark's daughter."

"Really? I had no idea. I mean, she may be but—"

"The strange thing is that when we spoke to Jimmy Clark's daughter she claimed to have no knowledge of Cara, she claimed never to have known anyone called Cara."

"I'm baffled. Why would she say she was friends with her if she wasn't? I don't understand."

"We need to speak to her," said Garibaldi, getting up to leave. "As soon as we've contacted Yasmin Marsh and got hold of Cara we'll let you know."

"Tell her to ring me," said Frank. "Please."

Frank sat in his chair, hands clasped tightly in his lap. He was looking intensely at the wall.

Garibaldi followed his gaze and saw that he was looking at a photo. In it a much younger Frank stood with his arm on the shoulder of a strikingly attractive woman. Garibaldi assumed it was Maria. Between them was a young girl. She looked fifteen or sixteen. Garibaldi assumed she was Cara.

He turned to look at Frank again. His eyes were still fixed on the photo as if he were trying to bring himself into it, back to the time when he still had a wife and Cara still had a mother.

Garibaldi stood up. "Before we go, Frank, could we have a quick look at Cara's room?"

"Her room. Why?" Frank's eyes filled with alarm. "Something's happened to her, hasn't it?"

"I'm not saying that at all."

"Her room? Well, OK. I've no idea what state it's in, but . . ."

He led Garibaldi and Gardner into the hall and up the stairs onto the first-floor landing, where he pointed at a closed door.

"That's it," he said. "I don't go in often. Ever since Cara moved back she's been, as I said, struggling. I've kept an eye but I've also wanted to give her space, so . . ."

Garibaldi and Gardner slipped on forensic gloves and went in.

The room was neat and orderly – a single bed, wardrobe, chest of drawers, a desk, and a bookcase. The only untidy area was one corner where a turntable and speakers sat on the floor in the midst of a scattering of vinyl albums. Garibaldi walked towards them and his eye picked out a few titles – Carole King's *Tapestry*, James Taylor's *Mud Slide Slim*, Bob Dylan's *Blood on the Tracks*, The Stones' *Exile on Main St*. He nodded his approval and went to the desk. As he did he noticed two framed pictures on the wall either side of the door – the cover of *The Freewheelin' Bob Dylan* and *Sergeant Pepper*.

Garibaldi turned to Frank, who was standing in the doorway. "Fond of music is she?"

"She is," said Frank with a rueful smile. "Got it from her mother. Most of those albums were Maria's and those pictures on the wall were hers as well. Her mother was a big music fan. Loved all the old stuff, particularly Dylan. Always had a soft spot for The Stones and The Beatles as well and Cara, well, she shared her enthusiasm. When Maria died it seemed to become really important to her. She started reading about it all, collecting stuff—"

"What did she collect?" said Garibaldi.

"Old albums mainly. I think it was her way of connecting with her mum. Music does that, doesn't it? It can be a real bond, and I think Cara found comfort in it. Since she's been back here she's been in her room listening to those albums a lot and she's been out to a lot of gigs as well. Not Dylan or The Beatles obviously but she's certainly been into her music."

Garibaldi looked at the prints on the wall and went back to the stack of albums. Ideas were running round his head and he was struggling to connect them.

"So," said Frank from the doorway, "when you've got in touch with Cara's friend..."

"We'll let you know as soon as we have," said Garibaldi, as he and Gardner followed Frank downstairs.

As they walked to the car, Garibaldi's phone rang. He didn't recognise the number, but took the call.

"DI Garibaldi."

"Something's happened," said a voice he recognised. "I think you'd better come round."

Hazel Bloom sipped a whisky and looked at Garibaldi and Gardner, her eyes wide with fear.

"I thought I was going to be killed!"

"It must have been a terrible shock," said Gardner.

"I mean—" Hazel turned to the window. Her lips trembled as she looked at the river flowing beneath Barnes Bridge. "The mask!" she said turning back. "I couldn't believe it. The Debbie Harry mask! My own mask, staring at me!"

"Are you sure it was the same mask?"

"Absolutely. There aren't other masks like that. Look, I'm not trying to do your job for you or anything, but those masks disappear from Jimmy's house and then first someone in a Dylan mask on Jimmy and now someone in a Debbie Harry mask on me. You don't have to be a genius to—"

"Let's take one thing at a time, shall we?" said Garibaldi.

Hazel took a slug of whisky. "Of course, I don't mean to..."

"Did this person say anything?"

"Nothing. As soon as I turned I saw the mask and then the water hit me. Right in the face. Right in the eyes. It sounds like nothing but, believe me, when you're not expecting it and it's close up—"

"And when you got inside you found this..." Garibaldi reached for the transparent evidence bag in Gardner's hands and held it up. Inside was a sheet of paper with 'RIP Frankie Dunne' typed in large black letters.

"I have no idea what they think I – we – anyone did, but can I say yet again that I have nothing to do with Frankie Dunne's death. I have no idea how he came to be there."

Garibaldi nodded slowly, as if giving his next question serious consideration. "So, Hazel, this gun—"

"Look, Inspector, I've never been shot before. I have no idea what it feels like. I saw the gun pointing at me and the next thing I knew was my face was covered with something wet. I thought it was blood. I—"

"Did you see where they went?"

"I have no idea. When I realised what had happened they'd vanished. What are you going to do about it, Inspector? It's all connected, surely? And what about this second set of masks? Bill told me about the second set of Okay Boomer masks delivered to Frankie Dunne. That has to be significant, doesn't it?"

Garibaldi kicked himself. He should have anticipated that Bill Bloom would tell his wife.

"It's forming part of our investigation."

"But what does it mean? Frankie Dunne's dead. It can't have been him in that Debbie Harry mask, can it?"

"As I say, we're looking into it."

"When I told the others they were freaked out. They couldn't make any sense of it."

"We'll be in touch, Hazel," said Garibaldi, nodding to Gardner and getting up to leave. "But if you remember anything more that might be relevant, any detail however small, do let us know."

"Of course." Hazel showed them the door and led them downstairs. "In the meantime, what am I going to do?"

"What do you mean?"

"What if this person tries it again?"

"You just need to take sensible precautions."

"Sensible precautions! What are you talking about? Is there nothing you can do?"

Garibaldi paused at the door. "We'll do all we can, Hazel."

"I've done nothing wrong, nothing at all."

"That may well be, Hazel, but that doesn't mean you're not connected."

Hazel shook her head in exasperation and closed the door behind them. Garibaldi and Gardner stepped onto the pavement and walked to the car, Garibaldi's mind trying to work out what kind of offence had been committed by the water-pistol wielding masked assailants and what, exactly, they were trying to do.

39

Larry Benyon was worried. It had been bad enough after the discovery of the body, but the bizarre assaults on Jimmy and Hazel had made things even worse and he'd been treading carefully ever since, being more watchful than usual when he went out and not answering the door unless he was absolutely certain who it was.

That's why it had taken him some time to let in the two detectives who now sat opposite him in his living room.

"So am I the next in line for a masked soaking?" he said to them. "Or will that be one of the others?"

"We advise you to be careful. There would seem to be a pattern but who knows?"

Larry gave an amused laugh. "Who knows indeed? I mean – do you have any idea who's behind it?"

"Do you mean the death of Frankie Dunne or the assaults?"

"Any of them. They have to be linked, don't they?"

Garibaldi looked irritated, as if he was on the verge of losing his temper. "We're keeping an open mind, but there would seem to be obvious connections."

"The most obvious being the masks. And now I hear there's a second set of them that were delivered to Frankie Dunne. What's all that about?"

"It's a significant development," said Garibaldi.

"I know that, but what does it mean?"

"Can we go back to the night after the Okay Boomers gig?"

"I can't believe I've anything more to tell you."

Garibaldi looked at Larry with a frown and said nothing for several seconds. He leaned forward. "Frankie Dunne died after all the band had left Jimmy's. That's right, isn't it?"

"I'd certainly left, and all the others say they'd left as well..."

"But what if you hadn't all left? You didn't all leave together, Jimmy didn't see you out, so there's a chance that one of you might have stayed in the house."

"Are you saying one of us hid in the house and then killed Frankie Dunne?"

"I'm trying to imagine possible scenarios."

"Well it's a possible one," said Larry, "but it seems pretty unlikely."

"And why's that?"

"Because it assumes that one of us would have a motive for killing Frankie Dunne. I've already told you I have no idea who he was and I should imagine the rest of the band have told you the same. That's certainly what they told me."

"There's another scenario for you to consider, Larry. Let's imagine that someone stayed in the house and then, some time later, they went upstairs looking for someone they knew was up there."

"But I've told you. We don't know—"

Garibaldi held up his hand to stop him. "Picture this for a moment. They, whoever they are, see someone in the Mick Jagger mask and they think they know who it is. It can only be one person, the man for whom the mask was made, the man who was wearing it on stage earlier that day at the Bull's Head. Who else could it be? Who else is in the house?"

"OK," said Larry, "so if that's the case – and I have to say I find it extremely unlikely — there's one big question you need to ask, isn't there?"

"You're absolutely right. Why would one of the band want to kill him?"

Larry took his time, trying to work out the best way to respond.

"I'm sorry," he said, "I can't think of any reason any of them – of us – would have for wanting to kill Jimmy."

"So you all get on well with each other?"

"Why else would we all play together in a masked band?"

"My thoughts exactly. But in my experience when you scratch below the surface of any group of friends you find all kinds of tensions. It's the same in marriages, isn't it? Some couples can look perfectly happy but below the surface ...in my line of work I've come across several murders of spouses where all friends and family have thought the marriage was good, that husband and wife got along fine."

"So you're saying that someone, one of us, hates Jimmy so much that they want to murder him?"

"We don't know for sure that he *was* murdered, but we have to consider the possibility. We have to consider all possibilities."

Garibaldi fixed Larry again with his disconcerting gaze.

"Look, Jimmy's no angel. I know he seems to be Mr Nice Guy but anyone who's been in this business knows appearances can be deceptive."

"So he could have enemies?"

"Enemies? Yes, I suppose so."

"Including the members of the band?"

Larry shook his head. "No. I can't see it."

"You can't think of anyone in the band who might have reason to—"

"To what? Attack him? Try to kill him?"

"Did anyone in the band have reason to dislike him?"

Larry paused. This was not the time to mention the *Crustie* article.

"I did hear one thing," he said. "It may well be just a rumour but someone told me . . ." He held up his hands as if stopping himself. "No, it's nothing. Forget it."

"I'd like to hear, Larry. You might not think it important but we need to hear everything."

"OK," said Larry, hoping he hadn't overdone the feigned reluctance, "I heard that when Jimmy was on a poetry prize judging panel he was very scathing about Craig Francis. I can't remember the details but apparently he was spectacularly rude. Something about Craig not being a real poet. But I can't believe that would make Craig want to . . ."

"You'd be surprised at what people do, Larry. I used to be surprised myself."

"I know poets are sensitive and all that, but I can't imagine that would make Craig . . . no, I don't see it."

"And yet you chose to mention it."

"I mentioned it because you asked if any of us might have reason to dislike Jimmy. Believe it or not, I'm trying to help."

Garibaldi gave him another silent stare. "There's one other idea I'd like to run past you, Larry, and it's to do with the mask Frankie Dunne was wearing when his body was discovered. What if I were to suggest to you that Dunne might not have been wearing that mask when he fell to his death and that it was put on afterwards?"

"Put on afterwards. By who?"

Garibaldi stifled the 'whom' before it passed his lips.

"Let's assume that Dunne wasn't killed in a case of mistaken identity, that it wasn't one of your band. And let's assume that whoever killed Dunne knew him and had reason to kill him, but decided afterwards to put the mask on to confuse things, to make the killing seem linked to your band."

"Who are we talking about here?"

Garibaldi said nothing and raised his eyebrows.

"You mean Jimmy?"

"Can you think of any reason why Jimmy might have wanted to kill Frankie Dunne?"

"He claims not to have known him."

"It would be foolish to assume that everyone's been telling the truth."

Larry took a breath. "OK," he said, "this is pure speculation, based on nothing I know myself, but some have said that Jimmy might have ...particular tastes."

Larry watched as the detective opened his notebook and reached for his pen.

Gardner strapped on her belt and pulled out of Larry Benyon's drive. "You know that idea about Dunne not wearing that mask when he fell?"

"What about it?" said Garibaldi.

"Where did you get the idea from?"

"Where? I don't know. That's the thing about ideas. You never know when they're going to come."

"The funny thing is," said Gardner. "I seem to remember coming up with it myself."

"Really?"

"Yeah, in one of our meetings I made the point that

Dunne might not have been wearing the mask when he fell, that someone might have put it on him afterwards."

As she said the words Garibaldi remembered the occasion. He also remembered that no-one had picked up on the idea.

"There you go," he said. "Great minds."

"But there's a problem with your other theory about one of the band staying in the house."

"What's that?"

"We have them on CCTV leaving."

"Oh I know that," said Garibaldi. "There's a clear picture of each of the Okay Boomers leaving. I'm well aware of that."

"So your theory's wrong then?"

Garibaldi laughed. "Not entirely. The front door's not the only way in and out of the house, remember? There's a side entrance as well."

"With no cameras."

"Exactly. So, as I say, a bit of a long shot, but you can't rule it out. But as for the mask being put on Dunne after being killed – that's still a possibility, and I think it's still possible that Clark killed him."

Garibaldi's phone rang. He checked the screen. Bill Bloom.

"DI Garibaldi."

"Those other masks, the extra set of Boomers. I think I've found out how they got ordered."

40

"It's fucking ridiculous!"

Craig Francis had had enough. He was fed up with speaking to the police; he was fed up with the whole thing. He might have been OK if he'd been able to deal with it all by himself, but that wasn't the case. Gina had wanted to be involved in everything, and her reactions had made everything almost impossible. She'd been suspicious enough over the dead man in Jimmy Clark's garden but she'd gone completely crazy when Jimmy was doorstepped by the man in the Dylan mask with the water pistol. And that was before Hazel was on the end of the same kind of thing.

The way Gina had gone on about it, you'd have thought that Craig was the one responsible. Nonsense, of course, but he was only too well aware that the recent stress had brought him very close to losing it completely.

He felt very close now as he faced the two detectives.

"I know it must be worrying, Craig," said the woman. She was much gentler than the one called Garibaldi who kept looking at him in an unnerving way, as if he knew everything about him.

"It's crazy!" said Craig. "The masks disappear and

then someone wears them to do that thing to Jimmy and Hazel – and what about this extra set of masks? Hazel told me about it. Okay Boomer masks delivered to Frankie Dunne. Does that explain why he was found in one of them?"

"It could do," said Garibaldi.

"But he can't be the one with the water pistol. It has to be whoever took those masks, doesn't it? They were there that night. We left them at Jimmy's on the table. If you find who took them—"

"We're looking, Craig," said Garibaldi, "and we'll find them. But I'd like you to consider something else. What would you say to the idea that it was Jimmy Clark who killed Frankie Dunne?"

"Jimmy? Why would he do that? I can't think why he — unless maybe if Dunne was trying to burgle his house and Jimmy came upon him in the act . . ."

"Came upon him in the act?" Garibaldi nodded slowly as if struck by the phrase. "An interesting possibility. Can you think of any other reason why Frankie Dunne might be in Jimmy's house at that time of night?"

Craig did his best to look as if he didn't know what Garibaldi was talking about.

"After all," said Garibaldi, "his wife was away for the night, he'd had an exciting afternoon and evening."

"OK. I know what you're saying," said Craig, "but there's no evidence of that, is there?"

"No evidence, no, but—"

"That kind of thing's not illegal, is it?"

"Of course not. We know that Frankie Dunne had a girlfriend, but we're trying to get the whole picture here."

"Have you spoken to the girlfriend?"

"Not yet, no. We hope to soon. One other scenario

I'd like to put to you. Do you think someone could have killed Frankie Dunne thinking that under the mask it was actually Jimmy?"

Craig puffed his cheeks and exhaled. "Why would anyone want to kill Jimmy? It doesn't make sense."

"Murder often doesn't. And sometimes it can be a small thing that triggers it. To the rational mind the motive can seem tiny and trivial when compared to the colossal significance of taking someone's life."

"I get all that, but...look, I know Jimmy may have made enemies along the way but he's never crossed me."

"Really?"

Garibaldi paused and gave Craig a steady stare, holding his gaze until he turned away in discomfort.

"Do you seriously think one of us killed Frankie Dunne by mistake, thinking it was Jimmy?"

"I'm just trying to work out the dynamics between you all. We have to consider all possibilities."

"So you want to know whether Jimmy has ever done something to me that would make me want to kill him?"

"Done something. Said something."

Garibaldi paused, giving the last two words space.

The longer the silence went on the more uncomfortable Craig felt.

"OK," he said, deciding to shift the focus elsewhere. "If you're looking for motives, there are people in the band with bigger motives than me."

"So you do have a motive then?"

"No. I'm not saying that."

"Bigger motives than me. Doesn't that suggest that you yourself have a motive but it's not as big as the motives of others?"

"I don't mean that at all."

"If you didn't have a motive, wouldn't you say, 'Unlike others, I haven't got a motive'?"

"You're being a bit pedantic, aren't you? It's just words."

"Just words? But you're a poet, Craig. Words are your tools."

Craig felt his anger rise. He tried hard to control it. "OK," he said. "Take Charlie. Did you know that Jimmy slept with his first wife? I know they're separated but you don't forget a thing like that, that kind of betrayal. Someone who smiles to your face when they're screwing your wife."

Garibaldi nodded, but said nothing for several seconds. He looked at his notebook and flicked over a few pages.

"So you're saying Charlie had a motive. What about Larry and Hazel?"

"Look," said Craig, throwing his hands in the air as if to say he'd had enough. "This whole thing is so fucking ridiculous! I can't believe you're so desperate that you're accusing us all. Have you really made no progress? Are you really so far away from finding out how Dunne died, not to mention the fucking water pistol attacks!"

"We're getting there, Craig," said Garibaldi, snapping shut his notebook and getting up from his chair. "In fact, we're very close. Very close indeed."

He gave a knowing smile to his colleague as they walked to the front door.

Craig closed the door behind them and leaned back against it, trying to imagine what it would be like to be confronted by someone in one of those masks. It had been one thing to wear one – it would be another to see it from the other side.

What would he do if it happened to him?

He felt the familiar feeling return, stronger than ever.

*

Charlie Brougham couldn't work out which he hated more – working on the ludicrous film or being interviewed yet again by the detectives. Sitting in an office at the studios opposite the short stocky one called Garibaldi and the younger woman whose name he hadn't caught may have got him away from the set, but he was beginning to think that delivering wooden lines and acting in implausible scenes in *Coming to Terms* was preferable to having to answer more questions.

He'd already raised his concerns about Jimmy and Hazel's encounters with the masked men, his anxieties over his own safety hardly quelled by the advice to 'be careful', and he'd just asked about the second set of masks Hazel had told him about, Garibaldi's answer convincing him that the detective had no idea what to make of it.

He now had to respond to the suggestions Garibaldi had just come up with.

Could Jimmy have killed Frankie Dunne? Could one of the band have killed him thinking he was Jimmy?

He knew he had to answer carefully.

"I can't see why Jimmy would do that," he said after a long pause. "Unless he found Dunne in his house and felt threatened."

"What about if Jimmy had invited Dunne?"

"You mean that old rumour?" He laughed. "I've heard it too, but in all the time I've known Jimmy I've never seen any evidence of it."

"But," said Garibaldi, "you have personal experience of Jimmy's, what shall we call it, wayward behaviour?"

"What do you mean?"

"I've heard things about something he did to you, or rather did to—"

"Who told you that?"

"I can't reveal my sources."

"You think that because Jimmy had an affair with my first wife I might have killed him?"

"I'm just checking that what I heard is true."

"Look, Inspector, it was a long time ago. It was in a different country, and besides—"

"And besides, the wench is dead?"

Charlie's mouth fell open.

"*The Jew of Malta*," said Garibaldi.

Charlie shook his head in disbelief. When he had started the line from the Marlowe play (remembered from a student production many years ago), the last thing in the world he had expected was for the detective to finish it.

"Or," continued Garibaldi, "if not dead then at least divorced."

"Look, I separated from my wife a long time ago."

"Even so, these things stick with you, don't they? I'm no expert on French law but I don't think *crime passionnel* has a sell-by-date. What surprises me is that, knowing this, you chose to be in Jimmy's band."

"It wasn't Jimmy's band. There was no leader."

"No leader, but he kept the masks. Sounds like a leader to me."

"OK, so I was in the band. But if you avoid people who've said things about you, or done things to you, you wouldn't get out much. Not in this business at least."

Charlie watched Garibaldi open his notebook. There was something unnerving about him. It wasn't just the way he had finished the quote, there was something else. Maybe it was the way he looked at you and held your gaze for several seconds before he spoke. Exactly what he was doing now.

"So tell me," Garibaldi said eventually, "can you think of anyone else in the band who might want to kill Jimmy?"

"Assuming that Dunne was killed in a case of mistaken identity?"

"Exactly."

What should he say? He had to come up with something – even if only to take the pressure off himself.

"Look," he said, "I don't know if this is true—"

"Don't worry about truth for the moment. If you've heard something or if you think something I want to hear it."

Charlie took a breath. "Well, I've heard that things haven't always been great between Jimmy and Larry. Very different backgrounds, of course, and very different politics. Someone once told me that Jimmy had written a particularly vicious article about Larry in that magazine for old fogeys. What's it called? *The Creakie*? No, *The Crustie*, that's the one. I wouldn't know myself as I never read it. Can't remember who told me but they said it was Jimmy writing anonymously and it was savage. I've no idea whether Larry ever found out—"

"But if he did he would have a reason to dislike Jimmy?"

"Not enough to kill him! I can't believe for one moment that he'd do anything like that. When you're as famous as Larry you have thousands, millions of people saying nasty things about you. It comes with the territory. It used to happen to me. Less so now. But look, I can't believe Larry knows. If he did, why would he have joined the band?"

"You knew what Jimmy had done to you and you joined the band."

"I know, but . . ." Charlie spread his hands in front of him. "What can I say?"

"What about the others? Craig? Hazel?"

"Craig? I can't think of anything. Hazel . . . well, now I come to think of it I did hear something some time ago from Hazel's husband Bill. I know him quite well because we worked together on a lot of films. You know, back in the day."

"What did he say?"

"He said he had it on good authority that Jimmy had blocked Hazel from being on some panel quiz show. Bill didn't tell me what he said, just that Hazel was furious about it. But look, this whole idea is ridiculous. None of us would . . ."

Charlie broke off. An idea had come to him.

"Look, I probably shouldn't say this, but if you asked me who, out of the band, is the most likely to have the capacity to do something crazy like that I'd say it was Jimmy. Your theory about Jimmy maybe killing Dunne and the attacks on him being revenge – that makes more sense to me than any of the band killing him."

Charlie had no idea whether or not he believed it. All he wanted to do was take the spotlight off himself.

Looking at the expression on Garibaldi's face, he couldn't work out whether or not he had.

41

"I'm still very shaken up," said Hazel Bloom, turning to the window of her first-floor living room and looking out onto the river. "I haven't been able to relax since it happened. To see that face. Debbie Harry. And it may sound silly, a water pistol fired at your face but, believe me, it was a huge shock."

"I'm sure it was," said Garibaldi. "But I'd like to ask a few questions about Jimmy Clark."

"You mean what happened to me isn't important?" Hazel wore the look of an actress relegated to a supporting role.

"Of course it is," said Garibaldi. "Not only were you attacked, but you received that note. RIP Frankie Dunne."

"I know what it said, Inspector. Was there anything on it? Fingerprints. DNA?"

Garibaldi sighed inwardly. With so much police drama on TV, everyone was now an expert.

"Nothing significant."

"What does that mean?"

"It means that there are prints and DNA traces but we have yet to match them."

"I see." Hazel looked unimpressed.

"If we could get back to Jimmy Clark, Hazel—"

"Of course. Look, there are a lot of people out there who don't much like Jimmy Clark. Yes, he's all very pleasant in public, but as I've said before, he has a dark side. We all have our dark sides – do you know what I mean?"

"I do," said Garibaldi. "Every Jekyll has his Hyde."

"Exactly. And there's a Deacon Brodie in every town."

Hazel looked at Garibaldi as if curious to see if he'd picked up on the reference.

"Ah," he said. "Deacon Brodie. Robert Louis Stevenson's real-life inspiration. The duplicitous locksmith."

Hazel's nod suggested she was impressed. "That's the one. The respectable man with the dark hidden alter ego. The thing is I've heard things about Jimmy over the years, things he's done, things he's said, that make you look at Mr Charming in a different way. You look at him and you see..."

"You see behind the mask?" said Garibaldi.

"The mask, yes." Hazel laughed, but her laugh was still nervous, as if she couldn't work Garibaldi out. "Well, as a wise man once said, we all prepare a face to meet the faces that we meet."

"Very good," said Garibaldi, "but leaving T S Eliot aside for a moment—"

"Of course," said Hazel, "it's a habit of mine. Just can't resist a quotation."

"I quite understand."

As someone who himself was not averse to the odd quotation or reference, Garibaldi understood perfectly. Unlike Hazel Bloom, though, his habit wasn't born of a desire to show off.

Or so he liked to tell himself.

"To get back to Jimmy Clark's dark side?"

"Of course," said Hazel. "Well, it was when you suggested that Jimmy could have killed Frankie Dunne, it just reminded me of some of the things I've heard whispered about Jimmy over the years. You must understand that, in saying this, I'm not saying Jimmy *did* kill Dunne, but it's been said that Jimmy has always had an ...let's say 'an appetite'. He may have stayed married to Sophie all this time but that doesn't mean he's necessarily been faithful. He has, apparently, put it about and still does."

"So you're suggesting that's why Frankie Dunne was in his house late on that Sunday night."

"If rumours are to be believed, then, yes, it's possible that's why Frankie Dunne was at his house."

Garibaldi looked at his notebook. "And why would he kill him?"

"I'm not saying he *did*. I'm suggesting it's a possibility."

"OK. So in this possibility why would Jimmy do it?"

"I have no idea. Money, maybe?"

Money. Why hadn't Garibaldi considered this before? Could Dunne have been blackmailing Clark?

"Or maybe it was some kind of sex thing? As you say, there's a possibility Dunne wasn't wearing the mask when he fell, that it was put on him afterwards. But on the other hand ..."

Garibaldi nodded. The first question he'd asked when Gardner told him the body had been found in a mask was whether it was a sex thing.

"OK, what about the other suggestion that it was one of the band who murdered Dunne thinking it was Jimmy behind the mask?"

"You want to know if any of us would have had a motive?"

Garibaldi opened his hands, inviting her to continue.

"Look, I don't for one second, for one nano-second, believe that any of us could do that to him. And I'm sure you don't need to hear this again, but one thing is certain and that is that *I* definitely didn't do it!"

Hazel paused and looked at Garibaldi and Gardner, her face set hard in absolute conviction.

She looked like she was waiting for them to nod in agreement.

"As in all aspects of this case," said Garibaldi, "we're keeping an open mind."

"So you think I *did* do it, do you?"

"I'm not saying that, Hazel—"

"Look, I'm going to tell you something, Inspector, that might surprise you. I'm saying it to you in confidence – I can rely on that, can't I?"

"It depends," said Garibaldi. "If it constitutes an important piece of evidence—"

Hazel waved a dismissive hand. "Well, I'm going to tell you anyway! And I'm going to tell you to show that I am absolutely innocent of the accusation, that I definitely didn't kill Jimmy. The thing is—" she leaned forward in her chair and lowered her voice, "—the thing is, I *do* have a possible motive."

She leaned back as if waiting for Garibaldi to ask her to continue.

"I'm not sure it's motive enough for a murder, but, as I've said, I'm puzzled about any motive being big enough to justify taking someone's life. An act of revenge, perhaps, against someone who's harmed a loved one, who's murdered a loved one perhaps – that I could understand, but—"

"Has Jimmy done something to you?" said Garibaldi, beginning to lose patience.

"Yes, he has. He said something about me that was very hurtful. I wasn't there when he said it, but I have it on very good authority and it has been confirmed by more than one source. It was in a meeting at some TV production company and Jimmy was discussing a possible game show, a panel quiz show thing, the sort of thing that Jimmy's always doing. They were talking about possible presenters and my name came up. And, apparently, Jimmy let rip. Said I was talentless and that – and this is what really got me — I had slept my way to the top."

Garibaldi tried to make his nod one of understanding rather than agreement. "I see," he said.

"I'm completely innocent and that's why I've told you. I wouldn't have told you if I wasn't!"

"Unless it's a bluff."

"What? I—" Hazel stopped herself, as if she hadn't considered this. "It's not a bluff! I didn't do it. I'm telling you because—"

"Because there were times when you thought you'd like to kill him?"

"That's what I'm saying. There have been times when I've really resented what he said, when it's really hurt. We all have those moments when we say to ourselves, 'God I could kill him' but we don't act on it, we just say it. I'm not bluffing, I'm just being honest with you."

"I appreciate your honesty," said Garibaldi, flicking through his notebook. "One thing puzzles me, though, and that's why, if you knew Jimmy Clark had said these things about you and you were so wounded by them, why you chose to perform with him in this masked band."

Hazel put her hands to her head. "I know! And I can't tell you the number of times I've asked myself the same question." She took her hands down and looked at Garibaldi with wide eyes. "It's just the way it is. You spend your life in this business working with people you don't like and having to make it seem that you do."

Garibaldi flicked through his notebook.

"What does your husband think of Jimmy?"

"Bill? I guess he thinks the same as me."

"He was the one who told you what Jimmy had said about you?"

"Yes — hang on, you're not suggesting that Bill had a motive as well? That he might have tried to kill Jimmy because he slagged off his wife?"

"I'm not suggesting anything, I'm just trying to establish the facts."

"You cannot for one second believe Bill has anything to do with all this. He wasn't even at Jimmy's house that night!"

"Doesn't rule him out, though, does it?"

"That's ridiculous! I've never heard anything so absurd!"

"I'm just considering possibilities, Hazel."

"And I'm still shaken up, Inspector. It may have been a water pistol, but it could so easily have been something else."

"It could." Garibaldi nodded his agreement and headed for the door, trying to suppress the thought that when it came to the Okay Boomers it wouldn't be a bad idea for them all to be assaulted with something other than a water pistol.

42

Deighton hooked her reading glasses off her nose and looked up from the sheet of paper she held in her hand.

"Cara Ferdinand."

She turned and pointed at a photo on the board behind her: a young woman smiling at the camera.

"An assistant at Bloom Productions. She rang in on Tuesday, said she had a sickness bug and hasn't been at work for the last five days. Her father Frank Ferdinand – yes, I know – says she's been living with him for the last year since his wife died but that she hasn't been off sick at home, she's been staying with an old friend in Brighton, Yasmin Marsh. We've contacted Yasmin who says she hasn't seen Cara for months and that she definitely hasn't been staying with her. So we have a missing person who we believe was Frankie Dunne's girlfriend with him at the Bull's Head on the night before he was found dead. Any questions?"

Garibaldi glanced at Gardner. Her hand shot up.

"When was she last seen?"

"At work on the Monday when Dunne was found."

Deighton turned and pointed at the picture again. "Finding Cara Ferdinand is our priority. We've activated the search but nothing so far, so let's have a look at where we are on everything else, shall we?"

Gardner went to speak, but to her visible annoyance, was beaten to it by DC Hodson.

"We've followed up the Bull's Head gig," she said. "Gone through the list of all those who bought tickets."

"Anything?" said Deighton.

Hodson shook her head. "Nothing."

"What about CCTV near the pub?" said Deighton.

"Nothing," said DC MacLean, "and I've been in touch with the people who sorted out the Okay Boomers equipment at the Bull's Head. All the instructions came from a Brian Jones and the payment from a James Clark."

"Brian Jones, eh?" said Garibaldi. "Sounds like Jimmy Clark was having a little Rolling Stones joke, doesn't it?"

Hodson and MacLean looked baffled. Garibaldi turned to the rest of the room, who looked equally confused.

"Brian Jones," he said. "He was a member of the Stones. Died in 1969."

Garibaldi saw a few nods. The team might not be making much progress in the case, but at least he'd contributed to their knowledge of pop history. One day, in a pub quiz somewhere, one of them might thank him.

"Thanks for that," said Deighton.

She fixed her eyes on Garibaldi, her expression shifting towards zero-tolerance. He held his breath. Was she about to lose her temper again?

Deighton turned away and the moment passed. "What about the extra set of masks?"

"Right," said Gardner, "Bill Bloom couldn't find anything in his records that showed an order of more masks to be delivered, but Guy confirmed that he'd received an email from Bloom that clearly asked for them."

Garibaldi turned to Gardner. "Did it ask for them to be delivered to Frankie Dunne?"

"It did, yes."

"But surely," said Garibaldi, "this Guy bloke would have remembered that when he heard that Dunne had been found dead in one of the masks. Why didn't he get in touch?"

"I asked him," said Gardner. "He was a bit sheepish but said he hadn't made the connection. The address he'd been given was for F. Dunne, so maybe he didn't register it."

Garibaldi gave a derisive snort. "Did he not ask why Bloom wanted an extra set?"

"He says not. Just thought maybe they'd lost them, or even liked them so much they wanted some more. He seemed particularly proud of that set of masks. Said they were the best."

"OK," said Deighton, "so this email . . ."

"Guy forwarded the email to Bloom who checked its date and time and it turns out it was sent when Bloom was out of the office all day. No trace of it in his sent folder, and nothing in his deleted folder."

"So," said Deighton, "someone sent it and got rid of it."

"Someone in his office," said Garibaldi, "with access to his computer." He pointed at the picture on the board. "So we're looking at—"

"Cara," said Deighton. "The Cara who's gone missing. The Cara who we think was going out with Frankie Dunne."

Garibaldi nodded. "And who, if she sent that email, wanted an extra set of masks sent to him. Why would she do that?"

A silence followed. "Maybe," said Deighton, "she didn't want the masks coming to Bloom's office in case he found out."

"I don't get it," said DC MacLean. "Surely Bloom would speak to Guy at some stage and it would come up in conversation."

"Yeah," said DC Hodson, "and it's hardly the most sophisticated way to do it – send an email and then delete it from your sent folder. Even if you empty your deleted folder it can be found. Digital forensics could do it in their sleep."

"All it will show, though," said MacLean, "is that it came from Bill Bloom's account, and we know that already."

The room fell silent again. Garibaldi looked around and saw confused faces. "The other question," he said, "is if the masks were sent to Dunne why weren't they found in the search of his house?"

Another silence. "Maybe," said Gardner, "Cara, for some reason, wanted them for herself but didn't want them to come to the office. So she got them delivered to Frankie and he gave them to her."

Garibaldi nodded. "Could be, but the question still remains – why would she want them?"

"This sounds a bit silly, "said Gardner, "but—" She broke off, as if losing confidence.

"Go on," said Deighton.

"Maybe she just liked them and wanted some for herself. They both – she and Dunne – liked music from the sixties and seventies, so maybe she just wanted some because they were so good."

"But made to fit other people's faces," said Garibaldi, "and look at the date they were ordered. It was before the Boomers had played, so how did she know about them?"

"If she could access Bloom's emails, she could have found out."

"OK," said Deighton from the front. "We're going round in circles on this one. What about the assaults on

Jimmy Clark and Hazel Bloom? Have we got anything from CCTV?"

"We're going through it," said Gardner. "But nothing from the cameras on their houses. Hoods up, masks on, and no distinguishing features. We're looking at footage from surrounding houses and shops in the time leading up to, and just after, the incidents."

"We do, of course, have prints and DNA from the 'RIP Frankie Dunne' note," said Deighton. "But at the moment no matches."

She paused and looked round the room.

Garibaldi sensed her frustration. "Let's not forget that there's still a chance Dunne was killed in error," he said. "If someone did kill him because they thought it was Clark behind the mask then there's no shortage of people with a possible motive. And when I say people, I'm talking about the Okay Boomers. Clark wrote an anonymous article slagging of Larry Benyon, he had an affair with Charlie Brougham's first wife, he apparently slagged off Craig Francis's poetry when he was judging a prize and he accused Hazel Bloom of being talentless and sleeping her way to the top."

"We know all this," said Deighton impatiently.

"I'm aware of that," said Garibaldi, "but I think it's important we don't lose sight of the basics."

Deighton looked confused. Basics weren't Garibaldi's usual habitat – he was more left-field ideas and obscure references.

"Let's also not forget," continued Garibaldi, "that if someone killed Frankie Dunne it could have been Jimmy Clark. Maybe something sexual was going on between them. They had an argument, they fought and he pushed Dunne to his death, maybe deliberately, maybe accidentally.

He could have put the mask on Dunne after he killed him just to implicate the band, to confuse us. Or, of course, Dunne could have been wearing the mask for other purposes..."

"But the post-mortem," said Gardner. "Did it show evidence that Dunne had been involved in recent sexual activity?"

"Nothing," said Deighton. "Or at least nothing that suggested he'd been involved in sexual activity that night."

"Exactly," said Garibaldi. "Nothing may have happened that night, but that doesn't mean there couldn't have been something sexual going on between them at other times."

"But it does mean," said Gardner, "that he wouldn't have been wearing the mask that night for sexual purposes."

Garibaldi shrugged. "Not necessarily. We have no idea what they might have been getting up to. Just because there's no evidence when it comes to Dunne, doesn't mean that Jimmy Clark didn't—"

"But hang on," said Gardner. "If Dunne was with Clark that night how did he get in?"

"Clark let him in."

"But there's no sign of Dunne on the CCTV."

Garibaldi nodded. "You're right, but, if you remember, the front door's not the only way in. There's a side entrance—" He glanced at Deighton. "—A tradesman's entrance. No cameras. Maybe that's the entrance Clark liked to use for that kind of thing."

"This is all well and good," cut in Deighton, "but—"

Garibaldi held up his hand. "There's something we need to consider. Remember what Oscar Wilde says about masks?"

Deighton's nod acknowledged Garibaldi's return to type.

"'A mask tells us more than a face'." Garibaldi turned to

the room. "So let's have a look at them. Dunne was found in the Jagger mask. Clark was attacked by someone in the Dylan mask and then Hazel Bloom was attacked by someone in the Debbie Harry. So which masks haven't been involved so far?"

"Bowie," said DC Hodson.

"And McCartney," said DC MacLean.

"Exactly," said Garibaldi. "And does that seem in any way significant?"

There was a short silence.

"Could it be," said Garibaldi, "that whoever is doing this is drawing our attention to something?"

"To what?" said Gardner.

"To the people who wore those particular masks" said Garibaldi. "Jagger was Clark, Dylan was Benyon, Harry was Bloom. Who was McCartney? Craig Francis. Who was Bowie? Charlie Brougham. So why have some masks been used and not others? Will the others be used?"

"I'm not sure what point you're making," said Deighton.

Garibaldi said nothing for a few seconds. "Nor am I."

"I see, well in that case—"

"And that's the point," said Garibaldi. "The point I'm making is that the masks have confused things. They hide and they distract and we've been in danger of being distracted by them from the very beginning."

"We can't ignore them, though," said Gardner. "The victim was wearing one. The attackers were wearing them. They have to be important."

"What I'm saying is that maybe someone *wants* us to be distracted, wants us to think about the band and the masks. When someone sees a mask what do they do? They wonder who's behind it. There's a dual focus. You look at the face but you think of another, of the face behind the mask."

"I'm still not sure what you're getting at," said Deighton.

"Then job done," said Garibaldi. "I've confused you all and that's what I think whoever's behind all this has been doing to us – confusing us, deliberately distracting us, deliberately leading us in the wrong direction."

"So what's the right direction?" said DC MacLean.

"I don't know," said Garibaldi. He pointed at the board again. "But Cara is crucial. Her boyfriend's found dead at Clark's house, she claims to have been friends with Clark's daughter but wasn't, and it seems she ordered extra Boomer masks and had them delivered to Frankie Dunne."

"I agree," said Deighton. "Our immediate concern is Cara Ferdinand. We need to find her..."

The words 'dead or alive' echoed in the silence.

43

Gardner walked towards Garibaldi's desk. "I've got something."

Garibaldi looked up. "Yeah?"

"Cara's phone records." Gardner leafed through the sheets of paper in her hands. "First of all, her phone was registered in the name of Lucy C Ferdinand, so my guess is she used her second name for some reason and that's why we couldn't trace her from Dunne's calls. The second thing is the last time her phone was used was on the Sunday evening of the Boomers gig at 6.34 pm."

"Who did she call?"

"A friend from work."

"And have you spoken to the friend?"

Gardner nodded. "Yeah. She says it was to confirm a drink on the Monday night."

"On the Monday night?" said Garibaldi. "So on Sunday she was planning a drink on the Monday night and by Monday night she'd rung in sick and disappeared."

"Looks like it."

"Where was her phone last used?"

"Close to the Bull's Head."

"And what about Dunne's last call?"

"A bit later that evening. 7.10. If you remember, it was to his football mate about music."

"Oh, yeah," said Garibaldi. "Little Feat with an 'a'." Gardner looked confused. "What about the rest of Cara's calls? Any pattern?"

"She called Dunne's number quite a lot. And her phone hasn't been used since she disappeared."

"Well, we know what that could mean, don't we?"

"One thing, though," said Gardner. "I've looked at all the calls she made on the day of the Chelsea–Man U game and, guess what, she called Frankie Dunne at 11.10 am."

Garibaldi nodded his approval. "So Danny was right. Cara called Frankie and asked him to do something. We don't know what, but whatever it was, Frankie left work to do it."

Gardner looked down at a sheet of paper. "One other thing about these phone records. It's not the last call Cara made, but the last one she received. It's from a number that doesn't appear anywhere else in her records. I've traced it and guess who it belongs to?"

Gardner paused, doing to Garibaldi what he so often did to her. "Eileen Dunne. Frankie's mum."

"What?"

"Not her mobile. Her landline. Crazy, isn't it? Why on earth would she want to ring Cara?"

Garibaldi looked at Gardner, his mind whirring with narratives and what-ifs.

"What time was the call?" he said.

"11.15 pm. I don't get it. Why would she call her that late? In fact, why would she call her at all? She says she's never heard of a Cara, so why would she ring her? Unless she's lying, of course, but—" Gardner's face jolted as the penny dropped. "It wasn't her, was it? Of course! I wasn't thinking. Frankie lives there, doesn't he? It was Frankie, wasn't it?"

"And if it was Frankie," said Garibaldi, "the question to ask is why would he ring her at that time of night on his mum's landline? After all, he used his mobile earlier that evening. Why would he use his mum's home phone instead of his mobile?"

"Could be out of battery."

"Could be."

"Or it could be broken."

Garibaldi stroked his chin. "Could be either of those, but there's one other possible explanation, isn't there?"

"What's that?"

"He could have lost it."

Garibaldi put his hands behind his head and leaned back in his chair. "Have we got the digital forensics report on Frankie Dunne's laptop?"

"I can dig it out."

"As I remember, it didn't flag up anything significant, did it?"

"Nothing unusual, no."

"Let's pull it up on the system, shall we?"

Garibaldi used 'we' but 'you' was understood. When it came to the digital world he was always happy to defer to Gardner's expertise.

Gardner came round to his side of the desk and hit a few keys. "Anything particular we're looking for?"

"I'm interested to see the last thing he did on his laptop. Can you find that?"

Gardner pressed a few more keys.

"Looks like the last thing he did was get on the website icloud.com/find-devices."

"What?"

"icloud.com/find-devices."

"I heard what you said. I just don't believe it. Why wasn't this flagged up? We spend hours going through phone records and we don't even know that hours before his body was found Frankie Dunne had lost the bloody thing! How could they miss it? It's ridiculous!"

"But there was no phone on him when he was found, was there?"

"So what? We didn't know that was because he'd lost it, did we?"

"Can we be sure he *had* lost it?"

"Why else would you go to a site like that? Of course he'd lost it! That's why he used his mum's phone."

"OK," said Gardner, "so if he'd lost it and this site told him where it was, could that explain how he ended up at Jimmy Clark's?"

"It's a possibility, but we can't be sure."

"But it's a good explanation for how Dunne ended up there."

Garibaldi sighed. "The question is, if his phone was at Jimmy Clark's, how did it get there?"

"Someone might have taken it."

"You mean deliberately?"

"Maybe. Or maybe they picked it up by mistake. Maybe it was one of the band. They were at the pub and we know they went back to Clark's."

"But they kept themselves hidden. When they weren't on stage they were out of sight. They couldn't have picked it up by mistake. It's a big *if*, but there's one other possibility we need to consider, and that's whether his phone could have been with Cara. He was with her all evening. If anyone picked up his phone by mistake she's the one most likely to have done it."

"And then we have to ask whether Cara could possibly have been at Jimmy Clark's."

"Exactly," said Garibaldi. "And Cara's missing and we've no idea why. If someone killed Frankie Dunne knowing it was Frankie Dunne, they had a reason. We've no idea what it could have been but there's a chance that Cara does. And that might be why she's disappeared."

"You mean for her own safety?"

Garibaldi nodded. "The trouble is it might not have worked."

"So you're saying —"

"It might explain why we can't find her. It might also explain why her phone hasn't been used."

"OK," said Gardner. "But if it was Jimmy Clark who killed Dunne—"

"We can't assume that."

"But he was there. We don't know if anyone else was."

"They could have been, though."

"But if they were, how did they get in? No signs of breaking in. Nothing on the cameras."

Garibaldi looked to one side and stroked his chin again. Something was nibbling at the edges of his mind, but he couldn't work out what it was. His mind whirred with possibilities and what-ifs, and he kept going back to his conversation with Hazel Bloom as if something she'd said had triggered it all. Something about Jekyll and Hyde, perhaps. Or maybe it was Deacon Brodie, the Edinburgh man thought to be the real-life inspiration for Stevenson's novel. Garibaldi smiled as he recalled the way smart-arse Hazel had been impressed by his knowledge of the respectable City councillor with the secret double life, the respected cabinet maker and ...

Garibaldi sat up with a jolt. "Shit!"

He moved so quickly that Gardner jumped back. "What is it?"

Garibaldi smacked his hand on his forehead. "Shit! Shit! Shit! How stupid!"

He jumped up from his chair. "We need to get the bag of what was found on Dunne's body."

"But there was hardly anything. Just his —"

"Exactly!" said Garibaldi. "Exactly!"

"Have you found who killed Frankie?"

"We're very close," said Garibaldi, standing in Doreen Amos's front room. "I'd just like to check a few things. Tell me, Doreen, you clean Jimmy Clark's house, don't you?"

"That's right. Once a week, sometimes twice."

"What time of day do you do it?"

"First thing in the morning; well, when I say first thing, usually about eight or eight thirty."

"And is there someone there to let you in?"

"Mr Clark is there sometimes but I have a key."

"A key? You have a key to the house?"

"That's right."

"Is that a key to the front door?"

"No, there's a door at the side. That's where I go in. Mr Clark likes it that way."

"So you keep that key with you?"

"Yes, it's with the others on a hook."

Garibaldi looked round the room as if trying to locate the hook. "And where—?"

"It's in the kitchen."

"Could we . . .?"

"You want to see where I keep it? Why, you don't think—?"

"If you could show us, Doreen, that would be great."

Doreen led Garibaldi and Gardner through the hall and into the kitchen at the back of the house. She went to a dresser and took a bunch of keys from several hooks.

"I do several houses and there's a separate bunch for each."

Garibaldi took the bunch of keys and examined them. Each key ring had a label attached.

He read the labels on each and held up one bunch. "So this is Jimmy Clark's, then?"

Doreen took them and read the label. "J.C. That's right. Two keys, one for the gate to the side alley and one for the door into the house."

Garibaldi looked round the kitchen as if searching for someone. "Do you live here alone, Doreen?"

"You mean could anyone else get hold of these?"

"I mean do you live alone?"

"Yeah. My husband left me years ago and Mark – you've spoken to him, haven't you – he lives in Hammersmith."

"Does he have a key to this house?"

"Yes—" Doreen stopped, realising where Garibaldi was heading. "You don't think Mark...he wouldn't do that!"

"I'm not saying he's done anything, Doreen."

"Do you think someone's taken that key?" said Doreen. "No-one would do that. How could they? No-one knows it's there!"

"You're sure it's always been there," said Garibaldi. "Hanging on that hook?"

"The only time it hasn't been is when I've been using it myself. I'd have noticed if it wasn't there."

"How can you be sure?"

Doreen looked nonplussed. "Well, I can't, I suppose, but no—I just don't see it."

Nor did Garibaldi. Not quite. Not yet.

44

Craig Francis sat at his desk, looking at the page on the table in front of him. It had not been a good morning – the Muse, if he she or it existed, had chosen to stay well away. Bad mornings like this were not unfamiliar to him – what was unusual, and a little alarming, was the way they were now coming one after the other and showing no signs of going. He'd always laughed at the notion of writer's block, but he was now beginning to think it was a very real thing and that he'd well and truly stumbled on it. He'd even tried to write about it but 'Stumbling Block' had got no further than the title.

He knew where to place the blame. So much had happened and so much was going on in his head that it was little surprise he was finding it difficult to put pen to paper. And added to that, Gina had been behaving more irrationally than usual, accusing him of all kinds of things to do with the Boomers, Frankie Dunne and masked attackers with water pistols.

It had all got so bad that there had been several occasions in recent days when Gina had come out with another ridiculous accusation and he'd felt close to snapping. That surge of adrenaline, that stomach-tightening anger, that sense of mounting force craving physical release had come close to overwhelming him and he'd felt the need to walk away before he did something he would regret.

"Craig!"

Gina was calling him again. His study door was shut but her voice was loud and shrill enough to be heard wherever she was in the house and however many doors were closed.

What was it now?

Craig felt it all again. Were things now so bad that the mere sound of his wife's voice could start it off?

Choosing not to respond, he got up, left his study, put on his coat and shoes and headed for the front door.

"Are you going out?" said Gina, as he was about to close the door behind him.

He thought of still saying nothing but, fearing that would make Gina even more suspicious, turned and said, "I need some air."

"Really?"

"Yes, really."

He closed the door and walked down the road, not turning when he heard the door open behind him and choosing not to respond to Gina's enquiry about where the fuck he was going.

Where he was going was the Leg o' Mutton, a nature reserve between Lonsdale Road and the Thames: a haven of quiet, home to a variety of wild birds and the perfect place to calm yourself. Ever since a particularly brutal murder there several years ago, people had been reluctant to visit, particularly when it was dark or when they were by themselves, but Craig had no qualms about it – the more people stayed away the more likely he was to find solitude there.

Solitude was what he was hoping for now as he cut through a quiet side-road and headed for the river.

If only he could clear his head properly. If only he could get back to writing ...

The tap on the shoulder surprised him.

He turned, expecting it to be Gina, having run out of the house after him.

But it was someone else.

Paul McCartney.

Craig felt that surge again and he knew nothing could stop him.

45

Gardner came up to Garibaldi as soon as he got back from visiting Doreen Amos.

"I think I've got something," she said.

"What is it?"

"These assaults. We've been looking at footage from cameras near where they happened and there's something strange. It may be nothing, but —come and have a look."

Garibaldi followed Gardner to her desk and stood by it as she navigated the computer keyboard.

"OK," said Gardner, pointing at a frozen image on her screen. "This is from a camera at the bottom of Castelnau." She pressed the keyboard and the image expanded. "What do you see?"

Garibaldi peered close. It was one of those moments when his relationship with Gardner went into reverse and she had all the power.

"It's a moped," he said.

"That's right. A red moped. And what else do you see?"

"Difficult to tell because of the helmet, but it looks like a man riding it."

"Okay. And what else?"

"Why don't you just tell me?"

"Look at the bag on their back. It's a Deliveroo bag."

"OK, so it's a Deliveroo driver. Where are we going with this?"

"This is at the bottom of Castelnau two minutes before the assault on Jimmy Clark with the water pistol, OK? Now—" Gardner pressed more keys. "Have a look at this. It's from the same camera, about a minute *after* the assault."

"The same Deliveroo driver, heading back."

"Exactly."

"So are you saying Jimmy Clark may have been assaulted by a Deliveroo driver?"

"I'm not saying anything. Now look at this." Gardner screwed up her face in concentration as she navigated to something else. "From a camera on a shop on the corner of Barnes High Street and Lonsdale Road just before – about five minutes before – the assault on Hazel Bloom. As you can see, it's the same moped and the same driver."

"OK," said Garibaldi, "and don't tell me you're going to show the same moped and driver going the other way shortly after the assault."

Gardner nodded and proceeded to do exactly that.

Garibaldi leaned towards the screen. "So are you saying that this is the person who committed those assaults?"

"I'm saying it's a real possibility."

"But where's the mask? Where's the water pistol?"

Gardner pointed her finger at the moped rider's back. "In the bag, perhaps."

"The Deliveroo bag—" Garibaldi peered closer. "But this one's not a Deliveroo bag. It's a . . ."

He screwed up his eyes as Gardner made the image larger. "I can't quite make out what's written on the bag, can you? Is that first word 'Barnes'?"

"Yeah. The first word's 'Barnes'."

"And the second?"

"The second's 'Athletic'."

"It's the same moped, right?"

"The same moped, but two different bags."

"Someone who rides for Deliveroo and who plays for..."

Gardner turned from the screen and looked up at him. "We know who that could be, don't we?"

"Yeah," said Garibaldi. "So let's—"

His phone rang. He reached for it. Not a number he recognised.

"DI Garibaldi."

"It's Craig Francis here. I've been done."

"What do you mean?"

"Someone in the McCartney mask with a water pistol."

"When was this?"

"Just a few minutes ago."

"And where?"

"Between my house and the river. Suffolk Road. But I got the fucker!"

"What do you mean?"

"I kicked him and landed a punch. Not on the mask but in the stomach. And he ran off. I chased but he was too quick for me – he ran fast all the way to a moped and then he was off."

Garibaldi looked at Gardner with raised eyebrows. "Did you say a moped?"

"Yeah he leaped on and he was gone."

"Was it a red moped?"

"Red? Yeah. But at least I hit the fucker. I hit him really hard."

"Right," said Garibaldi, turning again to Gardner when he ended the call. "Let's go."

46

"So here we are in a fucking hotel again!"

Sophie Clark stood in the middle of the room, hands on hips.

"At least it's a different hotel," said Jimmy. He sat at a table leafing through the papers. "And this time you *wanted* to get out of the house."

"I wanted to get out of the house because I kept hearing things."

"I'm well aware of that, dear. You didn't stop telling me."

"You heard them as well! That night when I was out you'd come down to check. Said you heard things and thought it was me."

Jimmy kept his eyes on the papers. "Your brain does strange things when you're frightened."

"So you're frightened, then?"

"Of course I am. What do you expect after what's been going on?"

"And what *has* been going on, exactly?"

Jimmy still didn't look up. "You know what's been going on."

Sophie gave a deep sigh. "The thing is, Jimmy, I'm not

sure I do. I'm still not convinced you've been telling me the whole truth."

"I've told you the absolute truth."

Sophie marched across the room, reached over Jimmy's shoulder and snatched the papers.

"Look at me when I'm speaking to you!"

She threw the papers onto the floor.

Jimmy lifted his eyes and slowly turned to his wife.

"Do you really need to behave like this?"

"Yes, I do. I want to know the truth! What was that man doing in our house? Who killed him? Who's been attacking you and the others?"

Jimmy rolled his eyes. "How many times do you need telling? I've told you everything."

"Of course you have. Just like in all our years together you've told me everything. Just like the way I've found out all kinds of things you've kept from me. That's the thing, Jimmy, isn't it? Everything's always been about you!"

This was the last thing Jimmy needed, but he'd come to expect it. Whenever he'd been in crisis Sophie, far from being supportive, had chosen to start huge rows. The more he thought about it the more remarkable it was that they were still together.

"You and your stupid fucking masked band! What on earth possessed you all to do it?"

"OK." Jimmy braced himself. Experience had taught him the need for steel and determination in times like this. "Let's get this straight, Sophie. I have been the subject of a ridiculous assault—"

"Yeah, by someone in one of those stupid fucking masks!"

"It seems it's related to the death of Frankie Dunne—"

"Of course it fucking is!"

"And I've been told by the police to be very careful. I suggested getting protection, but you wouldn't have that—"

"I don't want a bloody bodyguard in the house."

"It seemed sensible to me, but—"

"You and your stupid fucking masked band! All I want is for it all to be over."

"You think I don't? You need to calm down, you've always been over-sensitive."

"Over-sensitive! A dead body in the garden in a fucking Mick Jagger mask. Bob Dylan spraying you on the doorstep. Over-sensitive! What the fuck are you talking about?"

"Look, love, we just need to brace ourselves and wait until it's all blown over."

"And when will that be?"

"When the police have found who's responsible."

Sophie snorted. "The way they've been going about it that could be years."

"We need to be rational."

"I see. So I'm the over-sensitive emotional woman and you're the calm, rational man."

"I don't mean that."

"What? Like you didn't mean all those other things you've done? The trouble is, Jimmy, I just don't believe anything you say any more. I know I've given you ultimatums in the past, but this is the last one I will ever give you."

"What do you mean?"

"If there is anything to do with Frankie Dunne and with the attacks that you haven't told me now is your last chance."

"What do you mean last chance?"

"If it turns out there *is* something and you haven't told me I'll . . ."

Jimmy nodded. He'd heard the threat many times before and knew that her sentence would trail off.

"If I find out you've kept anything from me, anything..."

"There's nothing."

A long silence followed.

"I don't believe you," said Sophie.

"Well, that's your problem."

"Do you know what, Jimmy? I've had enough! I really have."

"I know. You've told me many times. And each time—"

Sophie picked up her bag and headed for the door.

"I'm off!"

"Don't be silly, dear. Where are you going to go?"

"I need to get out. If I stay in this room with you any longer, I'll—"

Jimmy watched as she opened the hotel room door, marched out. He flinched as she slammed it behind her.

At least this time there had been no flying flowers.

He picked the papers off the floor and carried them to the chair. He wasn't too worried. Sophie would be back when she'd cooled down. He even had some sympathy for her – given his track record, it would be odd if she wasn't suspicious and, given all they'd been through recently, it was no surprise that she was more emotional than usual.

And as for all that stuff about hearing things in the house, the truth was Sophie was right – he'd heard them as well.

He started to leaf through the papers.

An hour later Sophie was still out, but Jimmy was relaxed. She was probably taking a walk, or maybe she'd found a bar or café and was calming herself down with a mint tea. In terms of a Sophie storm-out it was early days.

After another hour there was still no sign of her and Jimmy was beginning to feel less relaxed. He was reluctant to give her a call – it had become a matter of principle not to be the first to make contact – but, given the stress of their current circumstances and the increased risk of her doing something silly, he thought this time he might.

He reached for his phone. As he did he felt it vibrate and heard the ping of the message alert.

He checked the screen and smiled.

It was Sophie.

At least he hadn't been the first to crack.

> I'm at home.

Jimmy typed:

What are you doing there?

> I came back to pick up some clothes.

Why did you do that? Are you OK?

> I'm fine, but you need to come back. I've found something.

What is it?

> Just come.

Tell me what it is.

> You need to see it.

What was going on? Jimmy started to type a reply but stopped, realising that the obvious thing was to give Sophie a ring.

It went to voicemail.

He called again and the same thing happened.
He called several times, but Sophie still didn't pick up.
What was going on?

I keep trying to call you. Why aren't you
answering?

>My phone's fucked. I can't make
>or take calls — I can only text.

OK. I'm on my way.

47

Garibaldi and Gardner stood outside the front door of Mark Amos's flat.

They'd phoned him several times but he hadn't picked up and they'd also rung his mother. She hadn't picked up either but they'd left her a message.

"Where the hell is he?" said Garibaldi, unable to hide his frustration. "All that good work of yours and we can't find him."

"Maybe we should wait."

Garibaldi checked his watch. "We've no idea how long he'll be out and we need to crack on. Maybe we should have another look for the moped."

Gardner shook her head. "If there was one we'd have seen it. He's probably out on it. Delivering, maybe."

Garibaldi stepped back from the door and went to peer through a window. "Maybe. Or maybe he's out there with the David Bowie mask in a bag on his back."

"Why Bowie?"

"Why do you think?"

Gardner thought for a couple of seconds. "Because it's the only one that hasn't been used yet?"

"Exactly." Garibaldi turned and walked back to the car. "Let's get back and see if we can track down that moped."

Back at the station, Garibaldi sat at his desk leafing through the media coverage. The story was still news. Everywhere he looked the words 'mystery', 'masks' and 'murder' were alliteratively linked in sensational headlines. The Sun had gone further with a double page spread under the headline 'The Masked Muppets' showing how each of the band members might have looked in each of their various incarnations.

The whole case irritated Garibaldi enormously. He'd had enough of the stars – their sensitive egos, their prickly defensiveness, their willingness to throw each other to the wolves – and he'd had enough of masks and water pistols. There was still no sign of Cara Ferdinand and they couldn't find Mark Amos or his moped to follow up what could be a breakthrough.

His phone rang. He didn't recognise the number.

"DI Garibaldi."

"Doreen Amos here."

"Hello, Doreen. Thanks for calling back. It's about Mark."

"Mark. Is he OK?"

"I'm sure he is," said Garibaldi. "It's just that we need to talk to him and we don't seem to be able to track him down. We've rung, but no answer and we've been to his flat but there's no-one there."

"Do you think something's happened to him?"

"No, it's not that. We just need to talk to him. Do you know where he is, or where he might be?"

Garibaldi sensed Doreen's anxiety in the silence that followed.

"No. I've no idea. He ... I hope he's OK. I've been

worried about him. He's found everything difficult since Frankie...I mean we all have. I went to see Frankie's mum yesterday and she's in a terrible state. I guess it's shock."

"I'm sure it is. But, Doreen, you have absolutely no idea where Mark might be?"

"I can't think, no. Look, I know you're busy and everything but is there any chance you could, you know, give Eileen a call or maybe go and see her? She'd like that. I think she just needs some reassurance so if you could tell her the progress you're making."

The progress you're making. Garibaldi considered the phrase.

"It might seem out of order of me, and I'll understand if you can't but—"

"No, Doreen, I'm glad you called, but I'm not sure I—"

"It's just that we've always been close, our families. The boys growing up together and everything. We were always in and out of each other's houses, looking after each other. Mark always knew where to go when he'd locked himself out. Same for Frankie – he always knew he could come to us for the key. It's like I've lost family. And seeing the body like that. I didn't know it was him at the time, of course, but to see him lying there ..."

Garibaldi's mind jumped gear. He'd been reluctant to visit Frankie Dunne's mother again but it suddenly seemed a very good idea.

He went over to Gardner's desk.

"Milly," he said, "can we pull up Frankie Dunne's bank card details again? I want to look at the day he left work after the phone call."

He went back to his notes and started to read through them again, but, with ideas forming in his head, he found it difficult to focus.

Ten minutes later Gardner came back, holding a sheet of paper.

"Dunne's bank details," she said, handing the sheet to Garibaldi. "For that morning he got the phone call and left work. Only one transaction for that time period."

Garibaldi scanned the sheet and looked up at Gardner. "Timpsons?"

"In the High Street, just along from M&S. They do shoe repairs."

"That's not all they do, though, is it?"

"No?"

"They also cut keys."

"You think—?"

"I think we need to pay them a visit."

"OK. There's one other thing. We've just had Cara Ferdinand's dad on the phone."

"Has he found her?"

"No, but he says he's got something for us."

Garibaldi sat down in the Ferdinands' living room, looking at what Frank was holding out towards him.

"It may be nothing," he said, "but when you told me about her saying she was good friends with Jimmy Clark's daughter I thought it might be relevant."

Garibaldi took the piece of paper and examined it.

"Where did you find it again?"

"It was in the pocket of my cardigan. I hadn't worn it for a couple of days and when I put it on again today I found it. As I say, it might be nothing, but it was on the floor upstairs about a week ago. It was the day when Cara went ...well when she said she was going to Brighton. I was going to throw it away, but when I saw the dates and things I thought I'd better keep it and check with her when she got back So I must have put it in my pocket. To be honest with you, Inspector, since Maria died I've had these forgetful moments. It may be age or it may be to do with the loss – anyway I forgot it was there and then when I put the cardigan on again there it was. And when I looked at it something jolted my memory about the band and the names they'd played under."

Garibaldi looked at the sheet of paper again.

Bull's Head	*Presidents*	*Trump*
Bull's Head	*Comedians*	*Eric Morecambe*
Bull's Head	*Players*	*Pelé*
Bull's Head	*Animals*	*Cow*
Bull's Head	*Boomers*	*Jagger*

He turned it over and printed in capitals was an address. It was one he immediately recognised.

"Can I take this with me?"

"Please do," said Frank. "Is it important?"

"I think it could be."

"And...Cara? Any news?"

"We're looking very hard, Frank. We'll find her."

"And do you think...?"

Frank looked at Garibaldi, his expression making it unnecessary to finish the sentence.

"We have to keep an open mind," said Garibaldi, getting up to leave.

"But what if——?"

Garibaldi held up his hand, half to reassure, half to stop the thoughts running through Frank Ferdinand's head. He headed for the front door, his own head spinning with narratives.

*

Whereas Frank Ferdinand's expression had been that of a

father whose child was missing but could still possibly be alive, Eileen's was one of a mother who knew only too well the possibility had gone.

"I just wanted to pop in to see how you are," said Garibaldi, his eyes looking round the room.

"That's good of you," said Eileen. "Have you found out what happened?"

"Not yet, but we're getting close."

"I still don't believe it."

"It must be very difficult for you. I hope you're getting support."

Eileen gave a vague nod. "I've got good friends."

"That's good. And you're friends with Doreen Amos, aren't you, Mark's mum?"

"Doreen? Yes. Doreen and me, we go back a long way. It must have been such a shock for her, going in there to clean and finding him like that. She didn't know who it was, of course, what with that mask and everything, but . . ."

"Mark and Frankie were very close when they were kids, weren't they? Always in and out of each other's houses."

"They were, yes."

"His mum says he always knew where to come when he locked himself out."

"He did," said Eileen. "He'd often do that and come round asking."

"So Doreen gave you a key?"

Eileen looked blank.

"A key," said Garibaldi. "Did Doreen leave her key with you – you know for emergencies or for when Mark locked himself out?"

"That's right. A key. I've always had a key. You know, holidays, emergencies, stuff like that. It's always good for someone to have a key."

"You still have Doreen's key?"

"Oh yes," said Eileen. "It's hanging in the kitchen."

"Do you think I could have a look at it?"

"Why do you want to see it?"

"I want to check it still works."

"Why wouldn't it?"

"It's nothing to worry about, Eileen, it really isn't. I'd just like to test it out."

Eileen got up and went into the kitchen.

Garibaldi followed and took the key ring that Eileen lifted off a hook. "Don't worry," he said. "I'll bring it straight back."

Ten minutes later he was ringing on Doreen Amos's front door.

There was no answer. Garibaldi rang again. When he had rung three times and no-one had come to the door he tried Eileen's key.

It worked.

"Where to now, boss?" said Gardner when he got back in the car.

"Timpsons," said Garibaldi.

48

As he sat in the cab on the way to Barnes, Jimmy wondered why Sophie couldn't tell him what she'd found.

He needed to know, and he was nearly home when an idea struck him – one so obvious that he smacked his forehead in exasperation at not having thought of it earlier.

The home phone. He'd forgotten about the home phone.

He dialled, but it went to voicemail.

He tried once more. Voicemail again.

He typed a message.

> Just called the home phone. You didn't pick up. Call me on it.

He waited for an answer but none came and when he called the landline several times more Sophie still didn't pick up.

Now, as he stood outside his front door and turned the key in the lock, he thought yet again about what Sophie might have found.

You need to see it.

That's what her message had said.

What could that mean?

He braced himself and opened the door.

"Sophie?"

No answer.

The house was so big that, depending on where they both were, it was difficult to hear the other calling – sometimes they didn't bother shouting and rang each other on their phones.

But this was different. Sophie was expecting him and would be listening out for his arrival.

"Sophie?"

He called louder this time and from the middle of the entrance hall.

Nothing.

He went into the downstairs rooms, calling Sophie's name before cautiously putting his head round each door. He half-expected to see her standing in the middle of one of them, brandishing whatever she had discovered.

But his calls met with no response. All the rooms were empty.

She had to be upstairs.

He went up slowly, calling her name once more.

Silence.

He paused on the stairs, reached for his phone and dialled Sophie's number.

A phone rang upstairs. Jimmy went up to the first floor and swivelled his head left and right as he tried to locate the source of the ringing.

It seemed to be coming from one of the bedrooms on the left. Jimmy moved towards it.

As he did, the ringing stopped.

He edged closer until he was by the door.

"Sophie?"

No answer.

"Sophie, are you in there?"

Still no answer.

He turned the handle, opened the door and put his head round.

"Hello, Jimmy."

His breath stopped.

Facing him, standing behind a chair in front of the window, one hand round Sophie's neck, the other hand brandishing a knife, was someone he recognised.

David Bowie.

Garibaldi and Gardner crunched across the gravel to the side gate.

"Are you sure we should be doing this?" said Gardner.

"They're not here," said Garibaldi. "They're in a hotel."

"I don't mean that, I mean coming here like this. Hardly standard procedure, is it?"

"I'll take the risk."

Garibaldi put on forensic gloves, pulled an evidence bag out of his pocket, opened it, took out a bunch of keys and, one by one, tried the keys in the lock.

"We need to find out whether any of these . . ."

The next key he tried clicked and turned. He looked at Gardner with a smile, pushed the gate open and walked through it to the side door where he tried the keys again, giving Gardner another smile when the first one he tried turned in the lock.

He held the door for her, followed her in, and closed the door behind him. They went through a utility room into the kitchen and from there to the entrance hall. Garibaldi stood by the front door and looked around. Hallways stretched to right and left and the large staircase spiralled up to the first floor.

The voices took Garibaldi by surprise. They were so distant and muffled that at first he didn't hear them, but when he did he turned to Gardner with his finger to his lips.

They stood there, still and silent, and strained their ears. They heard the voices again, louder this time.

Garibaldi took the finger from his lips and pointed it towards the top of the stairs. He moved towards them and, treading lightly, went up to the first floor, Gardner following behind.

49

"Come in, Jimmy, we've been waiting for you."

Jimmy looked at Bowie, the red and blue bolt across the white face under orange spiked hair. He looked at Sophie, her eyes wide with fear, her body rigid with terror, her hand clutching her phone.

"What the fuck!" Jimmy moved towards them.

"Stay back!" screamed Bowie. He held the knife to Sophie's throat. "Come any closer and she gets it!"

"Who are you?" said Jimmy.

"Who am I?" said Bowie. "That's a very good question."

Jimmy looked at Sophie. "What's going on? Why did you come back?"

Sophie made to speak but no words came.

Bowie pressed the knife against her neck. "Tell him Sophie. Why did you come back?"

"I—"

"Tell him, Sophie."

"I came back to pick up some clothes."

Jimmy moved forward again. "Let her go!"

"Don't!" Bowie pressed the knife again.

"Do what he says," said Sophie.

Jimmy stepped back.

"Very wise." Bowie moved the knife from Sophie's neck and waved it at the bed. "Tell him what you found when you came back, Sophie."

"I – I found my clothes."

"That's right, but what else did you find?"

"I—"

"Me. You found me, didn't you? There you were going through your clothes and suddenly there I was."

"What do you want?" said Jimmy.

"I want you to sit down."

"Tell me what you want!" said Jimmy. "If it's money, I can—"

"I don't want money. I want you to sit down."

Jimmy edged to the bed and perched on its end, facing Bowie. He tried to give Sophie a reassuring smile but his face wouldn't move. He tried to speak but no words came.

"I want you to sit there and listen, "said Bowie. "Because I'm going to tell you both a story. And then – well what happens then depends very much on you."

Jimmy opened his mouth. This time words did come. "Who the fuck are you?"

"You're going to know who I am very soon," said Bowie. "Don't you worry about that ."

Jimmy couldn't tell whether it was a man or a woman. The voice was strange, pitched somewhere between the two, and the body was hidden by the chair – he couldn't see enough to use it as a guide.

"You'll know who I am when I've finished, because when I've finished I'll take off my mask. How about that? A big reveal. Just like *The Masked Singer*."

"You won't get away with this," said Jimmy.

"And nor will you. That's the whole point."

"Jimmy. I—" Sophie was barely audible.

"I'd keep quiet if I were you," said Bowie, leaning down towards Sophie. "It's a good knife. You've got some good knives in your kitchen, I have to say." He lifted his head. "Are you sitting comfortably?"

He put the knife against Sophie's neck. "I said, are you sitting comfortably?"

Sophie flinched. "Yes."

"And you?"

Jimmy nodded.

"I didn't hear you. Are you sitting comfortably?"

"Yes."

"Then I'll begin."

Jimmy looked at Bowie. Behind the fixed, static Aladdin Sane mask he could see the movement of eyes and lips.

"OK." Bowie took a deep breath and let out a sigh. "This story begins with a dying woman. A woman who'd been suffering from a long illness and knew that her days were numbered. Sad, right? Very sad. And as death grew closer this woman decided there was something she had to do. It often happens, apparently. When the end's in sight, you want to set your house in order, tie up loose ends, settle accounts, that kind of thing. And this woman decided she needed to tell someone very close to her a truth she'd been keeping to herself for many years. The someone she needed to tell was her daughter, and this woman did it – she told her daughter what she'd kept from her for so long. When her mother died the daughter was distraught. Of course she was. She'd lost her mother. Sad, right? Very sad. But the thing is, it wasn't just losing her mother that caused her pain. That was bad enough but she also felt pain because of the truth her mother had revealed."

Bowie paused, his eyes fixed on Jimmy through the slits of the mask.

"Do you want to know what that truth was, Jimmy?"

"What do you want? Just tell me!"

"All in good time, Jimmy, all in good time. I'll ask you again – do you want to know what that truth was?"

Jimmy nodded.

"I didn't hear you."

"Yes."

"Or maybe I don't need to tell you. Maybe you already know this truth. In fact, I'm pretty sure you do."

Jimmy shook his head. "I don't know what you're talking about."

"I think you do, Jimmy. You see the truth this mother told her daughter was that *you*—" Bowie pointed the knife at Jimmy before pressing it back against Sophie's neck. "*You* were her father. For twenty-six years she'd thought her father was the man who had brought her up, the man she'd lived with as a child, the man who had cared for her and loved her. But no. He wasn't. Her father was *you*."

Sophie squealed. Jimmy avoided her eyes but sensed they were fixed on him.

"So this girl tried to find out more about you. She already knew a bit because you're famous, aren't you, Jimmy? Everyone knows a bit about Jimmy Clark. But to her you were no longer the Jimmy Clark that everyone knew – you were her biological father and she wanted to know more. And what she really wanted was for you to know that she was your daughter. You see, her mother hadn't told her whether or not you knew, and she wanted to make sure you did. But how should she do it? How could she get in touch to tell you? She tried via your agent, via your publisher, via the TV programmes you work on, but no joy. Then she had a stroke of luck. She discovered her friend's boss knew you quite well, had dealings with you. He ran a production company and her friend was his assistant. So she asked her friend if she could get hold of your contact details – she didn't tell her why – and her friend did exactly that. She found them in a list of names. Larry Benyon. Hazel Bloom. Charlie Brougham. Craig Francis. And next to those names was another list. The Comedians. The Players. The Animals. The Presidents. The Okay Boomers. And next to that was a list of dates."

"So it was her, then?" said Jimmy. "She—"

"Just listen!" said Bowie.

"Tell us what you want," said Jimmy. "We'll do anything."

Bowie waved the knife at Jimmy before putting it back against Sophie's neck. "Listen! Both of you, listen!"

Jimmy leaned back and held up his hands.

"So this girl – your daughter – got in touch. The first thing she did was send an email. Did you get it? She didn't know whether you did because you didn't reply. So she sent another, then another. Still no reply. She said the same thing in all of them – that she had something to tell you and wanted to meet. You may well have thought she was a nutter, a crazy fan. I expect you get a lot of those and maybe that's why you didn't get back to her. And maybe that's why, when she started ringing you to say the same thing, you stopped taking the calls and blocked her. So what did she do then? She wrote you a letter. A genuine old-style letter, handwritten, envelope, stamp, post box, everything. Funny, isn't it? In this high-tech digital age a letter might still be the best way to get through to someone. And in this letter she told you that she was your biological daughter. She gave you her contact details and waited for you to get in touch, but she heard nothing." Bowie paused. "Are you listening to this?"

Jimmy and Sophie nodded.

"I didn't hear you."

"Yes," they said.

"You didn't get back to this girl and it hurt her. She was grieving her mother, but she was also now grieving her father. The father she had just discovered. The father who'd rejected her. She was in pain, and the pain took her to a very dark place."

"I've got money," said Jimmy. "I can—"

Eyes flashed through the mask. "I don't want your fucking money."

"What do you want then?"

"I want you to acknowledge that you are this girl's father. And I want you to apologise."

"And if I do?"

Bowie took the knife away from Sophie's throat. "I let her go."

"And if I don't?"

Bowie moved the knife back. "You don't want to know."

"You just want me to say it?"

Bowie nodded.

"OK. I—"

The door opened.

All three turned.

"Police!"

50

"Police!"

Garibaldi stepped fully into the room with Gardner behind him.

They were all so still that Garibaldi thought he was looking at some kind of weird installation.

Jimmy Clark on the bed.

Sophie Clark in the chair in front of the window.

An arm round her neck.

A knife at her throat.

And David Bowie holding it.

"Get back!" said Bowie.

"Put down the weapon!" said Garibaldi, his chest tight, his heart thumping.

"Come any closer," said Bowie, "she gets it."

"Put down the knife!"

Bowie kept the knife on Sophie's neck.

Garibaldi inched further into the room.

"I'm warning you!" said Bowie.

Bowie yanked at Sophie's neck. "Stand up!"

Bowie pulled her up, keeping his arm round her neck and the knife at her throat.

He edged backwards, his mask facing forwards, and

pulled Sophie with him until he reached the balcony windows.

With one hand still pressing the knife against Sophie's throat, he stretched behind with his other arm to the windows behind him. He pushed one open and then the other.

Garibaldi inched forward. "You're only making it worse for yourself."

"Worse for myself? Really?"

"Help me," said Sophie. "Please!"

Jimmy moved towards her.

"Stay back!" screamed Bowie.

"Look," said Garibaldi, "whoever you are—"

"Whoever I am? Good question. Who's it behind the mask, eh? Who's behind every fucking mask?" Bowie backed onto the balcony, Sophie in front of him, acting as his shield. "Tell you what, why don't you ask him?"

On the word 'him' Bowie took the knife away from Sophie's throat and pointed it at Jimmy.

As soon as the knife left Sophie's throat Garibaldi leaped forward.

He had no clear idea of what happened in the seconds that followed, but he knew it was his hand that pulled the arm holding the knife further away from Sophie's neck. He may have been the one to wrench Bowie's other arm away from Sophie or it may have been Gardner. And it could even have been Gardner who pulled Sophie away.

Who it was who pushed Bowie over the balcony railings and onto the gravel below no-one could ever be sure.

In the strange silence that followed, all four stood on the balcony and looked down at the body on the gravel. It lay on its back, completely still, its face still hidden by the Bowie mask.

Garibaldi rushed down the stairs into the living room, threw open the French windows and ran into the garden.

He crouched by the body, leaning close, and turned to look up at the balcony where Jimmy Clark, Sophie Clark and Gardner were looking down.

His hands reached for the mask and he pulled it off.

51

Mark Amos sat opposite Garibaldi and Gardner in Interview Room 2, looking from one to the other with wide, questioning eyes.

"So have you found who did it, then?"

"We'll come to that in a moment," said Garibaldi. "At the moment you're our concern."

Mark held up his hands. "Look, I'm guilty. I'm not going to pretend I didn't do it. Hit me with whatever you want – if you've found which of those fuckers did it it'll be worth it. So just tell me." He spread his arms wide. "You *have* found out, haven't you? Was it that Jimmy Clark wanker? Wouldn't surprise me at all. Or any of them. Masked fucking wankers!"

"I know you're upset, Mark," said Garibaldi.

"Too fucking right I'm upset. That's why I did it!"

"OK, Mark, so take us through exactly what you did do."

"You know what I did."

"For the purposes of this interview, I'd like you to tell us again."

Mark sighed and rolled his eyes. "OK. What happened is we picked up each other's bags at training just before I went to Brighton. I had Frankie's and Frankie had mine.

Easily done, I guess, given that they're Barnes Athletic bags and they all look the same. Surprised it's not happened before. Anyway, I have no idea it's happened and the first I hear of it is when Frankie rings me and tells me he's got my bag and I must have his and asks if he can go to my place and get it. I mean, looking back, it seems a bit odd, like he obviously had something more than his dirty football kit in there but I thought nothing of it at the time. So I told him no-one had a key. Didn't realise he'd already rung my mum as well, seeing if she had one. Anyway, I hear what's happened to Frankie when I get back and I'm so shocked I don't think about the bag at all and then I walk past it and ask myself what I should do with it. I can't give it back to Frankie. Could give it to his mum, I suppose. Then I remember how keen he was to get it back and I'm curious."

"So you opened it?"

Mark looked defensive. "Yeah. Wouldn't you? I mean, why not? Frankie's dead so it couldn't harm him. So, yeah, I opened it. And there, beneath his kit was this big package addressed to him. And, yeah, I opened that as well. And there they were."

"The masks."

"The fucking masks. As soon as I saw them I thought of Frankie in that Mick Jagger one, then I remembered all I'd read about that fucking band, those stupid fucking celebrities."

"When did you decide to use them?"

Mark gave a hysterical laugh, shaking his head in disbelief. "I had no idea what to do with them. I just kept looking at them and the more I kept hearing stuff about that band and Frankie the more I thought about them." Mark paused and looked to one side as if trying to work something out.

He turned back to look at Garibaldi. "You know why I did it, right?"

"I'd like you to tell me."

"It was so obvious to me that they were involved with what happened to Frankie. I'd warned him to stay away—"

"Stay away from what?" said Garibaldi.

"His posh girlfriend. No good would come of it."

"What do you mean 'no good would come of it'?"

"It doesn't work. People like Frankie, people like me, we should keep to our own, not get above ourselves. This girl was good friends with Jimmy Clark's fucking daughter. It was obvious what kind of person she was."

Garibaldi leaned forward. "So tell me, Mark, the masks..."

"I wanted to teach them a lesson, remind them of Frankie but I also wanted..." Mark pointed his finger at Garibaldi, "... to remind *you*. Remind you of them and their fucking masks!"

"And the water pistols...?"

Mark laughed. "Yeah, ridiculous, right? Truth is I wanted to hurt each of them, really hurt them. But where would that have got me? I'm in trouble as it is. No idea what I'll get, no idea what my crime actually is, but it can't be as much as if I'd done something more serious. I thought if they want to play around with fucking masks I can play around too. Wearing masks like that, it's childish, isn't it? So I figured I'd do something equally childish."

Garibaldi nodded. There was something compelling about the logic.

"Tell me," he said. "How did you know where they lived?"

"Deliveroo. They've all used it. I've been on all their doorsteps before."

"And the note 'RIP Frankie'. Your prints were all over it."

"I didn't do it thinking I'd get away with it. Cameras. CCTV. I knew you'd get me. That wasn't the point. The point was to remind them of what they did to Frankie, to keep you on them." Mark stopped and spread his arms. "That's it. So now why don't you tell me which of those bastards killed Frankie."

52

Deighton looked at Garibaldi across the desk. "How is she?"

"Well enough to speak," said Garibaldi, "and we've had the whole story."

"So what was Frankie Dunne doing at Jimmy Clark's that night?"

"Looking for his phone. Cara picked it up by mistake when she left the Bull's Head. Frankie tracked it to Jimmy Clark's house."

"So Cara was at Clark's house? What was she doing there?"

"I'll get to that."

"OK," said Deighton. "So Frankie Dunne goes to Clark's house to get his phone, which is with Cara. How did they get in?"

"With keys to the side entrance. The entrance not covered by cameras."

"They had keys to Clark's?"

Garibaldi nodded. "Remember the day Frankie disappeared from work and his mate covered for him? He'd had a call from Cara and she'd asked him to do her a big favour. She said she was with Jimmy Clark's daughter and

Clark's daughter had locked herself out. She'd lost her key. No-one was home, she couldn't contact her parents and she desperately needed something from the house. Could Frankie help? Could he get hold of a key from Clark's cleaner, Doreen Amos?"

"And he did?"

"Yeah. Cara knew Frankie was friends with Doreen Amos's son and that Doreen was Clark's cleaner. It may have been one of the reasons she went out with him. In fact, it may have been the main one. So she asked Frankie to do this huge favour for Clark's daughter. Frankie was so keen to please her, so besotted with her perhaps, that he did it. Left work, went to his mum's house, took the key to Doreen Amos's, let himself in, took the keys to Jimmy Clark's house, cut a copy, met Cara and gave it to her and then put the keys back."

"Where did he get the key cut?"

"Timpsons, just a few shops down from M&S. I've checked their records for the day and I've checked his bank card details."

Deighton looked puzzled. "Why did he cut a copy? Why didn't he just get the key and go and let them in?"

"Cara asked for it. Said Clark's daughter had definitely lost it and she needed a new one. But that's not the strangest thing about Frankie's visit to Timpsons."

"What do you mean?"

"He cut an extra copy."

"Who for?"

"Himself."

"Why did he do that?"

"We'll never know for sure. What we do know is that when his body was found he had nothing on him apart from his keys. He'd come out in a hurry, he'd lost his phone, didn't have his cards with him or anything. Just his keys. And on that key ring were copies of keys to Jimmy Clark's side entrance."

"Right, so that's how they got in, but how does this—"

Garibaldi held up his hand. "The thing is, when Cara asked him to get a key she wasn't telling the truth."

"What do you mean?"

"She said she was with Jimmy Clark's daughter and that's why she wanted the key, right?"

"And she wasn't with her?"

"Well, she was in a sense."

"What do you mean?"

"Cara wasn't *with* Clark's daughter. She *was* Clark's daughter. Conceived in an affair with her mother when Clark worked with her on some TV thing. Cara's mother told her before she died."

Deighton pursed her lips in a thoughtful nod, as if everything was falling into place. "Did Clark know?"

"Oh, he knew all right. Cara got in touch to tell him but Clark was having none of it. Ignored her completely. Didn't want to know. And that was too much for her. She wanted to prove that Clark was her father. That's why she wanted the key – to get into his house to get what she needed for a DNA test. She hadn't had a chance to use the key yet, but on the night of the Okay Boomers gig she decided it might be a good night to try it. She'd had a bit to drink and wasn't thinking too clearly but she thought that maybe she could sneak in when the lights were out and they'd all gone to bed. So when she left the Bull's Head, picking up Frankie's phone by mistake, she told Frankie she was staying the night with her friend, Jimmy Clark's daughter—"

"And she wasn't," said Deighton, "because she—"

"Because she *was* Jimmy Clark's daughter. Exactly. She

went to Clark's house, hid herself on the other side of the road, waiting for Clark to return and for the lights to go out. But it didn't go as she expected. Clark came back but so did everyone else and soon it was clear from the noise that they were having a party. But far from putting her off it encouraged her. What better time to do it? More noise. More people. Less chance of being discovered."

"So she let herself in and tried to get the samples while the party was going on?"

"Yeah. She's upstairs looking round and thinks someone's about to discover her so she goes into a bedroom and hides behind a curtain."

"And that someone is Frankie Dunne, right?"

"Right. He's lost his phone and thinks it's with Cara. He locates it at Clark's house and that makes sense. She'd said she was staying with Clark's daughter, but he hadn't realised it would be at Jimmy's house. He rings her from his mum's landline but she doesn't pick up, so he decides to give Cara a surprise and go and get it."

"But the mask . . .?"

Garibaldi held up his hand. He enjoyed moments like this, when he could reveal the truth, or in this case the closest he could come to it.

"My guess is that Frankie was surprised and a bit pissed off to find a party going on. Cara said she was staying with a friend but it looks like she was going to a party. That's why she wasn't taking his calls. So he lets himself in and I don't know what happens next but it could be that he's worried he'll be discovered or he wants a bit of disguise, but he sees some masks . . ."

"And puts on the Mick Jagger one?"

Garibaldi nodded. "So Cara's upstairs looking for samples. She hears Frankie. Has no idea it's him, no idea he's come for his phone. She hides in a room, behind the curtains. Frankie, looking for her, comes in and pulls back the curtains. So what does Cara see? A Mick Jagger mask. A man in a Mick Jagger mask. Who had she recently seen in that mask? Jimmy Clark. Who did she think it was? Jimmy Clark. Cara says she couldn't stop herself. All the rage she felt overwhelmed her. Grief for her mother. Anger at Clark's refusal to see her. She rushed at the man, not hearing what he said, not hearing anything. She pushed him back towards the windows. A vase fell and broke. The windows flew open. She pushed him through onto the balcony and then..."

"So Cara pushed Frankie Dunne to his death."

Garibaldi nodded. "One push, maybe two. There was no fight, no struggle. Dunne's bruises were from the football match that afternoon – a disagreement with an opposition player."

"And this happened *during* the party? Didn't anyone hear?"

"It seems not. They were having too much fun. Making too much noise."

"No-one noticed the windows being open or the smashed vase?"

"Clark's wife was away. It was only him. He didn't notice it when he went to bed and discovered Frankie Dunne in the Jagger mask the next morning."

"So who took the masks?"

"Cara. She ran downstairs and picked them up off the table as she rushed out. Says she couldn't stop herself. The thing is, ever since she found out about the Okay Boomer masks she was fascinated by them. She was into old music – the sixties and seventies – just like Frankie was. Her mum was a big fan, especially of Dylan, and after she died Cara started to listen to all her mum's old albums more and more. Maybe it was a way of connecting with her. So she took the masks on impulse. She'd seen them earlier when the band wore them at the Bull's Head. She liked them."

"OK," said Deighton. "But what about the extra set? What was happening there?"

"Cara found Bill Bloom's diary, the one he kept in his desk drawer. He was out and she was looking for something and she came across it in his drawer. She opened it out of curiosity and came upon the details for all the band's performances – masks, costumes, dates. And when she saw the details for the Okay Boomers masks she was excited. That was her kind of thing. That was her mum's kind of thing. She'd really like to see them perform and she'd love to see those masks. In fact she was so interested in the masks she got into Bloom's email, found his correspondence with Guy Armstrong and ordered an extra set."

"And had them delivered to Frankie Dunne?"

"Exactly."

"Why did she do that?"

"She didn't want them arriving at the office and she says she also had the idea that Frankie, given that he shared her love of that music, might like them as well. I'm not sure I believe her, but she says she was going to give them to him as a reward for getting the key cut. Another reason why she took those masks off Clark's table – she wanted some of her own."

"OK, so she gets them delivered to Frankie but why doesn't he open them?"

"She told him not to. They were going out for a drink after training on the Thursday and she told him to bring the package along and give it to her then. As I said, I'm not sure she was going to give them to him at all. I think she wanted

344

them for herself. The problem is that after training Frankie picked up the wrong bag. He picked up Mark Amos's and Mark picked up his."

"So, hang on," said Deighton. "When Cara left Jimmy Clark's she had no idea who she'd pushed through the window."

"None at all. She picked up the masks, left the way she came in, and took an Uber home. When she heard that someone had been found dead at Jimmy Clark's in a Mick Jagger mask she knew it was the man she had pushed off the balcony. She thought it was the father who wouldn't acknowledge her, who refused to know her. She couldn't understand why he hadn't been named as Clark and then she found out why."

"She found out that she'd killed her boyfriend."

"Exactly. I don't know how much she felt for him. As I said, he was a convenient connection and it seems she strung him along, played him. But even so the shock must have been quite something. That's when she disappeared and tried to come to terms with it all."

"Where was she? Why couldn't we find her?"

"She told work she was sick, told her dad she was going to stay with a friend in Brighton and checked in to a bed and breakfast at the top of Castelnau. False name. She went off the radar. Stopped using her phone. God knows what was going on in her head, but she watched Jimmy Clark very closely. Obsessively closely. And she watched his house. Watched the comings and goings and when she thought the house was empty she let herself in with her key. She may even have done it sometimes when it wasn't empty. That might explain why Jimmy and Sophie Clark kept talking about hearing noises, thinking someone was there. And that's how she took Sophie Clark and held her at knifepoint.

She was watching the house, saw her go in and that's when she decided to force things to a conclusion."

"What did she want?"

"She wanted Clark to apologise – to acknowledge her, to say he was her father."

"So she took Sophie and held her."

"She put on the Bowie mask, held Sophie and sent Jimmy messages on her phone to get him there."

"And then you arrived."

"Courtesy of Deacon Brodie."

Deighton looked at him, puzzled. "Sorry?"

"You know Jekyll and Hyde?"

"I do, yes."

"The respectable Dr Jekyll who is also the evil Mr Hyde."

"I am familiar with the idea."

"Well a man called Deacon Brodie could well have been the inspiration for the whole thing."

"For what whole thing?"

"For Jekyll and Hyde."

Deighton's face flashed with impatience, as if her tolerance tank was about to empty again. "Stop playing around, Jim, just tell me."

"Brodie was a respectable man who had a secret life as a housebreaker. Copied keys using wax impressions. Had access to some of the wealthiest houses in the city and through his copied keys he was able to break into them, partly for a thrill and partly to subsidise his gambling habit."

"And your point?"

"Thinking of Brodie – it didn't solve anything, but it kind of, you know, unlocked it a bit."

Deighton leaned back in her chair, her eyes on Garibaldi, her expression thoughtful. She said nothing for a few moments, then let out a heavy sigh.

"Poor girl."

"Yeah," said Garibaldi, "What's going to happen to her?"

"Who knows? It'd be nice to think she'll get away with manslaughter, but the fact is she pushed someone through a window intending to harm them. Mistaken identity, yes. Diminished responsibility, perhaps. But we're looking at murder."

"Hardly seems fair, does it? When you think what she's been through."

Deighton nodded. "A life ruined. As for Jimmy Clark..."

"A career ruined," said Garibaldi. "I mean, we can only hope."

53

Garibaldi leaned back on the sofa while Rachel added up the scores. Experience had taught him to assume nothing when it came to Rachel's scorekeeping, but after such a good *Only Connect* performance (triple points) he had to be in with a chance.

"Ooooh!" Rachel's voice was full of a surprise.

"Go on," said Garibaldi. "Tell me."

"I thought you were going to win—"

"But I haven't."

"Yeah, one point in it. Just one point."

Garibaldi tried to look accepting, but his tight-lipped smile struggled to hide his frustration. He was tempted to ask to see the scoresheet, to see how it could be that he had lost by one point (one measly *House of Games* answer) but he restrained himself. The night on the sofa was still fresh in his memory.

"Didn't think that's how it would turn out," said Rachel, rubbing salt into the wound. "Just goes to show, doesn't it. You never can tell."

"Yeah, you never can, can you? How about I—?"

Garibaldi stopped himself in time. Asking if he could take over the scoring next week would not be a good move.

Rachel pointed the remote at the screen and pressed stop. She turned to him. "How are you feeling?"

"OK. There's always next week."

"I meant about the case."

"The case? Glad it's over."

"So she thought she was attacking the father who wouldn't acknowledge her and ended up killing her boyfriend. It's like something out of a Greek tragedy."

"Yeah. Greek tragedy's just about right. And you know what the Greeks were keen on when it came to theatre, don't you?"

"They were keen on a lot of things, as I remember."

"But particularly keen on masks."

"You're right, they were."

"I've been reading about it."

"You've been reading about masks?"

"Yeah."

"But the case is over, so why—"

"I'm interested in them, that's all."

Interested was good. Better than frightened.

"These masks," said Garibaldi. "They had loads of functions. They meant an actor could appear in several roles, they could help the audience identify sex, age, social status, they could help the men play women. They also had these really exaggerated expressions and features that could terrify the audience..."

He thought again of Nick Lowe and Los Straitjackets at Shepherd's Bush Empire.

"But the most important thing about masks is that they hide. That's what that band were doing, that's what Frankie Dunne was doing – they were hiding. Masks keep things hidden."

Rachel rested her head on Garibaldi's shoulder. "Well, I hope you're not wearing one."

"Me? Wearing a mask?"

"You're not hiding anything?"

"What you see is what you get."

Rachel snuggled close. "But I do like a mask. There's something about them."

Was now the time to tell her, or should he let the whole thing slip away quietly? Now the case was over, would they ever have a conversation about masks again?

Rachel moved even closer. "I sometimes think it might be fun to wear one when . . ."

Garibaldi shivered. He hoped Rachel didn't notice.

"Only joking," said Rachel, giving him a playful pinch.

Garibaldi gave a weak laugh as he tried to shut down the images in his head. "Sure," he said, trying to think of a diversion. "But you know me, always up for something different. And talking of something different, I might be up for a bit of jazz soon."

"A bit of jazz? Great!"

"Yeah, maybe it's safe to go back to the Bull's Head."

"OK, I'll check it out."

Garibaldi turned to Rachel and smiled. She smiled back and they looked into each other's eyes, holding the gaze, seeing the sparkle, sensing the warmth. He remembered the night when he told her about his mother and as he fixed his eyes on her for a second it seemed as though something had come over her face.

He shook his head and the image went.

"And how's work?" he said, reaching for Rachel's hand. "I've been so wrapped up in masks I've forgotten to ask. Still feeling the same about things?"

Rachel looked to one side, screwing her eyes up as she reflected. "Yeah, pretty much the same, but I think I'll stick it out. As long as—" She turned to Garibaldi. "As long as we're OK."

Garibaldi, not sure how to respond, said nothing for a few seconds. "As long as we're OK? You mean you have doubts?"

"No. No doubts. I just, you know, need to check sometimes."

Garibaldi squeezed her hand. "OK doesn't come close."

An idea had rushed into his mind, one that he'd had frequently in recent weeks but chosen to keep to himself. Was this the time to share it?

Maybe not.

"How about an early night?" he said, deciding to share the other idea that had just come to him.

54

Deighton raised her glass and clinked it against Garibaldi's. "Good health!"

"Cheers!" Garibaldi clinked her glass and looked round the wine bar that had become the regular venue for their nights out.

"And good work," said Deighton.

Garibaldi gave a modest shrug. "As always, a bit of luck here and there."

"We wouldn't get anywhere without a bit of luck."

Garibaldi sipped his whisky. "Can't admit to having enjoyed all those masks."

"Really? Do you have a thing about them?"

"I—"

Garibaldi stopped himself just in time. What was it with Deighton? Whenever he saw her like this, just the two of them over a drink, he couldn't stop making revelations.

He'd been on the point of telling her about how bad it had been – the way he'd kept seeing masks of his mother, that time in her office when Deighton had spoken to him from behind one – but was glad he'd stopped himself.

Now that the case was over maybe the whole thing would go away.

"One of the reasons I thought we should have a drink," said Deighton, "is because I think I owe you an apology."

Garibaldi's ears perked up. An apology from Deighton was a rare event.

"Yes," she said. "I'm conscious that in recent weeks I've snapped at you a few times, and I want to say sorry."

"You don't need to apologise."

"Well, I am, and I'm not trying to excuse it, but—"

"Really, there's no need."

Deighton held up her hand. "There is a need, so listen." Her voice had turned teacher-like, with touches of the authoritarian St Trinian's vibe that Garibaldi had always found strangely attractive. "As you know we – Abigail and I – got married last year. And I'll be honest with you, Jim, it hasn't been easy. It sounds silly but ever since we've been married it seems we've been getting on worse. And these last few weeks have been particularly stressful. That's why I've been on a short fuse and that might be why I snapped at you."

Deighton paused and took a sip of wine.

Garibaldi couldn't work out whether that was the extent of the revelation, but decided to probe. "Is it anything...particular?"

"I can't put my finger on it."

"Maybe it's stress."

"I'm a cop and Abigail's a teacher."

"I know. Just like me and Rachel."

"So you know all about stress. No, it's not that and it's not as if anything specific's happened. It's just this...unease."

Unease? This wasn't a word Garibaldi ever associated with her. Deighton had let her guard down on their previous nights out, but never to this extent.

"This is going to sound ridiculous," said Deighton,

"but I'm sure you'll understand. The thing is, since we got married I've kind of felt less secure about things. I can't pin it down, but I think it's something to do with the future. When you're married that commitment is somehow solidified. You think more about your future together. You make plans. OK, marriages can go wrong . . ."

Garibaldi gave an emphatic nod. He knew all about marriages going wrong.

"But you assume when you do it," continued Deighton, "that you'll stay together, that's the whole point. And recently we've found ourselves having to make decisions we hadn't really faced before."

"Like what?"

"Like whether to have a baby. Abigail's young enough for us to try and we've been seriously thinking about it, looking into it. And if I'm honest, it's all got to me."

"I really haven't noticed," said Garibaldi.

"I think you have and I don't want you to think I've suddenly had enough of your, let's say, less orthodox approach to things."

"Well, I'm not sure what to say but . . . you know, good luck."

"I think good luck's just about right. As I said, we wouldn't get far without it."

Garibaldi looked at his boss, trying to imagine what she was going through. He liked to think he had well-developed powers of empathy, but he found it difficult.

"And what about you?" said Deighton. "You and Rachel. I'm assuming you haven't been in similar conversations?"

Garibaldi laughed. Rachel may have been younger than him, but it wasn't something they'd ever considered.

"No," he said. "I don't think that's an option."

But as he said the words another option yet again came

into his head and refused to go away. He thought again of what he planned to do on Saturday. He'd see Alfie at the game and then when he got back to the flat, after the take-away curry and before *Match of the Day*, he'd do it.

There would be no going down on one knee and no expensive ring, but he very much hoped the answer would be 'yes'.

Acknowledgements

Thanks to: Laura Macdougall at United Agents, Sarah Beal and Kate Beal at Muswell Press, Laura McFarlane, Joe Keenan, Fiona Brownlee, Graham Bartlett, Venetia Vyvyan and all at the Barnes Bookshop, Nick Lowe and Los Straitjackets.

Special thanks, as ever, to Jo and Rory, and special thoughts, as ever, of Caitlin.